To my, Mary Jo Wetstein

Jerry Lemonds (Gerald)

The Lonely Paddler of the Missouri

9/22/14

James G. Lemonds

The Lonely Paddler of the Missouri

First Printing

ISBN 978-0-9740774-1-3

Published by JL Publishing Co.

www.timerpages.com

Printed in the United States of America
by Fidlar Doubleday, Inc.

cover design by Patricia Rasch
www.patriciarasch.com

ACKNOWLEDGEMENTS

"The Lonely Paddler of the Missouri" and "The Delta Lovers"

I give special thanks to my friend Tom Nugent, free-lance editor and coach for creative writing of Hastings, MI. He was my ally for my first three novels. Also, I thank my long-time Baltimore friend, Ellsworth Hall (ellsounds@verizon.net) for his counsel, knowledge and assistance in working with cover designer Pat Rasch (pat_rasch@comcast.net) in CT. Their knowledge and patience was humbling. Also, a huge thanks to Lori Perkins (lperkins@fidlardoubleday.com) in IA.

For the DELTA LOVERS, I extend special thanks to my cousin-brother, Dale Lemonds, who provided me with (sometimes) "not-too-gentle" critiques. Using such criticisms and research, I worked harder to depict the fighter, fighter-bomber, and bomber plan "dogfights" and crashes. Of course, I drew on my own meager experience in flying many times as a non-crewmember, enlisted man during my four years in the Korean War stationed at NAS, Chincoteague, VA. Dales' insistence to me that "You should think more about who you're writing for and understanding what you read in the research," and his four years of sea knowledge in the same war helped me tremendously.

Tremendous help came from Google, MSN Encarta, Wikipedia and other search engines for research information. That included the U.S. Navy's Historical Center, Washington, DC and others too numerous to mention. Please forgive me if I missed you. IN LOVE & WAR by Jim Stockdale, Admiral, USN (retired) and his wife, Sybil Stockdale, helped in recalling the trauma of the Vietnam War and POWs. My hero only spent a few months in a Japanese POW camp in Saipan. We tend to forget the heroes left behind identified (usually) with white crosses or those in POW camps. Stockdale's experience for 7½ years was humbling indeed. Please read his book.

For THE LONELY PADDLER OF THE MISSOURI, the Mountain Club of Maryland canoe trip leaders, Ted and Fran Sanderson, Bob Carson and others unknowingly helped in writing this book. They patiently helped me to learn how to canoe in all types of waters. They claim they pulled me out of the water a few times during the thousands of miles I canoed with them over the years in several states. They maintain I capsized in white water, lakes or other calm water and weather. Surely not!

In my shock, I failed to obtain the names of those two wonderful fishermen, who rescued me 22 miles past the Virgille Landing Ferry MT takeout I missed. They delivered me past the Search & Rescue Team into the angry waiting arms of the Sheriff and owner of Virgille's Trading Post. Try solo canoeing on the Missouri sometime and you will know why I became disoriented. I revised that section of the book to include spending the night on the bank covered in ice from heavy dew.

I want to thank Alan Spencer, Mike Neeley and Trampis Williams, Aaron Farmer and Joel Comp, III, rangers at Starvation and Kodachrome State Park, Utah. They, and staff, listened to my stories about canoeing the Missouri and dogfights.

Jerry Lemonds

THE LONELY PADDLER OF THE MISSOURI

A Novel

By Jerry Lemonds

It was raining again. Would it ever stop? Perched behind the wheel of his midnight-blue Camry station wagon, Jim Clark shook his fist at the Rain Gods. "Leave me alone! You've been following me across the entire State of Montana!"

He laughed then – a deep and rumbling sound, like thunder trapped in a barrel. Clark was a big man, a former defensive end who'd never missed a game during three bruising seasons at the University of Missouri. He was tough guy, but with a sense of humor. Playful at times, and even a little bit silly . . .

Still chuckling, the brawny driver patted the empty passenger seat beside him . . . until his fingers located the cellophane bag of Hershey's Kisses. *Gotcha!* The car radio played on – "It's been a hard day's night, and I been workin' like a dog!" – and Clark began to whistle. The Beatles! So what if he couldn't carry a tune in a Dipsty-Dumpster? Slapping the dash happily, he kept his keen eyes watching the road, while the windshield wipers clattered away and the rain-walloped tree branches danced frantically through the gale.

He was 22 miles west of Bozeman, when it happened.

Trouble.

Get serious, thought Clark. *You're kidding, right?*

But this was no joke. Not at all. A huge mule deer – tawny, with jet-black hooves and a rack of 12-point antlers dripping in the rain – loomed directly in his path!

Instinct took over. Clark's right foot went to the brake, slammed down on it.

The car pitched drunkenly to one side, and the abused tires began to scream. A moment later Clark found himself looking directly into the terrified deer's enormous eyes. Time slowed way down…and they held a leisurely conversation in which the driver said, *Don't worry, I'm gonna miss you by several inches,* and the mule deer sighed deeply and then moaned back at him: *I sure hope you're right, pal.*

He was. By about the length of a thumbnail. Amazed, Clark watched the Camry jet-ski through a 360-degree spin, while barely grazing the ass-end of the terrified stag. *Candy Kisses,* thought Jim. *Candy Kisses on a hard day's night!* A moment later, the drenched car was rocking back and forth, its front tires slung halfway over the edge of a jagged limestone cliff.

Jim Clark had begun to shake. His hands danced along the wheel like the hands of some manic puppet. Gritting his teeth, he fought for self-control. After a while his breathing slowed and the world stopped spinning. Still holding his breath, he managed to ease the car back to the gravel shoulder of the road, and back to safety.

He just sat there for a while. Shaking. Feeling the cold sweat trickle from his armpits to his shuddering ribs. What was life? *A matter of inches.* He shivered with the knowledge. How close had he come to the edge of annihilation? Another foot, a single foot, and those front tires would have cleared the cliff. . . .

He knew he was superstitious, and easily spooked. And yet he couldn't stop asking himself: What if the near-collision had been meant as a warning? What if he wasn't supposed to *put that canoe into the water?*

But that was ridiculous. Absurd! Besides, he didn't really have a choice; he needed the dough. The contract he'd signed would put $100,000 into his pocket, provided he accomplished one simple task:

Solo the 2,540 miles of the mighty Missouri River by canoe for Wild Rivers Magazine – and then write the story of his odyssey for 16 million readers.

Clark. The tough guy.

But not right now. Not after doing the Sudden Death Cha-Cha with a fear-crazed buck the size of a Winnebago. Not after coming so close to the cliff-edge that he could count the burrs in the Joe Pye weed growing along the shoulder of the highway. Like most people, Clark wasn't the least bit afraid of dying – provided the event wasn't scheduled for any time within the next 50 years or so. . . .

It took him nearly an hour to recover. He drank four cups of coffee and smoked half a pack of Marboros, while doing his best to forget his adrenaline-soaked staring match with 1,100 pounds of totally panicked venison.

Brutal? You bet.

But at last his hands stopped shaking and his vision cleared.

Screw it, he told himself as he turned the key in the ignition. *I'm not quitting. Not now, and not ever.*

He drove on – but at a placid 60 miles an hour, now – toward his next port of call: the Rocky Mountain Outfitters and Inn.

Gradually, his high spirits returned. After a few minutes back on the road, the big man even found himself whistling: "Raindrops keep fallin' on my head...but cryin's not for me, because I'm free.

"Nothin's worryin' me!"

All at once, he was laughing out loud again. Heck, life is *good!* Why not enjoy it? Why not take time to smell the windblown snow-drops, the yellow buttercups and the mountain laurel that everywhere bordered this winding, wandering road? Suddenly the Clark-man felt fully restored to himself, felt fully alive and interested in everything. Look at that mob of cud-chewing Hereford cows, pestered so relentlessly by that that rear-end-sniffing bull! Why, who could blame the horned intruder for wanting to ride every one of his "I'm-not-in-the-mood!" mates? Grazing contentedly, the animals stood silhouetted on a hillside, within easy ambling distance of their rust-streaked water tank.

As the car passed, Jim watched the attached windmill rattle in the mountain breeze. Smiling with delight, he eyeballed the gushing of the life-giving water pumped by the spinning blades, and the young calves frolicking through the burdock and the creeping thistle . . . while their nervous mommas pushed the laggards in a constant but doomed effort to maintain order among these youthful bovines.

Life swirled all around him. A squadron of vultures circled above, and he could hear the harsh cries of two crows squabbling on a branch. Glorious! *Look at that lucky bull,* Jim told himself. *He's got 20 cows panting for him, and what have I got? A male Lab in the backseat and a woman named Veronica who's 2,500 miles east*

in Baltimore! Why'd I leave that beauty behind? Iif brains were dynamite, Jim Clark couldn't blow his nose!

But then he laughed again. He couldn't help it. "Stop chewing yourself out," he roared with merriment, while the battered station wagon once gain began to pick up speed. "Your time will come again!"

Whistling contentedly, he drove on through the drizzling afternoon. And from time to time, his mind drifted back to former scenes, former raptures. He imagined the blonde, blue-eyed Veronica sitting beside him in the car, caressing his thigh, and her sweet perfume filling his nostrils. He grunted as he felt his libido stir. That blond hair shining on the pillow, and her back arching so tautly as her body strained to meet his gentle, probing touch --

Twenty cows! Sonofagun! He laughed out loud and slapped his knee and then asked himself: "How are you gonna be able to stay away from the womenfolk for 120 straight days?"

Well – he'd better, or Veronica would have his head!

Still laughing, he looked down at the onrushing road – and felt a needle of fear go stabbing into the tender space behind his eyes. The damn steering wheel had just jerked to the right! *Easy, fella . . . you must've ripped up the power steering during that showdown with Bambi's poppa.*

He laughed. Still, it felt pretty scary, after the close call he'd just had. And what about the tie-down ropes on that Tripper canoe? Had he even bothered to check them after that thrill-a-minute episode with the deer? He grimaced. *Better get your stuff together, cowpoke.*

A moment later, he was piloting the car off the highway and into a breezy cottonwood grove. He'd check the ropes right after he took a whiz. He could tell that Jack wanted to water the cottonwoods, and they were overdue for a break, anyway.

He was relieved to find the canoe still lashed securely to the roof. But he didn't know enough mechanics to diagnose the health of the steering. Not good. He'd have to get it checked by a professional at the Inn, first chance he got.

He drove with extreme caution after that, but the rest of the trip passed uneventfully. Two hours after leaving the rest stop, he was slipping into Three Forks. And he was feeling terrific, if the truth be told. His payday at the magazine would be huge, after all – why not take advantage of the windfall to marry Veronica and settle on down with her? Why not help her raise Little Henry – while providing her cute-as-a-bear-cub-son with all the love and attention a frisky 12-year-old could ever require?

He frowned, then, as he asked himself a couple of very tough questions: "Why not become a real father – instead of merely a part-time 'boyfriend?'"

And the second one, which was even more difficult: "What are you afraid of?"

Hey, lighten up, Big Man! You'll figure it all out, somehow, and Henry will be the better for it when you do. Relax for once in your life and enjoy something – because life is good!

The tires were crunching gravel by now, as the banged-up wagon eased along the circular driveway that flanked the rustic inn. Surrounded by a wide verandah

and lit up by a series of antique, gas-fed street lamps, the Outfitters was headquartered in an authentic Victorian-style mansion that looked as if it had been lifted from the pages of a Wild West shoot-'em-up. The only thing missing was a tin-star-wearing sheriff with a smoldering cheroot sticking out of his jaw.

"We're here, Jack!" Clark told the barking dog. "But where is the marching band, old buddy?" Chuckling, he pushed open the car door and strode toward the lobby of the Mountain Outfitters Inn.

Thirty seconds later, the snuffling reception clerk – poor guy had a terrible cold – was sliding an overnight letter at his newest guest.

Ah, the lovely Veronica! Recognizing the home address, he lifted the missive to his nose and sniffed it, hoping for even a faint trace of her signature perfume. And sure enough, there it was . . . that fragrant scent of woodland lilac he knew so well. "Wonderful," he told himself. "I'm missed already. She must be lonely as hell, without Big Jim sitting across from her at the dinner table!"

But then he frowned. And frowned again.

> **Jim, I feel like a coward, breaking the news this way---but you need to know that things have changed. I've gotten close to someone here in Baltimore. He's a fine man---a steady companion and friend, and very stable. (Also pretty exciting at times!) I just know he's going to make me and Henry so happy.**
>
> **I'm sorry this is so abrupt, but you've always seemed to enjoy your time with that dog as much as your time with me, and I really don't think**

you'll miss me or Henry too much. We'll always be friends, and now you'll be free to wander the wilderness---here's wishing you well!

Sincerely, "V"

*

He sat there, paralyzed with shock, turning the letter over and over again in his useless hands. Surely he would find one of her funny notes on the back – a bright yellow "smiley face" and a hilarious one-liner telling him that the "Dear John" letter he'd just read was just another of her silly jokes?

No such luck. The letter was for real. Though he looked for it again and again, he could find no scribbled note on the back of a page – no scrawled message containing the two words he most needed to hear: "Just kidding!" It was over. Finished. *Kaput.* He and Veronica were no longer an item – and the hard-charging Jim Clark was entirely on his own again.

He felt like he'd just been slugged in the gut – and as a former light-heavyweight boxer (at least on the amateur level), he knew the feeling well. He recognized the green nausea that swirled in the pit of his stomach, the dizziness that swirled like shredded cotton candy through the stunned silence of his aching brain. Finished! On the strength of a single, two-paragraph letter!

For a moment he tasted murderous anger, somewhere deep in his throat – the taste of green, corroded pennies, like some bitter and metallic acid flaring into his acrid throat. *The Witch*, he told himself, though he knew it was a cheap shot: *I'd like to slap that fickle broad; I'd like to slap her so she* stayed *slapped!*

But rage is usually followed by fear in the human psyche, and Clark was no exception. No sooner had his anger surfaced than he felt a blast of chilling anxiety go howling through the pipes that fed his now-battered heart. How in the name of Sweet Suffering *Jesu* was he going to paddle a canoe for several hundred miles, he asked himself, while using a single, eight-inch paddle – and without the dream of Veronica to see him through?

How would he survive the roaring rapids and foaming snags of the Muddy Mo, without the promise of her soft, enfolding arms at the end of his long, cold ride?

Jim Clark had just received the ultimate "Dear John Letter" – a Bolt from the Blue so unexpected and merciless that it seemed likely to freeze his heart and totally paralyze his pecker, and both at the same instant. The note had been so unexpected that for a moment he had nearly burst into shocked laughter. But there was nothing funny about *this* news, nothing funny at all. His world had crashed; it was that simple. His illusions had been shattered by a few quick strokes of her black Flair pen.

What a fool Jim Clark had been! What an idiot – to have imagined her as fascinated, enraptured by his career as a pro journalist! How had he missed it . . . the now now-obvious fact that she'd been looking for an exit, even as he deluded himself about their bright romance and their glorious future? Was there a bigger bozo on Planet Earth than the man who whose destiny would be to test the roaring waters of the Muddy Mo?

The worst part, of course, was his growing realization that when things had gone well between them, life had been nothing less than *terrific.* They'd spent two wonderful, action-packed years together, after all, between his many journalistic assignments. They'd skied across the Adirondacks (and made love while buried deep in a snowdrift, so Henry couldn't spot them). They'd hiked the Blue Ridge Mountain passes that Clark had always loved, and they'd backpacked their way across Maryland's tranquil and bucolic Eastern Shore – pausing only to watch the wild ponies of Assateague Island flow smooth as molten silver back and forth across the windblown sand dunes.

They'd spent many a night at Center Stage in downtown Baltimore, and Veronica had wept her eyes out at The Magic Flute and Madame Butterfly, during enchanted evenings at the Maryland Opera Company's immense auditorium on Cathedral Street. And little Henry? Again and again, the two adults had tasted the thrill of holding the excited kid up in front of the Chinese pandas at the Baltimore Zoo, or leading him – amazed and overjoyed and even a little frightened, to tell the truth – past the boa constrictors and pythons and hissing rattlesnakes who dominated the always crowded Reptile House.

Remembering it, Clark just shook his head. How could Veronica have turned her back on their shared life together? How could she have found something better? Was there a man on the planet more dedicated to Little Henry than Jim Clark? And when it came to supporting this proud, headstrong woman emotionally – hadn't he always been right there, eager to do her bidding, eager to give her a shoulder to cry on, or to laugh on, whenever a shoulder was required?

Yes, he'd been faithful, and loyal, and truthful . . . and this was his reward! To be tossed aside like an old shoe, the first time she found some *other* guy with a hard-on for her, some endlessly attentive, exquisitely thoughtful guy who was probably faking it, anyway!

All at once, the bottom line seemed clear: Jim Clark had nothing to wait for. Nothing to plan for. If he survived the river, there would be no warm embrace waiting for him, no sweet perfume to savor. No triumphant kiss. He closed his eyes for a moment, and the pain went through him like an electrical shock. When he opened them again, a single word hung glimmering in his tormented mind.

Jack.

It was the only thing he had left.

"Listen," he told the staring clerk, "I...I think I left something outside. I'll be right back, okay?"

A moment later, he was staggering across the lobby, headed back toward the car and his one remaining friend on Planet Earth. Shivering in the crisp May breeze – the sky had cleared during the past hour or so, had gone cold and hard as porcelain – he limped back to the station wagon and slid into the backseat, right beside the loyal canine. A lone vulture circled overhead.

"We gotta talk, fella!"

Jack regarded him calmly. Expressionless, the dog's neutral gaze seemed to say: ***Actually, Jim, I've been expecting this for some time now. I'm afraid you aren't very observant, my good man.***

Still groaning in his misery, Clark kept shaking his head. "How could I have been such a jerk, old buddy?"

A skilled diplomat, the black Lab did not choose to reply.

"I thought she was crazy about me, Jack. I really did. I thought she worshipped the ground I walked on! She told me I was the most exciting man – the most exciting human *being* – she'd ever met! She told me I got along with Little Henry better than she did! I tell ya, she acted like the sun rose and set on her man Jim Clark!"

Jack blinked, then frowned. Then he sighed heavily. *Live and learn, Jimbo. I can assure you that I saw this coming months ago . . . but for some reason, you refused to look.*

Listening to his best buddy think out loud, Jim realized that his understanding of Veronica and Little Henry might be incomplete – or even non-existent. Indeed, it was entirely possible, he now concluded, that Jim Clark might belong to that unhappy category of *homo sapiens* known as "total jerks without a single clue." Had his whole life been a raging, ass-backwards mistake? Had Veronica ever loved him at all? Had Little Henry really considered him the greatest single human being since Superman? But there was no time for such painful speculations; the station wagon was getting colder by the minute. The sky was still overcast, and the brisk Montana wind – it was still May, after all – cut through his light jacket like the teeth of a starved barracuda.

"Look at me, Jack – I'm shivering!" But the dog eyed him without compassion, since the temperature was still well above zero degrees Fahrenheit. "Let's get out of

here, Jack-o." Rising stiffly, and while doing his best to ignore the painful lump in his throat, Jim scooped up the duffel bag from the back seat and began humping it back toward the lobby.

The dog followed at his heels, doing his best to ignore the questions that poured from his master in a steady stream. "What should I do, fella? How about renting a room at the top of the Inn, and then leaping from the nearest window?"

The dog cocked his head, as if intrigued by the possibility.

"How about if I wrapped the lamp cord around my neck, plugged it in, and then stuck both feet in the shower?"

The results would be shocking, all right.

"Do you drink Johnny Walker Red, Jack? I could buy us a bottle and we could sit on the floor of our room and get shit-faced. And if I start blubbering, which seems probable, at least I know you won't be able to tell anybody that I cried like a heartbroken baby!"

Don't be so sure, buster-boy. I have ways of getting my points across.

Bent almost double under the weight of the heavy bag, Jim twisted his neck so he could look down at his loyal companion. "I suppose you're going to tell me that I've made my bed – and now I'm going to darn well have to sleep in it?"

Jack didn't hesitate. ***On target, Ranchero – and don't expect to find me curled up beside you. You got yourself into this mess, and you'll have to find the inner resources to get out of it.***

"You're a tough hombre, Jack."

I do my best, pal. And it's "cano," not "hombre."

"Speaking of beds, did I ever tell you about the great times Veronica and I used to have in the sack?"

Puh-leeeeeze! You're embarrassing me.

"It's true, Jack-o. I can't tell you how many times we spend the entire night laughing, cuddling, making love and caressing each other all night long."

The dog gave him a huge, gaping yawn: *Much more of this romantic stuff and I'll go comatose.*

But it was true. The two of them had been inseparable for days at a time. Clark knew he would never forget the moment of his farewell – standing there at the end of the driveway with the car's engine muttering and Jack leaping about hysterically on the backseat. "Henry and I are going to miss you *terribly*," Veronica had moaned in his ear. Clinging desperately to his shoulder, she'd wept as if her heart was about to break: "You won't forget us, will you, Jim?"

"Of course not, Veronica. How could I do that? You two are my life's blood. You're the reason I still get out of bed in the morning." He tilted his head back, so he could gaze deeply into her glistening eyes. "The time will go quickly, Vee; before you know it, I'll be holding you in my arms again, just like this."

Her lips trembled and twitched. "Do you promise?"

The liar! Why, she'd probably started working on the terms of separation before Clark's jam-packed station wagon had even reached I-70, en route to Frederick, Breezewood and the mountains of Pennsylvania!

It was hopeless . . . and all at once, Jim then let out one of his big belly laughs. What was the point of worrying – he couldn't *change* the situation by fretting about

it! "Jack," he said with another rumble of laughter as they pushed through the swinging doors of the lobby, "I want you to know that just talking to you has helped me enormously. I'm out of the doldrums, and ready for action. What the hell! I'm glad you were willing to listen – a lot of people would have written me off as a nut case!"

The dog stared at him, poker-faced: ***And with good cause, my man, with good cause. Listen . . . I don't mean to be rude, but have you completely forgotten the concept known as "eating dinner?" If so, I'd like to bring a simple fact to your attention: I'm hungry as a wild hog running loose in a turnip patch!***

Jim was laughing out loud now, with his spirits completely restored. "What's the matter with me, Jack? Why am I crying the blues nonstop? Don't I have a wonderful job,and you for a friend? So what if I've lost Veronica – don't you think I could provide a passing fancy for some lonesome babe out there, if I work at it?"

But Jack refused to be drawn in. ***What is this, pal – Twenty Questions? Sorry, but I'm not the Answer Dog. Are we having pork chops for supper, or what?***

"If there's anything I learned during my divorce, Big Dog, it's that I need to take care of business! Just do the important things, one at a time – and the I'd-like-to's will take care of themselves."

With that, Jim snapped his fingers and led Jack in a crazy dance in the parking lot of the Inn. Barking gleefully, the clever Lab bounced along on his back legs . . . and drew goggle-eyed stares from two elderly women who watched them pass. "Look at that dog, Marge," one cried to the other. "Do you think there's a circus nearby?"

*

They settled into their room without further problems, and within a matter of minutes, they felt like old roommates. While Jack wolfed down two cans of Premium Beef Riblets and slurped at his water bowl like a Slovakian cargo-hauler on a three-day bender, Jim sat down and banged out a quick e-mail to Spader: ***Arrived here safe and sound.***

Within 60 seconds, the publisher's reply was flashing onto his screen: ***Terrific! Looking forward to a great story---let us know if you need anything.***

When Jim looked up from his terminal, the over-fed Lab was already snoring hard enough to rattle the coffee cups in the kitchenette. The big man took one look at him and laughed out loud. "Go ahead, doze your head off, you no-count canine. Don't you know the cholesterol is piling up deeper in your arteries with every snore? Me, I'm going for a healthy walk, followed by a light supper."

A moment later, he was out the door and strolling along a pathway that led through a forest of red cedar and mountain pine. Night was coming on quickly now, and he could hear a barn owl hooting forlornly, way back on one of the ridges that flanked the Inn. The wailing sound filled him with melancholy. "Veronica," he told himself quietly as his solitary footsteps crunched across the pine needles, "I hate to admit it, but I really do miss your sorry –"

"Hello, stranger. How you gettin' by?"

Startled, Clark looked up from his shoe tops to find a slender, hawk-faced old man wearing a gray ponytail blocking the path ahead of him.

"I've been better," said Clark. He stuck out his right hand. "Jim Clark, from Baltimore, Maryland. And if you're wondering why I'm so far from home, I'll just tell you flat-out: I'm going to canoe the river. The Muddy Mo. The whole thing. Or at least, I'm going to *try*."

The elderly stroller gazed at him curiously. "Are you now? The whole thing? Interesting coincidence, Mr. Clark! You probably won't believe this, but my name is Buffalo Snake Rider. I'm a Lakota Sioux, and I know a thing or two about canoes and rivers."

Jim could hardly believe his good fortune. "Listen, I could use a good coach, my friend. I'm gonna need all the help I can get!"

Smiling, the Indian nodded at him in the gathering dusk. Was he mocking the white man from Baltimore? "I can tell you that I have canoed many miles of the River, and I have great respect for it and the people who try to conquer it. No one in my tribe would attempt to paddle the entire length to St. Louis, I can assure you of that."

Clark squinted at him. "Why not?"

"It's impossible. You will be exhausted within a few days; perhaps you will drown. But I like your courage, my friend. I will build our traditional smoke fire tonight and ask the Great Spirit to protect you from harm and becoming lost on your trip!"

Clark took a closer look at his new friend. Was this guy for real? Could he be trusted? But Buffalo Snake Rider had begun to chuckle by now; he could see that the white man in front of him was full of fear, full of disquiet. "Easy, my new

friend. Let me tell you something of my background; perhaps it will help you to know me better. My ancestors met Lewis and Clark on their expedition in the early 1800s. They were amazed that white men could be so resourceful, so full of courage. What Lewis and Clark did was beyond imagining at that time."

He looked carefully at his companion, then chuckled again. "Forgive me, I could not help noticing your last name. You are perhaps related to the great explorer, yourself?"

Now it was Clark who laughed. "I only wish," he said with a sigh. "But I come very a very different gene pool, Mr. Rider. Unlike my illustrious namesake, I have a tendency to stumble now and then. In other words: things don't always work out the way I plan them."

The Indian regarded him calmly. "You are afraid of failure? Is that what you are trying to tell me?"

"Yessir, it sure is. And for good reason. It's like my brother J.D. always used to tell me, whenever I'd mess something up. He'd shake his head and groan: 'Jimbo, when the good Lord gave out the brains, you thought he said *trains* – and you sure missed yours!'"

Buffalo Snake was gazing at the newcomer as if he'd just arrived from the dark side of the moon. "How's that, again? You are missing some brains?"

"Sorry," said Clark. "It's a white man's expression."

"A train-wreck, you say?"

"A lifelong *mess-up*, Mr. Rider. Or at least, that's what J.D. calls me. It seems that I'm always starting things – *big* things – and then I have trouble finishing

them." Clark looked at his companion in the last of the fading daylight, and saw confusion boiling in his eye. "Look, I'm fine, okay? No problems! I guess I'm a little scattered, mentally. I've had a brutal day, lemme tell ya. First I nearly went *mano-a-mano* with a suicidal deer. That was out on the highway. I actually grazed his hindquarters at about 70 miles an hour. And then, within two hours of the near miss, the one woman in my life gave me the boot. I mean big time. I got a classic 'Dear John' letter – and it nearly burned the shellac off my canoe paddle."

Buffalo Snake blinked calmly at him. "Your woman has turned away from you?"

"In a manner of speaking. She's shacked up with another guy."

The Indian sighed unhappily. "This is painful, I'm sure. Yet I have a good feeling about her. I am feeling that you will see her again."

Clark laughed out loud. It was not a pretty sound. "Not very likely, Mr. Rider. She's flipped for some sniveling *nerd-nick* who knows how to touch her deepest soul. The guy sounds like Mr. Total Sensitivity, if you know what I mean? He's warm, he's thoughtful, he's insightful – in short, he's all the things I'll never be. Compared to the nerd-nick, I look like Jack the Ripper with a really bad case of five o'clock shadow."

"*Nerd-nick*?" said the Indian. "Here I cannot help you, for I do not understand this term. Yet I sense that your heart is good. Mark my words – you will see this fine lady again, and when you least expect it to happen."

Moaning in his travail, the Clark-man shook his head. "I want to believe you, Buffalo Snake, I really do. But the odds don't look good. She thinks I don't

care about her and her little boy, little Henry – but nothing could be further from the truth.'

It was fully dark now, but Clark could still read the Indian's eyes. They were watching his face. "I wonder if she senses that you fear her," he said after a bit.

"*Fear* her?' Clark felt a flash of anger zoom through the space between his eyes. Who did this Indian think he *was*? But before he could reply, the man in the ponytail was stepping away from him.

"My friend, I must depart now. But I wish you the greatest luck. I have looked at your boat and you should do very well. Believe me, our birch-bark canoes are certainly no safer nor faster than yours. You are also welcome to take pictures of me and my people who live nearby.

"We are proud of our heritage, and all we ask is that you do us proud. We are not wealthy, but we have pride in ourselves. May the Great Spirit go with you!"

Clark found himself nodding eagerly. He needed friends, at this point in his journey, and he needed them badly.

"Mr. Rider, I most certainly will do my best to show you and your people as representing the great heritage of our country. I, myself, am one-eighth Cherokee and I have great respect for the Sioux people. It's obvious that you are a truly great representative of the Sioux Nation and the Native American Indians wherever they are."

Jim followed the old man to his village, where he spent two hours with the Lakota Sioux and even smoked a peace pipe with them, while also sharing their

tasty and tender nutritious meal of beef and potatoes. The friends of Buffalo Snake Rider gathered around Jim and wished him well.

An hour later, he was sitting over a cup of *Dunkin' Donuts Mocha Java* and scratching his muddled head. Cluttered with maps, brochures and piles of scrap paper, the motel room looked as if it had weathered a hurricane. Jim Clark was very good with his hands---especially when they gripped a canoe paddle---but he would not be winning any awards for Planning and Organization. Not in this lifetime, anyway.

"Okay, Jack---here's the lowdown." He licked the business end of his pencil once and began scribbling on the yellow legal pad in his lap. "I think we can average five miles an hour, with the help of the currents."

Jack lifted one eyebrow. *Are you sure about that?*

Jim stared him down. "Hey, fella---those currents run three or four miles an hour, day in and day out. Five miles is a conservative estimate! Anyway, five mph for seven hours each day... he was scribbling...we're talking about 35 miles or so each day we're out there on the water."

Jack lifted one eyebrow and made a dry, coughing sound, after which his human pal could almost hear him thinking: *I assume that estimate doesn't include any paddling on my part?*

"If you crunch the numbers, it looks like 12 weeks on the Mo, before we finally arrive in St. Louis. That's pretty ambitious, maybe...but it still allows us one day a week to rest and recuperate. And we're gonna need it---don't forget that we gotta

portage the dams and locks ourself, and we're gonna have to hire somebody to haul us over a few of the portages."

He paused for a quick slug of his *Mocha Java.* "But those land-crossings will be the least of our problems, Jack-o. Look, I didn't tell you this before---didn't want to spook you---but we'll be going up against some monster barges and some high-speed powerboats after we leave North Dakota." Now he turned and looked the dog in the eye. "Jack, I want to make something very clear: This little voyage of ours will not be for the faint of heart!"

The canine blinked at him for a moment, then snorted with derision. *I'll be fine, tough guy---I come from a long line of river-explorers. But not sled dogs. As far as I'm concerned, the biggest question mark on that river will be a guy named Clark!*

The World According To Jack

Allow me to introduce myself, please.

I'm Jack. Make no mistake: I'm the beautiful part of the crazy duo that has decided to paddle the entire length of the River. Even though I don't paddle particularly well, I expect to contribute as much as anyone else to the success of the trip. And although I dearly love Jim Clark, I expect to win an Academy Award for pretending to be "interested" in his endless, incredibly boring monologues.

Before I begin setting the record straight about "Jim Clark's Marvelous Missouri River Adventure," however, I'd like to make a brief disclaimer.

I am <u>not</u> responsible for the factual content in that human bozo's narrative of Life Along The Mighty Mo!

With all due respect (he is my master, after all), I must tell you frankly: Jim Clark exaggerates. No, it's worse than that. Jim invents. I'm sorry, but there it is. When it comes to making up stories out of whole cloth, the Big Guy ranks right up there with the nation's major-league bullshit artists – and I'm talking about such top-of-the-line, legendary hornswogglers as P.T. Barnum, Ronald Reagan and the Rev. Billy Graham!

Look, I'm not denying that some of the best times in my six-year life took place while I was hanging out with Jim, Veronica and Little Henry in Baltimore. They took me for runs in the park, where I retrieved thousands of sticks, tennis balls and frisbees (but only when I was in the mood).

Let's face it: I am clearly a major-league leader among frisbee- and tennis ball-catching dogs. And I also happen to be one generous canine, lemme tell ya. Example: During our years together, I often allowed the humans to accompany me on duck and goose hunting excursions along the Chesapeake Bay. We also went pheasant and quail hunting once or twice on game preserves – after Jim shelled out to get me some fine-tuning as a retriever, that is. I wasn't too impressed with his shooting, but boy, did I look good with a pheasant hanging from my jaws!

I don't like to sing my own praises, but there's simply no denying that I was one heck of a hunting dog! Sure, some of my canine acquaintances may be better at pointing game and fetching downed birds than I am – but inevitably, they miss more than they point! They also tend to chew up their birds something fierce. But not this Lab. I find my share of downed fliers quickly, and I bring them home safely every time. And why not? I may get to eat some of those tasty rascals, myself – so why mangle them up before they even start making the rounds in Chef Veronica's kitchen?

Okay, where was I? Oh, yeah – remembering the wonderful times we all spent together. Did we have a blast during our time in the City by the Chesapeake? Ask yourself: Does the Pope eat angel-hair pasta at supper in the Vatican? Henry and I rough-housed often on the plush living room carpet – and I was always careful to let him think he'd had gotten the best of me. Hey, I'm so good at everything I do, it would give Jim an inferiority complex, if I won all the time!

I'm not bragging, you understand, just stating facts – but like all well-bred Labs, I possess incredible stamina in the field and in the water. It doesn't hurt, of course, that I've been blessed with a broad head and muzzle, along with a powerful neck and body. And my webbed feet certainly give me a boost when it comes to swimming. Oh, and have I told you about my IQ? The scientists at Harvard pleaded with me to let them run some tests on my psyche, for their ongoing study ("Genius Canines: Is Their Brilliance Learned, Or Inherited?"), but I put my foot down. I'm a Labrador Retriever, not a guinea pig!

Say, have I told you about my two years with the Baltimore City Police K-9 Crew? I won a dozen citations . . . although there's no denying that I over-reached a few times, especially on crime assignments. You see, locating missing children and Alzheimer's victims (to say nothing of week-old corpses) was a breeze for me – but the challenges I faced while working on undercover drug busts were actually dangerous.

Example: I remember one particularly dicey afternoon when I found myself involved in a shooting standoff with a dangerous thug. John, my squadron leader, had instructed me carefully: "Jack-o, you cover the back door." That tipped me off to the guy's probable escape route – and when he burst out the door like a racehorse leaving the starting gate, I leaped on his back and took him to the pavement, sending his gun flying. Bloodied his nose, too. He was squalling like a baby! I kept on top of him – with my perfect teeth bared – until John arrived with his AK47.

They gave me the Bronze Doggy Star, for that one. And it was only the beginning of my career; later, I was even shot at twice. But I never faltered, and I never flinched . . . not even when some dipstick drug addict tried to run me over with his hot car. I stood tall, and refused to budge – and at the last moment the driver hit the wheel and went head-on into a giant billboard advertising Burger King: HAVE IT YOUR WAY!

After my tour with Baltimore's Finest, I was honorably discharged and given a "debriefing" that trained me to stop using force on human beings. After I demonstrated that I would never again go for anybody's jugular, they pronounced me "fit for discharge" and advertised me as a potential "family pet." And it wasn't long before I was settled in happily with Veronica, Little Henry, and their somewhat slow-witted live-in companion, a gentleman named "Clark."

The rest, as we like to say, is "canine history."

All in all, I believe I'm prepared – mentally, spiritually and in terms of basic motor skills – for our upcoming 2,540-mile adventure on the Missouri.

It was time to sink or swim. Time to face the Moment of Truth!

Standing knee-deep in an icy current, the bold explorer and his canine lieutenant eyeballed the vast expanse of river that lay before them. It was a cool, perfectly blue-sky morning in the middle of spring, with a porcelain sky gleaming above and a few puffy white clouds drifting past the golden eye of the sun.

Observing all this, Jim Clark waggled his hardwood canoe paddle and laughed out loud.

"This is it, Lieutenant Jack: we're off and running. Please note for the record that we launched at precisely 8:03 on the morning of May 15, --after a hearty breakfast of eggs, bacon, sausage, toast and coffee!"

The dog did not respond, however. Turning, Jim quickly read the disapproval in his fellow explorer's eye: ***Sausage and bacon, was it? I seem to recall some dry dog food poured from a dusty bag.***

But the human adventurer refused to be guilt-tripped on this august occasion. "Will you stop complaining all the time, you four-legged wimp? We've got some serious decisions to make, starting right now." He gazed uneasily at the over-loaded canoe. "Jeez, I sure hope I packed this sucker right. And what about that waterproof video camera I mounted in the bow? Do you think it will hold---or am I going to wind up fishing it out of the drink?"

Jack withheld comment. Ignoring his master, the irked Retriever gathered himself carefully and then went airborne. A moment later, he was perched on his seat in the bow and frowning darkly at the boss. ***Well? Are you going to stand on that riverbank all morning, or what?***

Moving cautiously, Jim nosed the slender craft into the edge of the river current, then eased aboard. A moment later, the two of them were gliding slowly toward the great American metropolis of St. Louis, some 2,500 miles distant. Jim felt a wave of euphoria sweep over him; they were finally en-route! "I wish I had a

bottle of champagne, Jack, so I could smash it against the stern! Really, I feel like giving a speech!"

I'm warning you, pal – you start making speeches and I'm overboard.

Already, they were gaining speed. The river – one of several snow-fed streams that combined to form the headwaters of the Mighty Mo – was famous for its rocks and its swirling, foam-crested whirlpools. And it didn't take Jim long to find out why. Not 200 yards distant, the first rapids were already racing toward them. Like wind-whipped ocean surf at the height of a storm, the angry waters rumbled and churned, boomed like a rapid-fire cannon against the rising sun. For a moment, Clark felt a blast of actual fear.

"Holy cow, Jack, hang onto your jockstrap. We're about to take a ride over Niagara!"

"Lean, Jack! Lean! Stay away from that big rock!"

Which rock? They're all over!

"You're getting me wet, Jack. Keep us straight and put the nose straight through the V's, helmsman."

Jim could feel his heart thumping wildly. He heard a loud, slapping sound – he'd almost lost his hat to a hemlock branch. Ducking away from the blow, he struggled to maintain his balance in the slender craft. The almost-industry vessel pitched forward and side to side, as it struck one huge rock after another, then bottomed out in a series of deep-rapid waves.

Jim's paddle was moving at eye-blurring speed now, and the slender shaft spun like a human-powered propeller as he fought to maintain stability first on one

side and then the other. A kayak paddle might have worked better, he thought – but at last he was able to make some adjustments in direction, in order to keep the canoe running parallel with the water . . . a critical requirement, if he hoped to remain afloat. Suddenly exuberant, he hollered through the flying spray: "I love this!"

And then it happened.

Without warning, a huge, flat rock – invisible in the boiling foam -- suddenly forced the canoe sideways, directly into another rock-strainer. A moment later they were airborne, en route to capsizing.

"Over we go, Jack! Ooooh, boy! Whee – who put the ice in the water?" He gasped as the gelid current pulled him under, then shot him like a human cork high into the bright sunlight. The rapids were frigid, brutally cold, even though he wore a skin-tight wet suit designed to keep a thin layer of water warmed by his body trapped next to his skin.

Clinging to his paddle, the big man clawed his way to the trailing painter rope . . . got it! But then a rock walloped his shoulder, and he was underwater again. Up and down he went in the icy water – just like the clown in the booth at the County Fair – *25 Cents, Dunk Bozo The Clown!* – and after half a minute or so, he realized that he was actually fighting for his life.

But at last the world righted itself. Blessedly, the line of rapids had played out . . . had dumped him in a shallow, sandy enclave beneath a line of budding cottonwood trees. He sat there for a few moments, numb with shock. He looked down – the back of his left hand was a ragged mess of torn skin, still oozing blood.

Then he remembered his companion.

"Where are you, Jack?" Panicked, he staggered to his shivering feet. "Jack, can you hear me? Where did you go?"

A moment later, he spotted a flash of black. Amazingly, the dog was already loafing along the riverbank, not ten yards distant. "Jack!" he roared, his voice breaking with anger and relief, "what do you think you're doing?"

The dog regarded him thoughtfully. ***I'm taking care of Number One, Bozo. You're on your own, my man – after all, you wrecked the thing!***

Armed with his great strength and webbed feet, the powerful swimmer had paddled directly to the nearest shore. There he'd kept pace with Jim along the bank – whining, watching, and listening for commands.

"I can't bbbbee-bee-*lieve* I let this happen," Jim shouted to his loyal canine. "What was I thinking, Jack?"

Even from a distance of 20 yards, Jim could hear the brute thinking out loud: ***That's the entire problem here, Jimbo; apparently, no thinking took place at all.***

But Jim fell silent, after that; his instincts and training had taken over by now. Still floating on his back, he hovered just upstream of the tossing and spinning boat. "Whoa, here! We're out of control!" He winced as the fluorescent-yellow painter rope sliced into one hand, and did his best to hang onto his paddle with the other. Meanwhile, he was eyeing the water-loaded canoe. A veteran paddler, he understood all too well that allowing himself to be caught between the boat and the rocks meant would mean serious injury – and maybe even death from crushing or drowning.

Still bobbing on the current, he gave himself stern instructions out loud. "Stay on your back, Clark. Keep your feet in front of you downstream. Let go if need be, but do not get downstream of the angry boat. Work hard, big man!"

Just when he was about to let go of the painter rope and seek safety on a rock or on the shore, the swamped canoe wedged between several taller rocks and stopped dead.

It did his heart good to see that Jack was still prancing along the shoreline, not ten yards removed from his human partner. "Good boy, Jack! Stay! I'll be there as soon as I can empty the boat and drag my sorry butt over there."

He went to work with the bailing can. A white-tail fawn, still young enough to be carrying his beautiful stripes, watched from the shoreline, as oblivious to Jack and Jim as he was to danger. After half of an hour of steady bailing, most of the canoe was dry again.

"Let's see what the damage is to my home." Jack watched and paced anxiously along the shoreline, as Jim tallied up the results of the mishap. "Okay . . . the largest dry bag with my tent, sleeping bag and pad, backpack stove, campstool and small semi-automatic rifle – it's still strapped in and dry. Good deal. And my two smaller dry bags containing food and personal items, clothing, space-age blanket and clothing are still sealed and tied to the thwarts."

Indeed, he had been very lucky. Everything looked dry as toast, and there seemed to be no damage. In addition, the spare single and the double-bladed paddle and aluminum canoe cart were still tied to the boat thwarts, and Jim's favorite paddle was in his hand.

"Hang on, Jack. I'll be there as soon as I can empty the water from the boat and load her up again!"

The dog said nothing – but his expression spoke volumes. *Man, you're slower than a herd of overweight turtles. Get with it!*

At last the human explorer managed to walk the canoe in close enough for Jack to reach it. "Okay, Big Guy, we're back in business. Hey, look up there – all those circling vultures have disappeared!"

Really? No more vultures hovering over us? Is that supposed to boost my morale, Jim? Somehow, I don't feel encouraged.

"Yeah, we've really been lucky today. We didn't lose a single piece of gear – and if things went as planned, the video camera took pictures throughout the entire episode. Wait until *National Geographic* gets a look at our footage – we're sure to nail down a Pulitzer!"

But Jack chose to ignore these bright pronouncements. Moving warily – *how long before I'm subjected to take another dunking?* – he clambered back into the canoe and hunkered way down, until he was almost hugging the deck.

A moment later, Jim was also on board, no worse for wear, and the two bold

He estimated the speed of the current to be at least four miles an hour. With his adrenalin still blazing, the veteran canoeist paddled the 15 miles through breath-taking scenic mountains to his camping destination in less than three hours. In spite of the heavy paddle work, he couldn't help noticing the stark beauty of the terrain. Framed by the indigo-blue of the distant crags, and punctuated here and there by breeze-tossed stands of white pine and paper birch, the landscape might have been

lifted directly from a nature canvas by Millet. And the title? How about *River Mist? The Lone Paddler?* Or maybe *Silent Boatman, With Dog?*

Was it any wonder that Meriwether Lewis of Lewis and Clark – as described in Steven Ambrose's *Undaunted Courage* – had reported on the mountains, flowers and trees of this amazing region with such breathless admiration?

Only once during their hurried progress did Jim pull off and speak to a fine looking gentleman and his female companion. "I am Oglala Lakota of the Sioux Nation," said the male half of the duo. "It is important to identify us as Running Deer, an Oglala Lakota. We are proud of our history. We helped Lewis and Clark in their expedition." Jim snapped a dozen photos, then turned to thank his new friends.

"I'll send you a couple of these pictures if you give me your name and address, Mr. Deer."

Soon they were back on the water, and once again racing toward their campground. All at once, the captain of the tiny craft found himself to be ravenous. And why not? Jim had eaten only two power energy bars and given Jack one before pushing off, soon after recovering from the spill. But now his blood sugar was rising in revolt.

"Jack, I don't know about you, but I'm getting some kind of hungry. I could eat the hindquarters off a thousand-pound rhino, and then line up for seconds!"

Really? Sounds delightful . . . but I think I'll go with a rack of charcoal-broiled baby back ribs, en brochette.

As they covered the last mile of their journey toward dinner, Jim reflected on the day's events. He was extremely grateful for the *Tripper* – and also for Jack's nervy, level-headed performance. "This boat's entire capacity of 1,100 pounds must have been exceeded today," he told his boat-mate as they passed under a covered bridge and shot into a clear, wide stretch of gleaming water, "yet it has somehow managed to keep its shape!" He chuckled out loud, remembering the bright red brochure he and Jack had pored over at the dealer's big lot in Northeast Baltimore: "The *Tripper* – it's what wilderness canoeing is all about!"

For once, an advertising blurb had turned out to be accurate.

Calmer now, the captain of the Muddy Mo watercraft did his best to mend fences with the miffed canine.

"Jack, stop pointing your nose in the air like that. I told you I was sorry, didn't I? Okay, I'll admit there was no excuse for turning over in the rapids like that. Hey, it just *happened*, fella!"

The dog was still looking away. His affronted gaze reminded Jim of photos he'd seen in National Geographic: *The Bleak World of the Arctic Tundra.*

"Look at me, Jack. Hey, it's not like I wasn't *concentrating*, you heartless canine! I could understand your attitude, if I'd been messing around out there on the water. But I was giving it everything I had today – and your sanctimonious attitude is starting to tick me off.

"If you have to blame somebody, why not blame that treacherous current? You remember how we scouted it – the junction where the Jefferson merges with Madison and the Gallatin, to form the Missouri? Anybody who eyeballed that

stretch would have reached the same conclusion you and I reached: Those V's between the rocks on the starboard side seemed almost certain to allow safe passage.

"Jack-o, you know that I've canoed whitewater-rated levels classes 1, 2 – and even a few 3's—for several years . . . not only in Maryland and Pennsylvania, but also in Maine, Virginia, West Virginia, New York, Arkansas, North Carolina and even Europe.

"I gave it a long, hard look, and I decided we were okay. *Mea culpa*."

Yeah, yeah, yeah. Go tell it to the Marines, Cap'n. All I know is, we went head-first into the drink – and it happened on your watch.

Sighing, Jim just shook his head. What a bum rap! Especially after he'd spent so many hours studying videotapes and practicing paddle strokes. Why, he'd even gone to the considerable trouble and expense of passing the official "Flat and White Water Training" course offered by the Red Cross!

"Okay, Jack – you can give me the silent treatment all you want. But the next time we go *mano a mano* with some Class 3 rapids, guess who's gonna be in command of the boat?"

He laughed out loud, then, and realized that his spirits had suddenly revived. Life was good, remember? He slapped his paddle gleefully, and almost at the same moment, the spruce pines and white ash that encircled tonight's campground came gliding into view.

"We're home, Jack. The campground, at last. "Dinner calls!"

For the first time in at least six hours, the dog actually looked at him – and even flapped his tail once or twice. ***Okay, pal, bygones will be bygones – provided you hurry up and get those steaks on the grill!***

Easing the canoe into a quiet patch of water among tangled roots, Jim felt a dagger of pain go slicing through his left shoulder. That glancing blow he'd taken from *Tripper* was surely the culprit. But Clark was accustomed to physical pain . . . how many times had he sat in a football locker room, just before kickoff, taping strained wrists and ankles in order to protect them as much as possible from the violent collisions that lay ahead?

It's just a little bit of a shoulder-ache, he told himself. So you turned the canoe over and banged up your shoulder – get over it! Long ago, as a four-year veteran of Uncle Sam's Navy, he'd learned the true meaning of that popular song: "I never promised you a rose garden."

Actually, he was far more worried about the canoe than his own corpus. The craft had been badly scratched many times in the past – but this deep gash in the keel would require surgery, and sooner than later. Still, Clark had learned from past experience that these fragile-looking boats could take a lot more punishment than most people imagined. On one occasion, he'd pushed a valiant canoe to the limit during a bruising, 100-mile trip through Ohio and Kentucky, via the mighty Ohio.

Other journeys had taken him through boiling rapids and thunderous gorges along the Allegash River in Maine, the rocky Shenandoah in Virginia – to say nothing of turbulent Deer Creek and the twisting, strainer-filled Gunpowder Falls

in Maryland. Clark had kept his cool during those wildwater forays, and the canoes he'd piloted had usually performed like thoroughbreds.

But the task ahead would not be easy. Great Falls on the Missouri was a treacherous canoe-killer, no doubt about that. And how would he deal with the annoying – maybe even dangerous – presence of the speed- boats and deep-draft cruisers that were plying the Mighty Mo in increasing numbers every year?

As he tied the canoe up and began to break out the shelter and cooking gear, he couldn't help ribbing his companion about the great challenge that now faced both of them.

"Jack, we're about to be tested to the absolute limit, old buddy. The way I see it, you've got two choices. You can lose some weight – or you can grab a paddle and help out."

The Lab made a wet, snickering sound: pure sarcasm. My friend, t*he day I pick up a canoe paddle will be the same day an honest politician gets elected to the U.S. Congress!*

Later that evening, while they sat above a crackling fire of hickory and water oak, Jim reviewed the coverage and the reportage that would be required for his 5,000-word feature on the Muddy Mo.

"Jack," he told the periodically dozing canine at his side, "we gotta make sure to touch all the bases, on this one – Spader will demand knockout copy, from start to finish. And rightfully so. *Rivers* is one of the best-read outdoor books in America, and its readers demand filet mignon on every page."

The dog woke instantly. *Filet mignon? I'm all ears, Jim.*

"It won't be easy – but the good news is that we've got some terrific story-elements to work with. For starters, the Missouri ranks easily as the longest river in the U.S., at 2,540 miles. And there's more, Jack-o. If you remember that the Mo links up with the Mississippi in St. Louis, you'll understand a key fact: the river that nearly drowned us today is part of a 3,800-mile watercourse stretching from the Rockies of Montana to the Gulf of Mexico at New Orleans."

Okay, pretty impressive – but can we get back to the filet?

Jim held up his scratch pad. "Listen up, hoss. I really need your input."

***Hoss?* The dog looked as he'd been mortally insulted.**

"Maybe I'm crazy," said Jim, "but I'm convinced that we can average five miles per hour in that three- and four-mile current. And I think we can keep it up for seven hours at a stretch – which would give us about 35 miles a day."

Well, I think I can agree with your opening comment, Jim – you're crazy!

But the weary canoe-pilot refused to be drawn into another brouhaha with his camp-mate. Instead, he dragged himself to his feet, then strolled past the fire to gaze at the majestic, snow-capped mountains on the horizon. "Jack, let's talk about provisions, okay?"

Whatever.

"I'm pretty sure I can pick up most of the supplies we need in towns along the Missouri. And in spite of your sarcasm, I'm also convinced that this schedule is *real.* We can do 35 miles a day, if we put our minds to it. But we're gonna have to throw some extra days in there – don't forget that I promised to shoot stills and video footage, along with conducting several interviews en route.

"We're also going to have to stop periodically to bundle all that stuff up and ship it to *Rivers.* All things considered, I figure we'll need at least 135 days minimum, from start to finish. According to my plan, our May 15 departure from Three Forks will allow us to reach St. Charles, Missouri, on the first of October. That will give *Rivers* and me 90 days to prepare the press releases, videos, photos, other announcements and interviews for the January issue."

Then, with a glint of fierce determination in his eye: "I know it sounds like an enormous undertaking, Jack."

The dog sent up a low, groaning sound. Derision? *Undertaking? Try under-tak-ER, you maniac. You're gonna get us both killed!*

THE RIVER: A Thumbnail Sketch From Jim Clark's "Mighty Mo Notebook"

THE MO: Part of the world's 4th-longest river system, and includes the 3rd-largest drainage basin on earth. Its drainage area covers 10 states and two Canadian provinces.

THE MORPHOLOGY: After Three Forks, Montana, the three rivers combine as the *Missouri* and wind eastward across Montana to North Dakota, before making a sharp turn southward into South Dakota and then southeast to Iowa and Nebraska. The Mo forms part of the boundary between South Dakota and Nebraska, then angles south at Sioux City, Iowa, to provide the dotted line between Iowa and Nebraska.

After that, the Muddy continues on as some of the Missouri-Kansas boundary, before looping eastward to join the Mississippi 20 miles west of St. Louis, at St. Charles. Big country. Big people. Salt of the earth? But some will be darker than that. Prepare yourself for unexpected. *Learn from Huck Finn.*

THE TOPOGRAPHY: Navigating the full length of the river means crossing six huge dams and numerous giant locks – each one large enough to allow monster-sized barges to change depth-levels. And while we're talking about "monsters" – how about them Buick-sized mosquitoes?

Popular joke about Missouri River mosquitoes: "Why, them skeeters got so big last summer that I swear I heard one of 'em ask a pal, as the two of them swarmed around my head: 'Say, do you want to eat him here – or wrap him up to go?'"

And how about those summertime thunderstorms? Winds of 80 miles an hour aren't uncommon, and five-foot waves are a frequent occurrence during such blockbuster storms. If you get caught on the water, the old-timers say, you can forget about paddling – just bend over and kiss your butt goodbye!

The topography will also include some tough-as-nails portages across rough-and-tumble, rocky terrain. Let's hope my aluminum cart holds up under the strain.

*

Within ten minutes after arriving at the campsite, Clark had a pot of water for coffee percolating above their cheerful campfire.

"Is this the life, Jack?" Slouched in his fold-up camp chair, the outdoorsman chuckled out loud. "Except for the mosquitoes, that is. Jeez, I've seen 747s that made less racket, taxiing down the runway!"

Will you please stop bitching and moaning – and start working on my cheeseburger?

He spent another ten minutes resting, then got busy. Some obscure instinct was at work in the back of his brain, and it told him to protect the gear. After scratching his head for a minute, he decided to move their camp farther back from the river – and also to hide the canoe in the trees. Moving quickly, he concealed *Tripper* in dry brush – a trick that had been invented by Montana's Blackfoot Tribe, at least five thousand years before.

Was he being too cautious? Maybe. Still, he was glad he had kept the camera, the binoculars and his small, semi-automatic rifle with him. It never hurts to be prepared, he told himself – and then felt silly, as remembered that he would be snoozing in Montana, probably the most crime-free state in the good old U S of A.

Darkness fell a few minutes later, and the night sounds – crickets, frogs, the occasional cry of a marauding owl – were soon underway. By then, Clark's tent was set up, his fire was roaring, and supper was crackling and steaming on the backpack stove. He opened a tin of beans and franks, brought it to a quick boil, then divided it equally. Then he slid Jack's portion toward him, encased in a metal skillet top he'd dug out of the pack.

The dog looked at the savory entrée, then back at his master. His face was a mask of stone. *What is this, please?*

"Whaddya mean, what is it? You know darn right well what it is. It's beans and franks – the same thing I'm eating, along with these saltine crackers. Do you want a saltine?"

I see. Beans and franks, eh? I think you know I had my heart set on something else, Jim.

Clark shook his head in disbelief. "You're kidding me, right? Turning your nose up at beans and franks? Where do you think we are, Jack – the Four Seasons? We're roughing it, for Chrissake!"

I see. Well, I was thinking flank steak, or maybe a smallish cut of tenderloin. In all honesty, Jim, the idea of "beans and franks" had not crossed my mind.

Jim opened his mouth for a sarcastic riposte – but then fell silent.

A twig had snapped in the distance. Then he heard another one. Soon they were listening to the sound of definite footsteps crunching through the underbrush.

Jim's eyes strayed toward the tent; his hunting rifle was hidden beneath his sleeping bag.

A rumbling baritone erupted suddenly in the shadows. "Halloo there, Partner! Are you needing some company?"

Jack's jet-black coat had gone stiff. For a moment, Clark was glad that the dog's coloring made him nearly invisible at night. Still growling, the dog edged closer to the tent, as if he were also thinking about the semi-automatic.

All of the other night-sounds had fallen away by now; even the hoot owls were silent.

"Stay, Jack!" Jim whispered.

"We're fine," he called out sharply. "We're just getting ready for supper here. Want a cup of hot coffee?"

"You bet, pard. I'd could use a cup of Joe!" With those words, the newcomer stepped into the circle of firelight. He was a large, bearded man in a greasy baseball cap. *Cleveland Indians.* His wet blue eyes were tiny – far too small for his broad, meaty face – and a soiled bandage hung from a laceration along his stubbled chin. The dog continued to growl, while the two men looked at each other.

"My handle's Kip," said the stranger. "I trap in these mountains in season. I was hoping you could give me an idea how the river's running."

Clark was on his feet now. His brain was skimming along on high-octane. *What's the deal, here? How did he find us in these woods? He must have decided to follow a lone canoe.*

But he said nothing. Instead, he poured the steaming coffee into a tin cup, handed it to the bearded Kip. "You want some sugar with that?'

Kip looked into the cup. His mouth split open in a smile, and Jim saw a row of yellowing, gold-filled teeth. What was that smell?

As the answer shot through his brain – *cheap whiskey* – Kip flung the boiling coffee toward his host's face and pounced on him. The dog roared and went airborne. A moment later the three of them were rolling around in the sand, perilously close to the snapping fire.

Jim felt the left side of his face go numb, as the intruder landed a stinging punch. The *Indians* cap had bounced away; now it was smoldering in the campfire. Fighting to break out of a vicious chokehold, Clark smelled cheap whiskey again,

then heard his adversary shout into the darkness: "Sam, come on and give me a hand!"

A moment later, a shadow detached itself from the surrounding darkness and leaped toward the two men who struggled on the ground. Jim took a hard shot to the ribcage, and for a moment he saw bright stars. But then he broke an elbow free and slashed it into the row of gold-crowned teeth. The shadow landed atop both of them, but Clark was lucky; the force of the collision knocked him clear for an instant.

Time slowed to a crawl, and Jim watched Kip pull a hunting knife from his belt. Fascinated, he saw how the firelight glimmered against the steel blade. He watched the cutting edge whistle toward him, even as he listened to the man's ragged laughter: "I got you now, smart guy!"

But he was wrong. Springing from his crouch, Jim delivered a swift karate kick that landed in the first attacker's groin. Kip went down in sections, like a capsizing ship. His eyes had rolled far back in his head, and he was making a strange whistling sound: shock and pain.

Jim roared for help with the other one: "Jack, go get him!" The dog whirled, sprang just as Sam was unloading a wild swing with a boat paddle. The lumber hissed through the air like an attacking snake, but Jack was too fast. In a flash, his bared teeth had sunk deep into Sam's shoulder. "I'll kill that black devil!"

A moment later, Clark had reached the open door of the tent. In less than a second he had the barrel pointed skyward and was pulling the trigger. He fired twice, and after each shot he blared at them: "Stop, or I'll kill you both!"

The two men had frozen in place. Absurdly, the enraged Jack continued to gnaw at Kip's trouser leg. "Easy now, Jack!" Jim waved the rifle. "Hold him, dog!" Jack relaxed his jaws from the man's pants cuff, but now his fangs were bared in Kip's face and he was snarling viciously at the pair all the while. For a few seconds, his ancestry had reclaimed him, and he might have been a wild dog or a wolf.

Now Jim was dialing 911 on his long-range cell phone. One-handed, he kept the rifle-barrel trained on the two invaders. "Dispatcher, can I report a crime in progress? Great!" The voice on the other end had started asking him questions. He frowned, waited, and began talking at a high rate of speed. "I was jumped by two men at my tent site at mile 81, just up from the lower end of Canyon Lake.

"What's that? Oh. Well, first this guy . . . he man identified himself as 'Kip,' then he pulled a knife on me. His partner joined in, but I was able to retrieve my .22 from my tent and I've got both of them at bay right now. My name is Jim Clark. I'm a writer from Baltimore, doing a story for Wild Rivers Magazine out of St. Louis.

"Can you send somebody up here, pronto?"

The voice in Clark's ear was cool, calm, under control. "No problem, sir. This is Sergeant Webb. We'll have a man at your camp site within an hour, Mr. Clark. Do you think you can hold them until then?"

"I'll do my best – but hurry!"

But Jim had made a mistake, and he spotted it too late. Foolishly, he'd allowed the thugs to sit with so much distance between them that he couldn't cover them

effectively with the rifle. A moment later, Kip was leaping into the dark and then rolling away from the camp. Jim could hear him cursing as he staggered through the brush and rocks. Had he been more prepared, he might have been able to send Jack after Kip.

"Hold him, Jack!" he bellowed now, pointing to the other intruder. Jack did as he was asked, and sat crouched with eyes trained on Sam while Jim pointed the rifle at him.

Gradually, the crashing sounds dimmed in the distance, as Kip made good his escape.

The men dispatched by Sgt. Webb were there within the hour. Corporal Davis said to Sam: "You have the right to remain silent – and you have the right to be represented by an attorney, as soon as we reach the jail. Meanwhile, you're under arrest for assault and attempted robbery. Put your hands behind your back so I can handcuff you."

After Jim signed the complaint, they took Sam away. The rattled canoer was astonished by the efficiency and speed with which the Montana Sheriff's Department had performed their duty in this remote area – and didn't hesitate to tell them so. He also took a couple of photographs for his story, although he kept the lens away from Sam's features.

The chief deputy was impressed. "Thanks for making our job so easy," he said with a chuckle. Then, more seriously: "Mr. Clark, if everyone who called for our help had things as well in hand as you and Jack, we'd sleep a whole lot better at night." Grinning, he gave the dog a congratulatory pat.

After the lawmen had departed, Jim examined Jack and himself for serious injuries. The dog showed no signs of pain that would indicate broken bones – although he'd obviously been hit pretty hard with the paddle. Jim hugged him like a proud parent: "You are one tough canine, Jack-o!"

The dog turned his head away, thoroughly embarrassed. *If you get mawkish on me again, I swear I'll jump in the damn river!*

Ignoring the predictable sarcasm, Jim went to work cleaning his own scrapes with alcohol-soaked cotton from the first aid kit. Moving quickly, he applied a cold, wet cloth to his bruises and wrapped his ribs with stretch bandages. He also took a double-dose of Tylenol for pain.

Then he looked across the clearing at his canine pal. "Hey, Jack Dempsey – could you use a little Tylenol for those bruises?"

When Jack didn't protest, Jim tilted his head back, opened his huge mouth and flicked two caplets toward his tonsils. They hit the hay right after that, but neither slept well; Jim tossed and turned throughout much of the night, constantly replaying the violent attack on the campsite. His dreams were stark, flickering landscapes peopled by masked figures with hands of fire – and he awoke several times to find his heart thudding with panic.

The assault had been deeply disturbing, but now it was over, and Jim assumed that he'd simply been the victim of a random crime of opportunity.

*

The two of them rested in camp until noon the next day, in order to allow their wounds to begin healing. But after a few hours, Jack's restlessness had become

palpable; his tail thumped steadily against the ground and his black eyes glistened with excitement. Jim took one look at him, and laughed out loud.

"Okay, pal, I'm getting the message. Time for us to take our act back on the road!"

Five minutes later, Clark was sliding the fully loaded canoe into the river, and groaning with the impact of the heavy lifting on his aching ribs. But they managed to climb aboard without incident, and soon they were making good time again. Without a head wind to confront, the canoe zoomed through the water – and with each powerful stroke, Clark was becoming more adept at using his new, twin-bladed kayak paddle.

"Take heart, Jack!" he boomed at his sprawled-out companion, as the slender watercraft shot past a series of camouflaged duck blinds, then through the charred remains of a burned-over stand of beeches and maples. "I'd say we're doing five miles an hour, easy. And how about that wildlife, fella? Ever seen so many eagles and ducks in one place together? Maybe you died during that showdown at the camp last night, and then went straight to Doggy Heaven!"

Doggy Heaven? Get real. Do you see any filet mignon or New York strip on the dinner menu?

But Jim's laughter was short-lived. As they approached the town of Ringling – located a mile off the lake and back on the river – two uniformed officers motioned the canoeist to the gravel dock. "I'm Sheriff Dolan," one said. "Please step out and keep your hands raised. Deputy Lee, hold the canoe and keep your eye on the dog."

Jim ordered Jack to "stay."

"Are you Jim Clark?

Jim nodded. The sheriff was a big man with a dirty blond crewcut and jumbo-sized ears. Beneath the Smoky Bear hat, his eyes were a bright, piercing blue.

"I have a complaint warrant for your arrest alleging that you and your dog attacked Kip Harwood and Sam Finch – two law-abiding citizens of the county – at the lower end of the lake. The complainants say the assault was completely unprovoked. You have the right to remain silent, but you must come with us."

Without another word from anyone, Jim was handcuffed and led to what looked like an unused grain bin. There were signs of rat infestation along the walls and a hole gaped from one corner of the enclosure. Jim stared in disbelief while they locked one of his cuffed hands to a ring on the side of the bin. For a moment, he nearly laughed out loud; the scene might have been lifted intact from a Grade B western.

"Circuit Judge Oscar Day will be here tomorrow," Dolan said tonelessly, "and that's when your trial will take place."

Jim just stared at him. "Is Jack under arrest, too?"

"Don't be a wiseacre," said Dolan. "I'm sure you don't want me to tighten those handcuffs before we leave."

They soon departed. Jack sat down beside his partner and gave him a fish-eyed stare: ***What is it with you, Big Man? Why is your life a non-stop, 100-mile-an-hour Chinese fire-drill? And why do I have to keep paying the price for your mess-ups?***

For once, Clark had no answers for the pooch.

After a few hours, the lawmen returned and escorted Clark to the town lockup. Jim was treated decently, and fed three straight meals that consisted of lukewarm hot dogs and stale potato chips. But there was no sign of any legal assistance. Nor was he permitted to make the mythical "single phone call." And his efforts to tell the jailers *his* side of the story fell on completely deaf ears.

His stomach rolled with dismay, each time he thought about the expensive equipment and the defenseless canoe. And that wasn't the worst of it – what if one of those cops decided to swipe the dog?

"Save it for Judge Day," the Sheriff grunted.

But when the famous court official finally arrived, Jim wanted to laugh out loud. Roscoe Day was a sawed-off little guy with a balding dome and pale gray hair-fringes flapping against his ears. "It's 10 a.m.," he barked at the defendant and the frowning Sheriff Dolan, "and this-here court is now in session. Make a note: I'm thirsty, so this case will be short. Also, the Sheriff tells me the person or persons filing the complaint didn't show up.

"According to the law, I can't hold a full-fledged trial – although the seriousness of your crime surely calls for it. Young feller, I'm sure you consider yourself innocent until proven guilty – but the Sheriff told me different, and his word counts for a lot around here . . . whereas *your* words don't mean nuthin. Are we clear?

"I'm goin' to dismiss the more serious charges, but I am fining you on a general misdemeanor case of disturbing the peace. You're guilty as hell, according to Sheriff Dolan, and that's good enough for me. Any questions?"

Dumbfounded, Clark blurted at him: "Your Honor, if you would only call the 911 operator who took my call, along with the two officers who handled the original complaint ..."

"Overruled," snapped Judge Day. "What the hell do they know? Any testimony they could give would only be hearsay – because they'd simply say what they heard! On the other hand, the Sheriff gave me the *facts* earlier, and I've never known him to lie about facts. You're guilty as charged – and if I hear any back-talk, I'll also fine you for contempt."

"Back talk?" sputtered Clark. "Why, I haven't even been allowed to testify!"

"Okay, I'm warning you," growled the miffed judge. His hair-fringes had gone stiff with outrage. "You try any of that fancy legal bullhockey on me, and you'll spend the rest of the summer behind bars of steel. I'm the law around here, and I demand respect."

He paused for a moment, then spat a gob of brown tobacco juice into a plastic Dunkin' Donuts cup a previous defendant had left behind. "You Easterners are making a big mistake, coming out here and trying to push the people of Montana around, while sicing your huge, vicious animals on them. Those two citizens could have been seriously injured, Mr. Clark. From what I hear, that brute of yours came at them like a rabid cougar!

"Maybe you can learn a lesson from this – while you're paying the $500 fine I'm going to levy on you in this case, along with the one day you already served in jail. And if you can't muster up the dough, you'll do another week in our slammer." He made a deep, burbling sound – was it laughter, or only rising gas? "I hope you enjoyed the hot dogs, Mr. Clark. Had enough of 'em, have you?

"If so, I'd pay the fine, and get on my way if I were you."

Fortunately, the "hanging judge" agreed to accept five of Jim's $100 traveler's checks. So much for Montana justice! But at least he was released, and free to go in search of the loyal Jack.

Leaving the renovated gas station that served as a one-room courthouse, he buttonholed the lawman. "Sheriff Dolan, could I get a word with you?"

The man in the Smoky Bear hat sent him a lazy grin. "What's up, Mr. Clark?"

"Can you help me locate my boat? And where's my dern dog?"

Dolan sighed unhappily. "Now, don't you get to cussin' and cursin', Mr. Clark. In case you didn't know it, using cuss-words is illegal in this town – and I don't want to have to arrest you again. Your canoe is tied up at the foot of the pier where we handcuffed you to the grain bin. I understand from Deputy Lee that your mutt has been guarding the vessel ferociously, and scaring off anybody who comes within a hundred yards of it."

Jim glared at him. "How do I know somebody didn't steal my gear before the dog went on duty?"

Before the sheriff could answer, Deputy Lee interrupted. "Here you go, Mr. Clark," he said as he handled the voyager a sealed envelope. "This here letter will probably make you feel a whole lot easier."

Jim tore open the missive and was startled by the words on the page: "Mister, I canoe often and I was worried about your boat and its contents. Everything you left

aboard is still there. I covered your supplies and your gear with your tarp, then tied it down securely. I'm watching over it until you get here. I'll take you right to it, if you'll just stop by my home ---106A Main Street.

"Sincerely, Joy Price."

Clark could hardly believe his eyes. Maybe these Montana folks weren't all thugs and hoodlums? Afraid to celebrate too early, he hustled across town with his heart in his throat . . . until he was finally knocking on Joy Price's home – actually a tiny apartment located above a delicatessen. Pausing in the yard, Jim noted the flashing creek that ran from her property toward the distant Missouri.

Apparently, she'd paddled his canoe home, after discovering it a day before. But what about Jack? Mystified, he knocked hard on the street entry door for 106A: "Hello, Ms. Joy! Are you home?"

His knock was answered within a few seconds.

Suddenly, he was looking into the deep, almond-hued eyes of a young woman with gleaming, auburn hair. One glance at her high cheekbones and coppery skin told him: Native American. She smiled timidly back at him. *Late 20's*, he told himself, *or maybe early 30's*. Either one was fine with him.

"Hello, ma'am. I'm Jim Clark."

She laughed softly – a musical sound, like a windblown chime. "Please don't call me 'ma'am, Mr. Clark! You make me feel like a spinster schoolmarm!"

"Sorry." He grinned foolishly at her, a scolded sheep. "If you're Joy Price, I want to thank you."

"I am, and you're welcome." She extended one slender hand, and he gathered it in his massive right paw.

"That was mighty good of you to write me the note. I've been having a pretty rough time of it, lately – but the minute I opened your envelope, I started feeling better."

She nodded, and he decided he liked the way her eyes took light each time she smiled. He also liked the tiny nest of golden-brown freckles that rode the bridge of her delicate nose. He liked her name, too. *Joy to the world . . .*

She took her hand back. Slowly. "Please come in, Mr. Clark, and get your dry bag and your clothes. Can I fix you a bite? I've been making chili all day long, and it's just about ready to serve. Baked a loaf of sourdough bread, as well."

"Fantastic," he said. "But only if you'll agree to call me Jim! And the chili sounds terrific. I haven't eaten anything but shrunken hot dogs for the past day and a half."

"Shrunken, Jim?"

"Jailhouse hot dogs. I think they boil them in the washing machines, along with the prisoners' laundry."

She laughed again, and the wind chime tinkled in his ear: *Ping*.

"Okay, watch your step, and follow me."

She led the way up a long, narrow staircase. On each of the big man's steps, the ancient boards groaned in anguish. After a few moments, she looked back over one shoulder: "Say, I'm sorry I didn't put in the note that I also was keeping your dog. I'm sure it would have relieved your mind."

"You've got *Jack* here?" Jim's smile could have illuminated the center stage at Madison Square Garden. But there was no need for Joy to answer; a moment later, the hysterical canine had launched himself skyward, barking loudly with delight at the return of his master.

Clark had gone to one knee, and just in time. "Jack, it's great to see you, buddy!" Their frantic embrace – part bear hug and part flailing, licking tongue – threatened to knock both of them back down the stairs Jim had just climbed.

"Jack, you're the best friend a man could have – and I nearly lost my mind worrying about you!"

The dog zipped through his favorite victory dance, while the young woman looked on in wonder.

A few seconds later, she was guiding Jim to the rear window of the one-room efficiency, where she pointed to *Tripper.* The canoe had been covered and securely lashed to the wooden dock. The backyard creek glittered here and there beneath the mellow, late-afternoon sun. *God's in His heaven, and all's right with the world!*

He turned back to thank his rescuer again, but she was gone. "Chili's on the boil!" she shouted from the kitchen, and Clark took a quick look at the dog. Jack's happiness was written all over his doggy grin: *Chow at last! Hey, I haven't eaten anything since the double- cheeseburger those two jerks interrupted at the campsite!*

For the first time in what seemed like a year, Jim's felt a current of hope go surging through his chest. *Life is good!* What was it about this Indian woman and her chili pot that made him feel so splendid? Pausing for a moment, he surveyed the simple but elegant room in which she lived. He liked the way she had decorated

this place with lots of curtains and lace and a quilt on the bed. Heck, he even liked the way it smelled – that whiff of aged cedar, with a tang of coffee and apples floating somewhere along the edges.

They sat at a simple wooden table covered with a red-checkered cloth. The meal was simple, but it tasted like a banquet to Jim; each time he scooped up a helping of the rich, meaty chili or buttered another steaming, crusty slab of the sourdough, he wanted to slap the table and roar at her: "Best grub I ever ate!"

She had stopped eating now. She was watching him carefully. "So tell me, Mr. . . . Jim: What brings you into our fair county – and how in the world did you ever end up in Sheriff Dolan's slammer?"

He grinned at her. Something strange was in the air; the curtains flapped merrily in the window, and bright shadows danced across the floor. "I was camping near the river," said Jim with a chuckle, "and a couple of minor thugs came after me and Jack. I reported it . . . but instead of locking up the bad guys, they made me spend 36 hours eating rubber hot dogs in Judge Day's pokey."

He put his spoon back on the plate. "I was mad as heck, back in the jailhouse – but not now. Meeting you was worth the wait!"

She wrinkled her nose, and the freckles scattered everywhere. "I suspect it's the chili you've flipped for, Jim." *Ping.* "You know, this batch didn't turn out half-bad!"

"I'll say."

"You know what I like about chili?"

"What's that?"

He was leaning toward her now; the curtains flapped and flapped.

"You can make a big pot of it, all at once – and it only gets better from day to day! I like simple things like that, don't you?"

He nodded slowly at her. He was concentrating on the amber specks in her almond eyes. *Joy to the world*. . . "You bet," he said at last. He felt as if he were drifting along the bottom of a green, sunlit pool. His movements had become strangely effortless, entirely natural. "I guess it's why I fell in love with canoeing," he said quietly. "When you're on that river, all the complications fall away. Everything is simplified. An oak leaf floating on the water – it's simply an oak leaf, that's all."

She was watching him intently. "On the river," he continued, "little things become magnified in a wonderful way. Tree shadows, for example. I've spent entire afternoons just staring at the shadows of trees." Weirdly, his eyes had suddenly filled with tears. "I don't know . . . you must think I'm a major-league nut case."

She laughed, and the room shook with music. "Not at all, Jim. Don't forget, I'm half-Native American." She looked up at him impishly, then wrinkled her nose again. "We specialize in oak leaves and shadows!" She turned away then, and gave her long, auburn hair a gentle shake. "But seriously, I'm curious . . . why in the world would a guy from Baltimore decide to break the North American endurance record for river-canoeing?"

He thought about it. "Good question," he stammered after a bit. "I guess the only honest answer is – they're paying me! Do you know *Wild Rivers* Magazine?"

"Sure. I read it almost every month. Don't forget, I've got a thing for paddling, myself."

He nodded. "Well, a couple of months ago, the executive editor phoned me with a proposal. How would I like to make the Guinness Book of Records? I didn't believe him at first. I said: 'What do I have to do – jump off the Sears Tower without a parachute?'

"But the guy just laughed. 'All you gotta do is canoe the longest river in America – non-stop and alone. If you make it in 90 days, you win the jackpot: $100,000. If you *don't* make it, we pay you our standard fee for a 5,000-word, first-person feature. Ten K, to be exact.'"

She shook her head. Not once but twice. "Jim Clark, you have to be the craziest canoe-jockey in the West. Do you know what happens to you, after a couple of weeks out there on the Big Muddy?"

"Nope. Will the alligators eat me?" He was buttering another slice of her sourdough – he was addicted for sure. "Look, I just figured, what the hey, I'm gonna get paid for the feature, anyway. What's the diff? Maybe I'll get lucky and grab the brass ring, while I'm at it."

"I see." She still looked pretty skeptical.

Jim hesitated and decided to risk a little bit of honesty. "Okay, I suppose there was more to it than just the Guinness thing. The truth is, I was ready for a break from my situation in Baltimore."

She raised one delicate eyebrow. "Your situation?"

Jim frowned. *Oh, nuts! What to say next?* "Well . . . you know. Life in the city – the traffic, the noise, the pollution, the crime . . . in the summertime, it's like being locked up inside a filthy laundromat in the heart of Calcutta. And I had some personal issues, as well."

This time she didn't speak. Expressionless, she was waiting for more.

"Okay," said Jim. Why hadn't he kept his mouth shut? "The thing is, I was living with this woman – an interior decorator named Veronica – and her seven-year-old boy. Henry. Jack lived with us, too."

Joy blinked steadily. "Married, you mean?"

"No, no," he stammered. "Not *married.* No way! Although . . . what I mean is, I . . . I wasn't ready."

"I see."

"Not that she wasn't a great lady, mind you! But something got in the way of marriage. It just didn't feel right, if you know what I mean."

She was frowning at him now. "Were there conflicts? Is that it? Misunderstandings between you and Veronica?"

He picked up a crust of bread and stared at it, as if the crust might provide an answer. "We had lots of fun together, but I just couldn't handle the idea of marriage. I'd tried it once, you see – and things hadn't gone too well. A nasty divorce, and she took the kid. I wound up living at the Central YMCA, drinking low-end vodka out of a Styrofoam cup."

Joy reached over and patted his hand. "You poor guy."

He pulled the hand away in a flash, as if he feared being bitten. "Hey, no need to feel sorry for me. I did fine! Had another girlfriend within two weeks. But the experience did leave a mark. That's how I see it, anyway. I've always felt like I was . . . *branded*, somehow. Branded by that early divorce." He sighed wearily, then shook his head. He laughed, but it was very faint, as if the laughter couldn't get out of his throat. "There was a popular song in those days – but that's been 25 years ago." Suddenly fearful, he shot her a look: "Am I weirding you out with all this stuff, Joy? Be honest."

Now *she* was laughing. "Not hardly, Mr. Clark. Not hardly. Wait until you hear about *my* nightmare." She reached for his hand again and this time he let her have it. "I like listening to you, Jim, regardless of the words. I guess I just like the sound. Go ahead. What was that popular song?"

He looked at her for a moment, then surprised himself by actually singing out loud:

Young and soft and tan and lovely,

The girl from Ipanema goes walking –

And when she passes,

Each guy she passes goes . . . aaaaaaah!

Neither of them moved. The white curtains flapped and flapped in the window. Joy's voice had dropped, almost to a whisper. "Is that how you thought of her, that first wife?"

"Something like that." Jim realized that he was holding his breath.

She picked up his rough, calloused hand, brought it to her lips.

"Jim," she said. "Jim, Jim."

He waited. He saw how the late afternoon sun lay in bands of gold across the Formica sink. He could hear a blue jay calling harshly, somewhere in the distance. *Graaaakkk!* Her breath was warm against his fingers. "Listen," she said after a few moments. "Let's not talk too much, you and me? Let's be different than we were with the others."

He nodded. "All right, then. I hear you, Joy. I'm tired of all the talk, myself."

A car passed on the street outside. For a few seconds, the radio blared an old Everly Brothers hit from the sixties: *Never knew what I missed, until I kissed ya!* They listened to the sound of the tires hissing against the asphalt, then fading, fading. . . .

Somehow, both of them had risen to their feet. Her breath was against his neck now, and it was moving faster. He looked down and watched the shifting light tremble against her hair. A green, sun-bright pool, located somewhere at the bottom of time . . .

They glided across the sun-warmed floorboards toward her bed. He would be very gentle with her, for all his strength; some instinct of wisdom told him to move slowly, carefully in everything he did. Soon they were stretched out on the pale yellow comforter. He looked into her eyes and saw a world there – the promise of another world than the dark and frightening place he had always known.

"Look, Joy –"

But she had covered his mouth with one slender hand. "If we don't talk," she said calmly, "we won't destroy the moment."

He put his mouth on hers, and he began to hear the surf rolling up the beach. One great breaker unfolded after the next, each one bearing the promise of some distant, unimaginable thunder. Time collapsed, the air went red and fragrant, and they remained deaf to the blue jay who still called and called from his distant tree: *graaaakkk! Graaaakk!*

He was on the river again, riding the surge of restless currents, being carried against his will toward some inescapable, inevitable collision that he knew would change him forever. Yet he didn't mind. Didn't mind at all. He watched his paddle bite into the green-glass surface of the Muddy Mo: *River, river, carry me on home, carry me all the way home. . . .*

Locked in each other's arms, they finally slept.

*

He awoke to find the bedroom full of shadow, and cold sweat bathing his forehead. What was that sound? That hollow thumping? That rattling, banging noise – was it inside the bedroom, or merely inside his head? He lurched up to a sitting position, then stared wildly around the layout. Nothing. Only Joy sleeping quietly beside him, her breath rising and falling peacefully . . .

Dirt.

That was the sound. Dirt falling on a mahogany casket. He'd been dreaming again – dreaming of his dead brother, Johnny Clark, the Marine Corps hero of Khe Sanh. Dreaming of that long-ago afternoon on which the old priest had intoned the ancient rite of passage:

Ashes to ashes, and dust to dust –

And with his miniature shovel, the cleric had thrown a handful of dirt into the open grave. And the bit of earth had rattled against the box in which Johnny would lie buried forever. *Vanitas, vanitatum*, chanted the old Irish priest, *all is vanity that liveth under the sun.*

That morning at Arlington Cemetery had changed Jim Clark forever, and he knew it. Standing near the pile of red clay and watching Father Mulcahy sprinkle holy water into the grave, he'd felt the last of his boyhood Catholic faith evaporating. Religion – what a joke. The world was war – not sheep and a loving shepherd! The reality was dog eat dog, not love thy neighbor! He kept remembering the times he'd spent with Johnny at the Dairy Queen on Padonia Road, his upper lip mustachioed with strawberry milkshake –

Or Johnny swinging at a hanging curve ball during a Little League game, and driving the pitch all the way to the fence –

Or Johnny, five years older than Jim, learning how to mount a horse at their uncle's place out near the Gunpowder Falls: "Ride 'em, you rodeo cowboy!" And then reading his letters from boot camp, at Parris Island: "I shot 211 on the Rifle Range this morning, and the D.I. grabbed me down at the Target Line, told me, 'Well, Private, at least you're not a total screw-up!'"

And then the letters from Khe Sanh, at the height of the 1967 siege: "Jim, don't let them feed you a line about this war. We're doing a hell of a job over here – we're holding the line against some mighty tough *hombres*, believe you me." And then that rainy afternoon the next January, right in the middle of the Tet Offensive, when the gray Ford sedan had pulled up in front of the house and the two warrant officers had climbed out and trudged gloomily toward their front porch –

"What's the matter, honey? You look like you've seen a ghost!"

He whirled toward her. Joy was up on her elbows, her youthful face a mask of frowning fear. "What is it, Jim? You scared me. You were making this moaning sound – I thought you might be getting ready to scream!"

He tried to smile. Did his best. But his lips were twisted strangely, and when the words finally emerged, they were full of stammers and empty air. "I'm okay, babe. Just shaking off the cobwebs. Bad dream, I guess."

She was studying him carefully. "You don't look so hot, sweetie. Why don't you hang out with me tonight, right here at the *Maison Price*? I'll make you a French omelet you won't believe – and we can drink some wine and tell each other some lies."

But she saw that he was frowning, and alarmed. "Don't worry, I won't lock you up! Jack can stay out in the kitchen, and the two of you can be on your way first thing in the morning. Hey, I can even help you – I know the river around here inside and out." Her eyes widened and a smile briefly touched her red mouth. "Shoot, maybe I could even go *with* you, at least for part of the trip."

She reached across the bed to stroke his chin. "If I paddled my own canoe, would that break the rules of your contest?"

He had to laugh, in spite of himself. "Jeez, Joy – you sure move quick, don't you? If I'm not careful, *you'll* wind up collecting that prize money in three months."

He chuckled again, and reached for her toes. But she was serious: "Jim, I haven't had a chance to explain this yet, but I'm an officer in the Montana Natural Resources Department and I've had training and experience in photography, dictation and canoeing. I'm also pretty strong. I can paddle very well, and I'm tough enough to portage a canoe. I have a leave of absence from my job now."

Clarke thought it over for at least five seconds. Who could resist having a beauty like this one in the next canoe? "Well, I *am* required to paddle solo to St. Louis by contract," he mused aloud, "but I sure don't want to say goodbye. Maybe we could do a side-by-side in separate solo boats for at least part of the trip, since you're on leave from work?"

Jim was trying not to be too pushy. Having driven Veronica off with his endless activities and compulsive outdoor rambles, he was fearful of spooking the half-naked beauty beside him. Strange to say, he hardly knew this woman – and yet he found himself hungry to be with her, night and day and all the time in between. "Joy," he said at last, "I think I must be the luckiest guy in the entire State of Montana, right now. I spend a day and a half in the local lockup – and then wind up in the arms of the most gorgeous female on the Great Plains!

"Of *course,* you can come along on the trip – I wouldn't have it any other way!"

Although he'd just met this amazing woman, Jim already felt as if he'd known her forever. Why not enjoy the pleasures of canoeing along with the soaring pleasures of her embrace? Was he being insensitive, taking up with another woman so soon after the loss of Veronica? But wait a minute – Veronica had dropped *him*,

hadn't she? Why should he be feeling so much guilt, after being dumped for another guy?

Hoping to resolve his doubts by acting – a familiar behavior pattern for him – he turned back to the new woman in his life: "Okay, Joy, quiz time. Have you got a canoe, a sleeping bag and some camping equipment?"

She frowned unhappily at him. "Sorry . . . but when I left the ranch two months ago, my partner refused to allow me to take our canoe and equipment. However, there's an outfitter here in town who sells and rents new and used canoes. Why don't I just buy one? "

"Sounds good to me," said Jim. "I always carry an extra, smaller tent for storage and we can both sleep in my larger tent. Provided that you promise not to sexually assault me, that is."

She aimed an elbow at his ribcage, but he ducked it.

They embraced, and Jim realized that he'd never felt happier in his life. He was certain that he'd be happier and far more effective in his journalism work and in paddling the long miles, if Joy accompanied him. He also enjoyed the prospect of teaming up with a competent companion who owned a feminine touch. "Say, this just might work out, Joy! If you're willing to take the risks – and I'm sure you know all about them, after living in Montana – then so am I. But you'll need a warm sleeping bag, heavy socks and a cap – because it will get pretty chilly out there on that water."

She shot him a glowing smile, and he turned to the capering Jack. "Okay, fella, whaddya think? Should we let her do most of the paddling – maybe even let her tow us some – while we just settle back and enjoy the river, the woods and the wildlife?"

Good plan, Jim. I'd rather look at her any day than at you. As if on cue, the canine prankster held out his left front paw to his new companion.

Jim was laughing out loud. "Look at that, Joy. Jim is eager to have you along – he knows you'll be far less boring than I am. I predict that he'll spend most of the time stretched out in *your* canoe."

Jack snickered loudly. *Most of the time? How about ALL the time, Big Guy?*

Joy laughed out loud, but then became very businesslike: 'Okay, guys, the bank is located in the first block and the outfitter backs up to the stream, right beside it. Let's get cracking – I can't wait to get started on this epic journey!"

They went to work. While the Indian maiden made preparations to pack her belongings for storage before joining him, Jim hustled down to the bank and cashed a couple of his Traveler's Checks. He was also careful to note the signs on the window of the outfitter's store: "Traveler's Checks and major credit cards accepted for purchase."

Moving fast, he was back in the apartment within 20 minutes. Together, he and Joy hurried back to the outfitter's busy emporium, where they spent the best part of an hour shopping for another canoe and additional supplies.

Jim pointed to a sleek cruiser suspended on racks above their head. "How do you like this used canoe, Joy? Our trip-leader in my Baltimore canoe club has one of these, and he says it works just great."

Responding, Joy lifted one end of the boat, then smacked its hull several times. Jim had to laugh: "You look like a used-car customer kicking a spare tire!" But she liked the way the streamlined hull responded, and they decided to go ahead with the purchase of the Camper canoe. Along with the boat, they picked up the required license – along with two sturdy paddles made of mountain ash, a kayak paddle, and some vital equipment and supplies. The list included one large and one smaller dry bag, a small cooler, a life jacket, a helmet, some painter lines and a dipper with sponge.

Joy also stocked up on clothing, camping gear, sun-block and insect repellent, while Jim stood nearby, firing off wisecracks: "Good idea, on that bug repellant – where we're headed, the mosquitoes are bigger than Winnebagos!"

She slapped at him, but he managed to duck the blow.

Fortunately, they were able to paddle *Camper* back to Joy's apartment, where they chained and locked it up next to *Tripper*. "Now listen here," chortled Jim, "we haven't talked about food. Nothing – and I mean nothing – is as important as food, when you're out there paddling the Mo all day. We need some of those juicy Montana steaks for the trip . . . and I could use one myself about now, Miz Joy!"

No sooner said, than done. They bought several frozen eight-ounce steaks, along with some insulation wrappings, bagels, some powdered potatoes and two 12-ounce fillet beefsteaks and potatoes for their supper that night. These last savory items they obtained from the downstairs deli – where the owner, a slender young woman with enormous green eyes named Angela, became even more excited than

Joy about the upcoming trip. "I envy you, Joy. Imagine spending a month or two on the water with a handsome dude like this one!"

Then, digging a friendly elbow into Jim's ribs: "Just be sure you don't get so caught up in the hanky-panky that you capsize the canoe!" And they left the store with her raucous laughter still ringing in their ears.

Jim and Joy returned to the apartment, then got down to the serious business of broiling steaks and baking potatoes. Before the food was half-cooked, however, they found themselves back on her bed and lost once again in the fiery sea of their growing lust for each other. Joy was without shame. Panting and moaning, she wriggled under his touch like a school of flashing, panicked minnows – then suddenly climbed on top and began to undulate with the single-minded intensity of some intoxicated Egyptian belly dancer. . . .

They remembered the steaks just in time – "Fire in the broiler!" – and leapt from the bed, shrieking. Naked as cavorting seals, they raced into the kitchen and barely managed to rescue their feast from the licking flames. Twenty minutes later, they were sitting back at the red-checkered table, feeding each other bites of steak and potato and salad, and dreaming of the new Life of Total Freedom that would soon be theirs. "Joy, if it gets any better than this, it would have to be Heaven!"

She nodded and smiled, and then fed him a mushroom with her fork. "I can't believe I'm shacked up with a jailbird! What would my dear old momma say, if she knew that you walked straight over here from the pokey and then poked *me*?"

They roared. They ate slabs of strawberry-slathered pound cake drenched in vanilla ice cream. They drank steaming cups of *Cappuccino* while Elton John sang

about the "Tiny Dancer" on her stereo, and Jim pounded on the rattling table as if it were a musician's drum. Then, right at twilight, a mighty thunderstorm broke around their ears. They sat on the porch and reveled in the sweep of gusting wind, the curtain of cleansing rain that blasted across the creek to drench the deli and the surrounding cars. "Don't you just love this kind of weather?" Joy hollered above the clatter made by a wind-powered trashcan, as it rolled along beneath their porch.

"You bet!" shouted Clark. "Wait until we catch our first storm out on the river. Nothing like it, Joy. I've seen four-foot waves more than once, during river squalls. And the rain slashes at you like flying gravel. It's fabulous . . . provided you know how to find shelter quickly."

She eased across the space between them, settled onto his broad lap. "Jim, I haven't been this happy in 15 years."

He didn't say anything. Just smiled at her. Why break the spell of the moment? But a tiny anxiety had begun to nag somewhere at the back of his brain. *Veronica*. What if she changed her mind about "the new guy?" What if she called out to him suddenly, out of the blue: "Jim, I need your help; you have to come now!"

Had Joy already shattered that old world forever? If Clark had to, would he be able to find his way back home? And where *was* that home, anyway?

"How do you like your eggs?" Jim was preparing a huge and delicious breakfast of eggs, beefsteaks and toast.

"Over and easy – just like I am with you, Jim," she laughed from the other room, as she wrapped sandwiches in insulated baggies for their lunch on the water.

Jim chuckled at her sense of humor. Within 15 minutes, they'd downed the nourishing breakfast, grabbed the dry bags and headed down the stairs.

"I'll run down to deli, Jim, and wrap things up with Angela. I'll also leave money with her for the next two weeks' rent, as well as the keys to the apartment. I really appreciate Angela – she's been just great. She offered to store my boxes and other personal items for me. I've promised to call or write her as soon as we can, and I also left your cell phone number with her."

Joy gave him a wistful smile. "You know, Jim, Angela told me she was going to miss me. She says I've become a very dear friend . . . and that my kind is badly needed in this town, quote-unquote!"

Jim nodded. "She sounds like a great pal, Joy."

They packed Joy's boat first – and Jim was careful to set her up with a comfortable kneeling pad to be used whenever they went through rapids. Then they tied in the dry bags, dipper, helmet and camera, water jug and snack bag containing snacks, sun block and insect repellent. Joy also lashed the kayak paddle to the thwarts and the two painter lines to the front-and-back grab handles.

Watching her work, Jim was impressed. When the last detail had been attended to, she picked up a paddle and waggled it at him. "Watch me in a couple of paddling techniques, Jim, and let me know if I need any adjustment." A moment later, she was going through her paces as a veteran canoeist. Once again, Jim found himself impressed. This feisty female was obviously quite good at balancing (trimming) the load in her boat, and she was no slouch when it came to the muscle-power required for effective paddling.

Smiling, he watched her demonstrate her strength in the forward-and-back strokes, the draws and the pries. Getting the hang of paddling solo with nothing more than a dead weight in the front seat would take some time, he was sure.

All things considered, Jim couldn't remember being happier or more at peace than he was at that moment. "I love being with you, Joy!" he blurted at her . . . and she responded by setting down her paddle and taking his hand.

"Jim, I promise not to get syrupy, but this is from the heart: I've never met anybody quite like you. I'm 29 years old, and I thought I'd seen everything. But what we have isn't just good – it's off the charts!"

He laughed easily, and reached for his own paddle. Suddenly, he wasn't missing Veronica as much. Why waste time fretting over the past, when a brand-new sun had just arisen in the middle of his present? He suspected that the ache for Veronica and Henry would return soon enough – but right now, he simply wanted to bask in the mellow, healing sunlight that poured from a very good-looking young woman named Joy Price.

Will you quit lolly-gagging around and get this show on the road?

He looked down to find the faithful Lab pacing in tight circles between the two canoes, and obviously ticked off.

"Jack!" he roared at his shipmate, "I'm sorry . . . we forgot all about you – almost left without you!"

Oh, yeah? Your loss, pal. Who do you think has gotten you this far, if not Good Old Jack?

They spent the rest of the day in easygoing practice sessions. Joy worked on her strokes until she became comfortable paddling solo. Soon she and Jim were ooohing and aaahing over the majestic scenery, while their two canoes drifted effortlessly

past plunging waterfalls and cliffs of wind-scoured granite. "I'm counting the hours until we set up camp, Joy!"

"Same here," cried his elated partner. "But watch out for those rocks at one o'clock, or we'll never get there in one piece!"

The hours passed slowly. Skimming along the surface, they marveled at the porcelain-blue sky above, the pale green water below. "Look there," hollered Joy, pointing with her paddle toward a floating log that carried five baby snapping turtles. "It's a *nursery* for turtles, Jim! I wonder why their momma isn't with them?" But even as she spoke, a dark, oval shadow emerged from beneath the log, with her beak snapping loudly: Momma had been riding herd on her brood, after all.

Twenty-five miles west of Helena, they passed a series of gleaming sand bars. Here the shallows were patrolled by stately great blue herons – stilt-legged creatures with knife-like beaks that probed the silt relentlessly in search of frogs, minnows and water bugs. The creatures were gorgeous to look at, but ruthlessly efficient; Joy looked away more than once, as their frog-victims were swallowed whole, while wriggling frantically.

Somewhere near the middle of the day, they stopped and enjoyed a half-hour respite from paddling. Joy broke out the water jug and the sandwiches she'd been carrying in her small cooler. They sat on a flat rock, bodies touching, and shared a few quick hugs and stolen kisses.

Once back on the river, each was aware of the other, and not concentrating on paddling. "I sure do like your moves, Joy," he joked. Like Jim, she was now

discovering that paddling a 16-foot canoe from the stern is quite different from paddling with a partner. But it didn't take her long to learn the "J" stroke quickly from either side. This classical canoe maneuver helps keep the canoe straight – without requiring the paddle to continuously be switched from side to side of the boat.

Joy was soon adept at the move. And Jim saw how her bra-less breasts pushed against her denim blouse, with the nipples outlined teasingly through the fabric. "You're looking mighty good, sweet."

"Your moves aren't bad, either," Joy responded. "But I bet you're so tired from paddling that you couldn't get it up right now, even if we were stretched out on the river bank."

He laughed out loud. "Try me."

She peered at him. "You're kidding."

"Not at all. Pull over beneath that overhanging grove of willows, and I mean this instant, young lady. We'll see who can get it up!" With a series of hard sweeps, they zipped easily into the tree-shade and beached. Pulling an easy-to-reach ground cloth from one of his dry bags, he stepped onto the gravel and sought her hand. Together, they spread the cloth and grasped each other hungrily. A moment later they were tearing at each other with gusto.

Jim chuckled with delight, as she nibbled at his defenseless ear. "Say, Joy – do you think we might be over-sexed?"

"Naah . . . I think it must be something in the water!"

Once back in the boat, they were surprised to discover that their lovemaking had actually energized them, rather than tiring them out. Paddles flashing, they zoomed along the river almost without effort – and they logged the 35 miles required by Jim's daily schedule without even breaking a sweat.

Moving quickly, Jim set up the two-person, double-side room and the storage tent. Then he dispatched a quick e-mail to Jay Spader at *Rivers:*

Ran into some unavoidable delays, and they won't be easy to make up. But things are going quite well, all things considered – will send you regular updates as I move down the Mo.

But he was careful not to mention Joy, or the fact that he was now traveling with a partner.

"Will chicken fillets be okay, Jim, or have you been spoiled on beef filets?" He grinned and shot her a thumbs-up. While he was doing his report and taking some notes on the River, Joy cooked chicken and vegetables over the campfire, using the portable grill. They each had a small cup of coffee with the meal. "Let's not absorb too much caffeine," Jim warned her. "We don't want to spend a whole lot of time roaming around in the dark, looking for a bathroom – not with all those black bears on the prowl out here!"

Joy was studying his face carefully. "You're kidding, right?"

He chuckled. "I wish. They're not too aggressive, when it comes to human beings – but I wouldn't want to startle one in the wee hours before dawn."

She nodded slowly, and Jack made a small growling sound somewhere in the back of his throat: *What a wimp! Hey, they're only bears, for chrissakes – I say bring 'em on!*

As soon as they'd finished their java, they went to work placing food scraps, toothpaste and soap and other aromatics in a tight metal container tied high in a tree. So far, so good. Yet they remained a tad nervous. They realized the odds were high that mountain lions and bears would give them a wide berth because of Jack's presence. . . .

Probably. But they also knew that if a bear gets hungry enough, anything can happen. Only a few days before, in fact, Jim had been amazed to hear a news story on the portable radio about some badly rattled campers in northern Montana. While sitting in their cabin at dawn on a recent morning, the five trout fishermen had gotten the shock of their lives – when a huge bear came crashing through a window right into their kitchen!

The fishermen fled in panic, but the bear remained calm and focused. Ignoring their terrified screams, he walked thoughtfully around the table . . . pausing only to paw-scoop the slices of bacon and the hotcakes still cooling on their plates! Then he tore several cupboard doors from their hinges, and went on to devour a five-pound box of cane sugar and a giant sack of pancake flour.

Delicious! Burping contentedly, the 600-pound behemoth had strolled back to the window . . . and then gracefully exited through the smashed frame. The bear-invasion had lasted less than 90 seconds, and yet the kitchen was completely devastated.

Smiling as he reached the end of his story, Jim took Joy's lovely hand. "Honey Bun, I've got a riddle for you. All set?"

"Fire away." She was watching the moonlight glimmer on a log, perched just outside their open tent flap.

"Where does an 600-pound grizzly bear eat his dinner?"

She thought about it. "Okay . . . I give. Where?"

"Why . . . anywhere he *wants* to!" And once again, the big man howled with delighted laughter.

Their loving-making that night was quieter, yet somehow deeper and more intense. Lost inside her voluptuous body, Jim found himself adrift among endless sea caverns – vast, underwater spaces where coral glittered on sun-washed reefs and mermaids curved through waves of shimmering light. What was it Shakespeare had said about life and love and human sexual desire, in that ultimate sea fantasy,

***The Tempest*?**

We are such stuff as dreams are made on,

and our little life is rounded with a sleep!

They dozed for an hour or two, then woke to the sounds of distant thunder. A spring storm, far upriver, rattled faintly out over the water and then moved off. Lightning forked once or twice and faded. They listened to the chatter of the crickets, the solemn cry of a wandering loon. The air smelled of river weed, wet pine, black mud.

"Jim, are you awake?"

"Sure am, babe."

"Are you enjoying all of this as much as I am?"

"Probably more. Remember, I came here from Beautiful Downtown Baltimore."

"City life?"

"In spades. Imagine being locked up inside a giant Dipsty Dumpster with thousands of exhaust-spewing cars. Imagine the summertime pollution – 98 in the shade, and you're breathing asphalt fumes and scorched creosote. Imagine the crime, the drugs, the blaring boom boxes on every street corner. Not fun. Honest to God, I hope I never see that place again!"

She had begun to wiggle her toes against the calf of his nearest leg. "Poor baby. You know, I never imagined that two people could fit together so well. It's like we were cut from a single mold, then attached to each other at the head and shoulders. Do you think we'll be able to keep it up?"

He smiled and scratched his nose. "Sure, why not? The best part about being out here on the river is that you can keep everything simple. You paddle your canoe, you build your campsite, you eat, you sleep."

The toes wiggled faster against his leg. "Hey, don't forget that *other* thing we do."

"How could I? Making love to you is like plugging into a 5,000-volt battery-pack. Pow! If we keep at it much longer, somebody's going to get electrocuted. I wake up each morning totally exhausted – and totally excited about what the new day will bring. And it's all happening because of you, Joy."

She was snuggling against him now, half-asleep. "Jim, I feel like Adam and Eve, before they made the mistake of touching that apple. The river seems so clean, so pure. All that sunlight, and the wind in your face – it makes you wonder why human beings would ever want to pave a highway, or build a shopping mall, or start a war."

They awoke to find a loud-mouthed blue jay making a racket no more than ten yards from their sleeping bags.

Joy reached across the space between them and patted his cheek. Then she winced. "Ouch, you need a shave."

He grinned up at her. "Actually, I was thinking I might never shave again, Joy. Could you handle it if I changed my name to 'Bushy Beard' and simply threw all my Shick blades in the river?"

"No way! I didn't sign on for the Mountain Man, Jim." She waved a tiny fist under his nose. "You see, I happen to like your smile. It's the best thing about you – and I don't want to see you hide it beneath a lumberjack's beard!"

Chuckling, he crawled up to one knee. "Okay, you win. Tell you what – I'll get the fire started for some oatmeal, and I'll break out my trusty razor at the same time. How'd you sleep, tiger?"

She made a comical growling sound. "Like a pampered baby, big man. You wore me out on that riverbank, lemme tell you. Think you could do it again today?"

He winked at her. "Does it snow in northern Minnesota in the wintertime? Does a wild bear lick his chops over the honey pot? If I were you, I'd stay out of arm's reach – or you could end up flat on your back, kicking at the sky."

"Promises, promises."

They both laughed, and then set to work. While Jim brought the oatmeal to a boil, Joy got busy taking down the tents. She was an expert camper, as it turned out, and needed very little help. After gobbling up the hot cereal, they sprayed each other liberally with sun block and insect repellent. A few moments later, they went to work removing the protective tarps on the canoes. The heavy canvas was wet with dew. As they settled into their fragile boats, Jim took a deep, luxurious breath.

"God, but I love that smell. River mud and dew-soaked pine – it's like ambrosia must have been for those Greek gods."

"Same here," said Joy. "Hey, I think you oughta write an article about the smells to be found on the river! Think about it. Mud, weed, fish, sun-baked pine needles, flowers – the works. They say that odors are the key to memory, Jim. Why not call your book: *Odors Along The Mighty Mo!* You'd have a bestseller, for sure."

The two canoes were launched, by now, with a still-yawning Jack sitting tall in the bow of Jim's craft. They moved off slowly through the rising mist. "Odors of the Mo!" boomed Jim, and hooted with laughter. "Joy, you never cease to amaze me. Before this trip is over, I predict that *you'll* be running Spader's magazine!"

Most of the day was devoted to speed-paddling – but they also called frequent "time outs," during which they used the dippers for giant water-fights that left them soaked and gasping.

There were quieter moments, however: brief interludes of peace and calm in which the current rippled gently against the hulls and the river birds hovered

silently above their gliding passage. Clark found himself chuckling out loud at times, utterly content to live in the moment.

"Look, Jim." She was pointing with her paddle at a bright cluster of flowers on the riverbank. "Don't you just adore the mountain laurel blooms all along here?"

"Sure do, babe. Talk about beautiful! My guidebook says most of the flowers on this stretch of the Mo will bloom in late May or early June." He shook his head in wonder. "This is what the garden must have looked like, before those two idiots took a bite of the apple!"

She nodded and then laughed. "You oughta get a look at yourself, Jim. You're sopping wet, and I'm totally dry!"

He grinned at her. "And your point?"

"My point is that I'm obviously a better water-fight marksman than you'll ever be."

"Oh, yeah?" His right hand shot out, scooped up a puddle of river and then flung it at her. "Wake up, sweets. Can't you see that I've been letting you win? And why? It's easy – I look so much better in a wet T-shirt than you do."

"Yeah, right." She was smirking at him.

"And there's another reason. As long as I stay wet, I stay cool. Which means that I can keep myself – barely – from jumping your bones on the riverbank. Keep dousing me will you, or we'll never get to our campsite."

But they arrived soon enough, and settled in for another unforgettable night beneath the stars. They feasted on garlic-broiled beef fillet, washed down with hot tea. They enjoyed feeding each other bites of the food, followed by kisses. And they

could hardly wait to crawl in the tent . . . where they could escape from the jumbo-sized mosquitoes, while also wrapping themselves securely in each other's arms.

"Aren't these zipped-together sleeping bags great?" whispered Joy. "You know, skin-to-skin all night cuddling is something I've never experienced before."

"Same here," smiled Jim.

"I wonder why not," said Joy.

Her companion thought about it. "We're *skin*-deprived, Joy!"

She reached over, swatted the top of his head. "Stop kidding around. I'm serious. Do you ever feel like you've missed out on an important part of life? The intimacy part? Like maybe you've never been really close to another human being because you were too afraid of what would happen?"

Jim reflected. "Say, you *are* serious. And you're asking *way* too many questions. Weren't you the one who suggested that we stop analyzing things, and just enjoy the ride?"

She nodded. "*Touche*, Monsieur Clark. Forget the seriousness – how about telling me a chilling ghost story, while I watch the fire."

"A ghost story?" He fell silent for a moment, and she noticed it. "What's the matter, Jim?"

"Oh . . . nothing." He looked away. There were plenty of ghosts in his past. There was a ghost named Johnny, for example, who had died in the middle of a mortar barrage. But this wasn't the time. This wasn't the place. He'd tell her about his brother later, when he knew her a little better.

"Okay . . . here we go. It was a dark and stormy night . . . "

She nestled against him. The red fire crackled against the pine logs, and the glittering stars hung motionless above their campsite. A hoot owl called through the darkness and he felt her shiver with the sound. The night was quiet; the world was at peace.

But tomorrow would come soon enough. It always does. And what would the daylight bring?

*

"How do you like this beautiful scenery?" Joy shouted over the rushing sound of the current. They were in the middle of their third day out. "The vegetation has changed, Jim. And how about those snow-peaked mountains in the background? We could make a fortune in the picture-postcard business, if we decided to settle down here!"

"Tell it, babe. I want to hear all the details – as soon as we get past these ragged rocks!" Frowning with concentration, the big man leaned forward and manipulated his paddle for all it was worth. The two canoes threaded their way through the churning foam – while Jack glared angrily from his perch in the bow of Jim's slender craft: ***Has it occurred to you that I might be getting thoroughly soaked up here, dorkus?***

"Hang on, Jack-o!" roared the captain at his peeved mate. "Another half hour or so, and we'll be cruising through clear water!"

Oh, yeah? Another half hour of this routine, and I'll have double pneumonia.

In spite of Jack's continuing complaints, the trio soon eased out of the whitewater and into a smoother stretch. After pulling the boats ashore, they spent the better part of the day hiking around and taking pictures of the White Cliffs – a deep, rugged gorge where the Missouri had cut through the sedimentary floor of an ancient sea. Steep, eroded cliffs reached a depth of nearly 1,000 feet, and their scarred surfaces formed a map of 10 million years of geological history.

Joy was beside herself with the beauty of the scene. "My Gosh, Jim, look at what the wind and water have done." She pointed with her paddle at the massive crags of sandstone looming everywhere above them. Like castles from a majestic fairy tale, the gnarled monoliths moaned and whined fitfully beneath the shifting wind.

"Unbelievable," said Jim. "Montana! You know, Joy, we haven't even begun to scratch the surface of this amazing State."

Joy turned to face him. "I remember you telling me how you hiked across Glacier National Park for that outdoors magazine. I'll bet it couldn't hold a candle to the White Cliffs."

"They're both pretty amazing, I'd say."

She was shaking her head. "Tell me, could you see yourself as a Montanan, Jim?"

He didn't hesitate. "You bet I could. This is wonderful country, Joy. Some of it's pretty wild, but it's all beautiful, and it's the real deal. This is the place to go, if you want to get away from it all."

After a few more prayerful moments, they boarded the two canoes in silence and set sail. An hour passed . . . and then the two watercraft began to pick up speed. Jack's ears had begun to tremble and twitch; his radar had locked onto something important up ahead.

The heard it before they saw it: The deep bass rumble of approaching rapids. *Big* rapids . . . as in "Class III, Better-Fasten-Your Seatbelt Rapids."

But Jim didn't seem very alarmed. "Okay, Jack, better settle back and prepare for some turbulence. Got your airline bag at the ready, in case you experience any nausea?"

The dog shot him a look of total disgust. *I'm already nauseated, and your wise-ass remarks aren't helping matters any.*

The roaring grew louder . . . louder. Was that really the sound of water they were hearing – or the sound of a Boeing 747 approaching the main runway? Jim didn't like it. He didn't mind taking a risk . . . but not a foolish risk. He held up one hand, motioned Joy to pull up beside him in her canoe.

"We better scout this baby on foot, Joy. It sounds like the 3:40 to Albuquerque! I want to know where all the holes are, *before* we drop over the edge."

She nodded. Within a minute, they were tying the boats off at the foot of a sprawling red cedar. "Come on, Jack!" The dog stared at him for a moment – *What? Are we canoeing, here, or are we hiking?* – but then clambered from the watercraft onto the rocky bank, and the three of them set out on foot.

As soon as he eyeballed the mile-long rapids, Jim was glad he'd decided on an advance look. The stretch of whitewater loomed before them like a runaway buzz saw – a howling tunnel of surf that boiled and crested between boulders the size of pickup trucks. The three of them shook their heads in amazement.

"Pretty hairy, huh?" Jim tried for a light, relaxed tone, but the other two could hear the uncertainty in his voice. "Hey, nothing to worry about," he sought to reassure them. "We'll just paddle hard, sweep and J-stroke our way around the holes and dodge the boulders as we go."

"Sure thing," said Joy, but the words sounded faint, distant.

"I'm sure glad we brought along the helmets and the wet suits," said Jim.

Really?* Jack had turned to face his master. *And what am I supposed to wear – a parachute?

"The key thing is to make sure we spot the 'open-armed Vs' through the rapids," said Jim. "And the good news is, most of the turbulence seems to be on the port side of the narrows. If we just bear to the right, the current will do half our work for us."

Joy was doing her best to smile. "That water looks like it's moving pretty fast, Jim."

He put an arm around her shoulders. "That's right, babe. But the speed isn't what will hurt you. The real danger is getting wedged against a boulder in a strong current like that. If that happens, you might not be able to break free. And if you're pinned with your head underwater . . . "

Jack was glaring at him. ***Like . . . you might experience a noticeable shortage of air? Count me out, bozo!***

"Joy, I want you to go first. I'll follow right behind, so I can help you if need be. Don't forget to keep your paddle in the water at all times – and never, ever grab the gunwale. Remember: that paddle in the water is your friend; it will guide you safely to where you want to go. It will also provide a brace to keep the canoe from tipping over.

"Just keep taking quick looks ahead, and pay attention to rocks and other strainers that might tip you over. If in doubt, paddle like crazy! And if you capsize, wait for me to pick you up. Stay upstream of the boat. If you can't hold the boat or have difficulty holding onto the painter, let it go, as well as your paddles. Take care of yourself first. Crawl onto a big safe rock or onto the bank if you can.

"Above all, never get yourself downstream between the boat and rocks. Tons of water will crush you. I have a rope rescue throw bag I can toss to you, if necessary, but it's difficult to throw or grab at times. You probably know everything I'm saying, but a review can't hurt. I'll give you a 10-minute head start and then I'll push off into the rapids. Of course, we must both paddle on our knees in order to better *feel* the water currents."

He smiled calmly at her. "Do you think you have all of that?"

"No problem," she smiled back.

But Jack wasn't smiling. No way. ***I'm outa here, starting this very minute – you guys are both raving maniacs!***

"All set, Joy?"

"Sure am, Jim."

They embraced for a moment. "You go easy, now – and don't take any chances. You hear me?"

She smiled back at him. "Sure do."

"If you get into trouble, just let the canoe go and make your way to the riverbank. We can always buy another boat – but we won't be able to purchase another Joy Price!"

She nodded, then settled herself in the stern of *Camper*. A moment later, she was pushing away from the red cedar roots and joining the fast-moving current. She looked back at him – just once and just for an instant – and he caught a strange look in her eye. It was part triumph, part fear, part sheer exhilaration. Her expression said: "Whatever happens next, I'm glad I did this!"

Then she was gone.

"Okay, Jack. This is the tough part, fella. All we can do now is wait."

For once the dog showed no expression. He looked almost as nervous as Jim felt. But a moment later, the big man got a surprise.

"How you doin', mister?" He turned to his right, was startled to see that a Mad River canoe with two people in it had floated into his backwater beside the tree. It was a couple, probably man and wife, in a boat loaded down with camping supplies.

"Where you headed, pal? How far you solo-canoeing?" The man in the stern wore a violet-hued life preserver and a floppy straw hat.

"Well, I'm actually going all the way to St. Louis."

"Wow!" The hat bobbed sideways as it owner held up his paddle in salute. "Hey, the best of luck to you, my man. That's way out of our league, but I wish you well."

Jim nodded and smiled. "Thanks for your support. I'm sure I'm going to need it."

The other couple drifted away, and soon vanished into the maw of the rapids. Jim grasped his paddle. Gritted his teeth. "Jack, are you ready to rock and roll?"

The dog made a low, moaning sound. Fear? *Couldn't we try something a little less demanding – maybe a slow waltz?*

But the time for hesitation was past. *Tripper* was on the move now, and gaining speed with every second. Had Joy made it successfully past the giant boulders and the seething strainers that lay in wait, directly up ahead?

Jim was about to find out.

Soon they were racing into the teeth of the drop. Amazed in spite of himself, Jim studied the terrain that lay ahead – the roaring caldron that was about to consume them. For a moment, his vision clouded with doubt and fear. Could he really negotiate this wilderness of waters, the thunderous currents and boiling whitewater of these Montana rapids?

He shook his head to clear it, then gritted his teeth.

A moment later, they had vaulted over the edge of the drop and into the howling chasm below.

Riding the whitewater in a fragile canoe – it's a little bit like playing football.

For starters, time slows way down. Let's say you're playing defensive end for Mizzou, the way Jim Clarke had played it, and the Colorado quarterback takes the snap, and he starts rolling down the line, and he fakes a hand-off to the fullback, and the fullback dives into the line, but you don't bite on the fake –*you do not bite!* – because you know he's pretending. The QB is only pretending, and the play has just begun. You're drifting along the line of scrimmage in slow motion, and fending off the block of an onrushing tackle, and he goes by like the 4:40 to Wichita, missing you completely, dream-like. You're still drifting out toward the sideline, with the quarterback in front of you. If you don't bite on the fake, he'll have to make a decision – is he gonna pitch it to the trailing back, or keep it himself and try to slice past you into the secondary? If you string the play on out – just keep it moving toward the sideline, you'll jam up the works and pretty soon the Colorado QB is running out of real estate and it's too late for the pitch to the trailing back, and then you can come up and put your helmet right on his numbers: ka-*plooey*, and he goes down all at once, face-first into the muddy turf, collapses faster than a tin outhouse caught in the middle of an Arkansas twister –

That's how it is in the whitewater.

Like football. Time slows way down, and you can count the boulders coming toward you like semis on a crowded freeway, and you can gauge the strainers one by one, and you just keep doing the J with your paddle, and whistling between your teeth, and watching the boulders and avoiding the whirlpools and riding out the open-armed Vs, until finally you're back out of it, riding free and easy and clear in

the open water, the flat, unruffled water, and you're feeling real good and whistling between your teeth – and then it hits you, *where's Joy, where the hell is Joy* –

And then you spot the blue skin of Camper up ahead, capsized, and riding the current, and glistening in the sun –

But no Joy, *where in heck is Joy*, and your heart freezes, it just plain freezes. . . .

Almost afraid to paddle in closer, he approached the overturned canoe with his heart in his throat. Yes . . . no doubt about it. This was *Camper* – but scan the flat-water as he might, he could find no sign of her presence. And it took him nearly half an hour to beach his own boat, just above where *Camper* was lodged, grounded upright and still full of water.

Now he studied the marooned vessel, and his heart sank. Her extra paddle was still tied to the frame, along with her dry bags . . . but the second paddle had vanished. Mystified, he turned to the dog. "Where is she, Jack?"

But the canine looked as befuddled as Jim felt. Increasingly frightened, he called her name and blew on his whistle – and then groaned out loud, as he saw how his frantic efforts were drowned into silence by the roar of the nearby rapids. And where were the *other* canoes? Not a single boat was in sight. Had the couple in the *Mad River* craft beached for the evening, or what?

Baffled and heartsick, he watched a Great Blue Heron and some noisy ducks feeding several yards downstream. For a moment he felt an irrational envy – those birds were *together*; they hadn't been driven apart, isolated by the cruel surge of the inhuman rapids! Angry now, he shook his head and tried to order his thoughts. No Joy in sight. Think! Had she been hurt when *Camper* went down?

Or had she actually drowned?

After several more minutes of useless speculation, he decided to begin using his head for a change. Moving carefully, he examined the mud along the bank of the river . . . and got his first break. After less than a minute of searching, he came upon two sets of fresh, muddy tracks leading into the brush. The footprints clearly belonged to a man and a woman, and they had obviously been walking together, less than 50 yards from the capsized canoe.

Excited by the find, he whirled to face the dog. "Come on, Jack, we gotta find Joy! We'll follow these tracks – and I want you to pick up her scent! Uh-oh . . . what's this?" Suddenly he was looking at some deep gouges left in the mud by four heavy tires. Probably a four-wheeled SUV, he told himself. You could never get a standard automobile through here – too steep and too slick.

Amazed, he stood motionless, gaping at the tire tracks. What did they mean? Had Joy been driven away from the downed canoe in an emergency vehicle, after being injured somewhere in the rapids? Or had she been abducted by some maniac at the wheel of mud-slashing, bouncing Ford Explorer? Heart racing, he grabbed his cell and dialed 911 again and again . . . only to get a maddening recording that told him: "We're sorry, but your call cannot be completed as dialed."

In an agony of suspense, he tried several other numbers . . . and at last managed to reach Angela, back at the delicatessen.

"Hello? Ringling Deli. How can I help you?"

"Angela? This is Jim Clarke, out on the river. I've got a little bit of a problem . . . wonder if you can help. Joy's canoe turned over, it capsized on her – and now she's vanished from the scene."

"Really? Uh-oh. That sounds bad. Sounds like it could be domestic trouble, Jim."

Clark stopped breathing. "*Domestic* trouble? What the hell are you talking about, Angela? I'm telling you, we went through some rapids, and Joy's boat capsized . . . and by the time I got there, she'd disappeared. I found some tire tracks _"

"I'm talking about her husband, Jim. He was here two days ago, looking for Joy, and he was mad. He swore he was going to find her, even if he had to search the entire Missouri River. And he said that when he found her, he'd either kill her or bring her back home!

"Sounds to me like he must've caught up with her on the Muddy Mo, while your back was turned."

Stunned, Clarke fell silent; for at least 30 seconds, he was completely unable to speak. He sensed real danger now, and his breathing came more rapidly as his fear increased. A sense of gloom for all his losses was blossoming deep inside, like some dark, sinister orchid. *First Jeanne and Sean*, he told himself with mounting dread, *then Veronica and Henry. And now Joy?*

Half paralyzed with anxiety, he hung up and stumbled back to the capsized boat. After struggling for several minutes, he was finally able to tip the canoe enough to pour the water from it. Moving slowly, painfully, he found that he could

walk Camper along the river's edge and past the rapids by holding onto the painter lines.

After clearing the rapids, he tied her canoe to his own. Then he and Jack floated very slowly to Helena. It was a mournful passage, to say the least. Head down, he felt as if his naked chest had been bruised by a gigantic stone.

As soon as got into town, he reported the missing – abducted? – Joy Price to the sheriff, and also to her supervisor with the Montana Forestry Agency. They promised to send a Jeep to the site – and also to dispatch a series of flyers via e-mail that would ask the entire staff to be on the lookout for her, starting immediately.

He was headed for the door when the sheriff called him back. A witness had just reported seeing a Chevrolet Blazer with all-wheel drive, driven by an unidentified male accompanied by a woman passenger. She had appeared to be in a panic, said the witness, and was attempting to attract the attention of people as the SUV went racing through a nearby town. "I took down the license number and called 911," an alert and sharp-eyed woman told the law enforcement officer.

Three hours later, the Blazer, which had been reported stolen, was found abandoned on the outskirts of Helena. A crumpled and scratched note was found on the backseat, where it had obviously been flung in haste. The note read: "Jim, I love you---J."

Once again, Jim felt icy claws at work behind his eyes. Was he cursed, or was he simply unlucky? Had the Fates set him up to take a giant fall – first by

introducing him to the most wonderful woman he'd ever met, and then by arranging this uncanny sequence of events and stealing her from him?

Grim-faced with determination, he rented an SUV and spent the next two days driving every back road he could find that led to the river from the highway between Helena and Great Falls. He grilled other drivers, horseback riders, cattlemen, shepherds, road workers, storekeepers, canoeists, fishermen, hikers and just plain "walkers." He asked one and all if they'd seen a woman who looked like Joy. *Nada.* And more *nada.* They told him nothing he didn't already know.

Utterly devastated and nearly ill with worry, he sat for hours in roadside diners, nursing cold cups of coffee and trying to analyze his next move. If only he'd asked her to tell him more about her ex-husband! But that was water under the bridge . . . too late to worry about it now.

At last he decided on a truly desperate move: He would hire a private detective. After making a few phone calls and scratching his head for a while, he wound up on the eighth floor of a downtown highrise, watching a fat man name Les Anderson smoke a *cigarillo* and scribble notes on the back of a yellow envelope.

"I'm truly sorry for your trouble," said the chunky gumshoe, "but that's my line of work. It's what I do. If she's out there, I'll find her."

Clark stared quietly at him. "I hope so," he said quietly. "But I already spent two days hunting for the thief who stole the Chevy Blazer. Didn't come up with a thing. The sheriff struck out, too. What makes you think you'll do any better?"

Anderson made a bright, chuckling sound. He was obviously enjoying himself. "Let's just say I have my ways, Mr. Clark. I have my ways." He took a long pull on the mini-cigar, then settled back in his swivel-chair. "I ain't bragging on you, but I've been chasing missing folks for more than 20 years. And sooner or later, I found 'em all – although seven happened to be dead by the time I got to 'em."

Clark winced. "I certainly hope that won't be the story this time."

The heavyset sleuth shot him a cheerful grin. "Naw . . . not a chance. Don't worry about it. These missing-person cases follow certain patterns, is what I've learned. If you've seen one, you've seen 'em all. In your situation, for example, the first thing I'd want to know is: Are you sure the husband was looking for her, right before she vanished?"

Clark was gazing at the carpet. "Yeah. But it's not the way it sounds."

"Oh, it never is. Never." Anderson put the *cigarillo* back in his mouth. He was smiling cheerfully.

"I mean it," said Clark. He could feel the veins beginning to stand out in his neck. "Joy left the guy a long time ago. And then . . . for some reason, he shows up again. She couldn't stand the man – she told me that several times."

"Uh-huh."

"My fear is that he might have abducted her."

"Right. That's always a possibility." The detective knocked a gray worm of smoldering ash into his *Dunkin' Donuts* coffee cup. "Of course, the statistics say it's much more likely she simply decided to shack up with him again. No offense."

"Really? Well, in this case, the statistics won't help us. I know Joy inside and out."

Anderson smiled. Cigarillo smoke trickled lazily from one nostril. "Experienced shows that the statistics don't lie, Mr. Clark."

For a moment, the big man wanted to reach across the desk and slap the stogy out of his mouth. "I don't care about the statistics, detective. Do you understand? I know this woman pretty well, and I'm telling you she was finished with the hubby. He must've snatched her, out on the road."

"If you say so."

Clark looked up now; he'd had just about enough. "Can I tell you something, detective?"

"What's that?"

"I don't like you worth a dern. Got it? I don't like your midget cigar, and I don't like the swirley flower-pattern on your cowboy boots. Got it? But they told me you're the best detective in Great Falls, so here I am."

Anderson winked at him. His right eye opened and closed rapidly, like the eye of a thoughtful lizard. "Well, they got that part right, mister. I *am* good. And that's why I charge $500 a day, plus expenses."

Clark was on his feet now. "Fine. I'll pay it, for the next few days at least. And as soon as you find her, you get another $1,000, on the spot."

The detective dropped the remains of his smoke into the cup. He was on his feet. "I can't wait to start spending it, Mr. Clark."

Could things get any worse? Yes, they could. Within an hour of the showdown with the detective, Clark found himself reading a very abrupt and no-nonsense e-mail from Jay Spader.

What's going on, Jimbo? I don't understand these delays at all. If you don't pick up the pace – and I mean pronto – you'll never make St. Charles on deadline. How about bringing me up to date on your current situation and schedule?

Gritting his teeth, Clark sat down at his Notepad and cranked out an e-mail riddled with lies. ***Jay: Tore a hole in the bottom of my canoe on some Class III rapids near Great Falls. Delicate surgery required, or the boat won't survive the trip. But the repair guys tell me she'll be ready in a couple of days – and I'll make up the time and distance, don't worry. Otherwise, everything is going well. I've done some knockout interviews and taken some river-photos you won't believe. More updates to follow.***

He hit the "Send" button, then shook his head. "You liar," he muttered at himself. "Look what you've gotten yourself into, by including a female in the action. Won't you ever learn?"

He stood up and walked to the window of the EconoLodge motel room. It had begun to rain; the dirty glass was streaked and beaded with wet. On the other side of panes, a paper birch tree spread its weary limbs into the gray twilight. He watched a few dripping leaves flutter through the drizzle. What a mess. Now that Joy had vanished, he found that he was missing Veronica and Henry more than ever. ***Figure that one out.***

He knew he would have to move on soon. He'd give it one more day – and if nobody came up with any new info about her, he'd resume the voyage at dawn the very next morning. He didn't want to eat, but he knew he would have to keep his strength up. After a miserable supper of fast-food cheeseburgers and fries – the Burger King motto on the side of the bag made him grind his teeth with frustration: ***Have It Your Way!*** **– he fell at last into a broken, tormented sleep.**

The dream came quickly, the same dream that had tortured him for the past decade.

His brother was calling to him: "Jim, Jim, you gotta help me!"

Terrified, Clarke staggered toward the sound of the voice. Somehow, he had wandered into a dank, steamy jungle full of harsh bird-calls and deep, sinister shadows. "Johnny? Johnny? Can you hear me? Where are you, Johnny?"

Nothing at first . . . then he heard a thin, wailing sound directly up ahead. "I'm here, Jim. I'm right here. Won't you help me? Won't you *save* me?"

He hurried forward. Gasping with fatigue, and soaked with perspiration, he fought his way through ankle-deep muck toward . . . the silhouette of a man sitting on a downed cypress log. A trooper wearing jungle fatigues. He was perched on the log with his back to Clark, his M-16 leaning against his hip –

Jim rushed forward – grabbed the man's shoulder from behind – shook it: "Johnny, I'm here to help you. I'm here!"

And then it happened. The moment his hand touched Johnny's shoulder, the trooper was transformed into a pile of dry, windblown sand!

Horrified, Clark watched the sandman collapse into the muck, watched the dry sand blowing away on the jungle breeze: "Johnny, Johnny!"

He awoke with his heart racing and a cold sweat trickling along his spine.

It was dawn. But this was no tropical jungle. His brother was a million miles away. Heart clattering in his chest, Jim Clark found himself stretched out on a lumpy mattress, in Room 227 of the EconoLodge. . . .

He lay there, paralyzed with dread, for at least 15 minutes. Deep down, he knew he'd never gotten over his brother's death in Vietnam – and he suspected that he never would. Johnny had been such a playful, devil-may-care youngster . . . a

bright-eyed, sandy-haired practical joker with a countywide reputation for pulling outrageous pranks.

Who would ever forget that immortal moment, ten years before, when Johnny and his daredevil lieutenants had actually succeeded in releasing a 1,000-pound dairy cow into the basketball gym at Parkdale High School? They'd all been seniors that year . . . a bunch of high-spirited kids with a huge lust for life – and it had taken them only a few weeks to set up what most local commentators still referred to as "the greatest single practical joke in the entire history of Parkdale High."

First Johnny Clark (as always, the ringleader) had managed to swipe the gym teacher's ring of keys during morning basketball. Then he'd slipped the ring through an open window at the back of the gym – straight to a waiting accomplice who'd already "called in sick" that day, and who wouldn't be missed. Without hesitating, the accomplice had then raced into town . . . straight to the Ace Hardware Store on Jefferson Street, where the sales clerk had quickly machine-tooled an exact copy of the key for him.

So far, so good. Next step: During several discussions with students from outlying farms, Johnny and his aides had pinpointed a farmer who always left his dairy barn open at night. "Like taking candy from a baby," said Rex Krongard, Johnny's top advisor on the project. "All we have to do is show up before dawn. We'll park the pickup at the back of the barn, where nobody will see us. . . ."

The whole thing had gone like clockwork.

A legend! At 8:15 on a Tuesday morning in October, 1987, the senior girls' volleyball class had entered the gym for required phys ed . . . only to find the panicked dairy cow mooing frantically, while sliding back and forth in about 20 pounds of recently expelled cow dung and milk.

"Mr. Hewlett, Mr. Hewlett! There's a cow running loose in the *gymnasium*!" Unforgettable!

But the man behind the legend had turned out to be all too mortal. Stretched out on his rack in the Great Falls EconoLodge, Jim Clark once again found himself mentally reading the letter that had come from the Pentagon on that rainy Saturday morning, ten years before:

The United States Army and the Department of Defense regret to inform you that your son, John Edward Clark, died in the line of duty in January 20, 1968, while valorously defending his position from an enemy assault with mortars, artillery guns and rifles. . . .

Clark sat on the side of the bed. He watched the rain falling against the motel room window. Long ago, he had stopped hoping to "get over" the loss of his brother. Long ago, he had simply begun to accept the loss as a fact of life – like slowly losing your hair, or your hearing. Some things, you didn't get over.

And then he remembered Joy. Sighing, he stood up and limped toward the sink. *Traveling solo again*, he told himself. *So what else is new? Better stop feeling sorry for yourself, pal – you've got a lot of work to do.*

He spent the day making preparations for departure. First he transported Joy's canoe – the faithful *Camper* – to the storage yard of a well-known outfitter. After explaining the situation in detail, he deposited $100 with the owner, along with

a careful set of instructions on what to tell Joy if she come looking for her missing boat.

Next he provided the owner with a tentative schedule of his travels along the river. "Mister," he told the bearded man in the *Wilderness Outfitters* slicker, "I know all of this must sound a little strange, a little wacky to you. But I'm hoping she just got called away, or wound up having to take care of some urgent business.

"Will you please help me with this?"

"Of course I will." The owner gave Clark a sympathetic nod. "I'm sorry for your trouble, sir. But don't you worry – we'll keep a sharp eye out for her, and if she does show up, we'll have her contact you immediately."

Jim shook his hand several times. "That's real good of you. I'll phone you from time to time, and here's my cell number, if you do hear anything."

As he eased the car out of the outfitter's pebbled driveway, Clark felt like he was leaving his heart behind, once again.

Moving as quickly as he could, he hauled his gear to a public access ramp that flanked the main county road. In less than 15 minutes, he and Jack were pushing away from the asphalt landing strip, and heading for open water. For a few moments, he sat staring at his own reflection in the river below the canoe.

What was it the old Chinese sage had said? *The longest journey begins with a single step.* He sighed once – and then dipped his paddle into the swirling water. It was time to go.

For once, Jack didn't offer any commentary. The dog just sat there in the bow, head down, obviously sharing his master's deep melancholy.

And now the canoe sprang forward, as Clark drove his kayak paddle into the Muddy Mo again and again. For the next three days, he would paddle almost non-stop from dawn to dusk, pushing himself toward the edge of exhaustion as the canoe darted among a endless series of Class I ripples & Class II rocky rapids. During this painful journey, the big man would sleep only four hours a night, right on the riverbank. He would eat ready-cooked foods or snacks on the go, and nothing else.

In the end, he would canoe 150 miles in three days . . . before finally realizing that this pace would kill him, if he tried to keep it up. Late on the third afternoon, he pulled *Tripper* onto a strip of sand a few yards from the purling current, then set up his tent. After commanding Jack to "stay," he sank into a black, bottomless sleep that lasted for more than six hours.

Then a growl of distant thunder woke him. Somewhere far up the river, a spring thunderstorm rumbled ominously, then faded. Coughing and blinking, the dazed Jim Clark rose to one knee . . . then caught his breath.

The canoe had vanished from its mooring spot along the riverbank.

And the loyal Jack was nowhere in sight.

Stunned, Clark staggered to his feet and spent the next few minutes racing frantically back and forth along the shoreline.

It was no use. Both the dog and the boat had disappeared, without leaving a trace behind.

Badly rattled by the discovery that both his dog and his canoe had vanished, Clark staggered back toward camp. How could Jack have been abducted without barking an alarm? And if the high-volume canine *had* launched a warning bark during the abduction, why hadn't Jim heard anything? It didn't make any sense. For nearly half an hour, he paced around the smoldering campfire, weighing his options and lamenting his fate. What a trip! Could anything *else* go wrong? Yes, it could: As if on cue, the lowering clouds opened up and it began to rain. Within a few minutes, the ground was soaked and the once-bright campfire was ancient history.

Shivering in the drenching wet, Clark debated his options – and soon discovered that each seemed worst than the last.

***Option A*: He could telephone the nearest office of the State Department of Natural Resources Police and beg for help: "Somebody swiped my canoe *and* my dog: Please come quickly!" (Right. And how would the DNR cops respond? They'd probably give him the Dumbest Camper of the Year Award, right there on the spot! Forget A.)**

***Option B*: He could spend a few hours exploring the riverbanks and nearby tributaries, while calling loudly for Jack every few minutes. (Good plan. Why not waste the afternoon digging through some local haystacks, instead, in a futile search for Rumplestilskin's golden needle?)**

***Option C*: Why not simply crawl into the river and hold his head under until he drowned? (It was easily the most attractive option, at this point – but then, who would take care of Jack, if the dog suddenly reappeared?)**

Irked and already coughing furiously (bulbar pneumonia?), the skin-soaked adventurer eventually realized that he didn't have a choice. *Option B, here I come.* Feeling utterly ridiculous, he spent the next hour and a half wandering along the Mo's muddy banks, where he periodically stumbled over tree roots and other obstacles, then toppled head-first into the mud.

"Jack, oh Jack . . . where are you, boy?"

No, it was not a fun time. But the powers of fate sometimes smile on even the dumbest among us . . . and around three o'clock, Jim Clark finally received two decent breaks. First the rain lifted, and the sun came out to quickly dry his sopping clothes.

Then, even as he was celebrating his meteorological good fortune, he heard a crashing sound in the underbrush, about twenty yards father up the riverbank. Had a whitetail deer somehow been spooked – right here in the middle of the Wednesday afternoon?

No! It was Jack! Airborne, the joyful Lab hurtled the last 15 feet of space between them – and landed with a mighty impact on the big man's mud-splattered chest!

"Jack, where in blazes have you *been*?"

But the joyful dog was in no mood to answer questions; he was too busy trying to lick the whiskers from his master's chin. After a struggle of more than a minute, Jim finally managed to get his four paws safely back on *Terra firma*. With the dog under control, he could turn to the crucial question he now faced: Where is *Tripper*?

Two plus two equals four, correct? If the canine had finally turned up, the canoe couldn't be far behind! It took Clark several minutes to calm the Lab down, but he finally managed to get his message across: "Use your nose, Jack! You gotta run the riverbank and pick up the scent of that canoe for us, bloodhound!"

Once the dog got his assignment straight, he went straight to work. And it didn't take him more than 45 minutes to pinpoint the abandoned watercraft . . . which had been dragged into a swampy tributary and wedged between two decaying logs. Camouflaged by brush and surrounded by over-hanging willows, the canoe could not easily have been found – not unless the searcher owned an All-America nose for detecting day-old scents above a moving stream, that is.

Jim was half-delirious at the discovery. "Jack, you are the King Creole of tracker-dogs! You are the Sherlock Holmes of the woof-woof world! You are smarter than Einstein, smoother than Houdini – "

But the dog was glaring at him now. Glaring hard. ***Knock that stuff off, and I mean right now – you're embarrassing both of us.***

Properly chastised, the big man backed away and began to look for evidence that might have been left behind by the canoe nappers. "I don't get it, Jack. Whoever swiped my boat – and you – wanted it to stay hidden for a good long time. That's obvious by the way everything has been so carefully camouflaged.

"And yet they didn't steal anything! Why? It's as if they wanted me to find all this stuff after awhile . . . as if they were only trying to slow me down for some reason. It doesn't make any darn sense!"

Hey, don't look at me, pal; I gave up the effort to understand human motivations a long time ago.

Frowning, Jim stared at the marooned canoe, the decaying logs. And then it hit him – right between the eyes.

"Holy cow, Jack – it's the prize money! Somebody wants to keep us from reaching St. Louis in time to claim that $100,000!"

Should he e-mail Jay Spader immediately and warn him that someone was attempting to sabotage their story?

Maybe. On the other hand . . . it seemed pretty clear by now that the saboteur – whoever he or she was – had to be someone familiar with the project. And except for Joy and Veronica, Clark hadn't told anyone the details of his epic assignment. Frowning, he sat down on the trunk of lightning-blasted pin oak to deliberate. . . .

Maybe the e-mail to *Wild Rivers* wouldn't be such a hot idea, after all – since it now seemed quite possible that the sabotage was coming from someone in Spader's office. What a mess! Nodding grimly, he decided that it was too early to tip his hand; he needed more evidence before deciding that the project was being attacked by insiders at the magazine.

At the same time, he also realized that he didn't want to tip his hand with Spader – not yet, anyway. Clearly, the best move was to keep paddling, while doing his best to make up lost time and reach St. Louis before the deadline expired. But that wouldn't be easy; he'd already lost another day, and he was at least *four* days off the pace by now.

Could he make up the difference? Moving quickly, he slapped the canoe into the water, loaded Jack and the scattered supplies back into position, and set sail once again. From now on, he would remain vigilant – a hungry hawk who knew that there forces arrayed against him out there on the fast-running water.

Jaw set with determination, he spent the next ten days skimming downstream, while dodging an endless series of rocks and strainers. The weather was improving now, as summer inched toward him, and the days were full of glittering sunshine and cobalt skies. Each evening he pulled *Tripper* ashore, all the way up to his campfire. After cooking a quick, simple meal, he slept the deep, dreamless sleep of an athlete whose endurance is being tested to the max.

On the afternoon of the tenth day, the next disaster struck.

He saw the tree strainer ahead, but felt sure he would have plenty of time to avoid it, even if he had to duck at the last second. But he wasn't prepared for the hidden-from-view drop that lurked just *before* the strainer.

There was time for a single, shouted warning – "Look out, Jack!" – and then in a single flashing moment of pain – the lights went out and the world went utterly dark.

Stretched out flat on his back, and with the loyal dog barking frantically, the man in the green-painted canoe hurtled unknowingly toward the next set of rapids.

*

He came back to consciousness slowly, like a deep-sea diver who returns to the surface in slow, painful stages.

Where was he? And why did his forehead feel so damp and sticky? He reached out to touch the painful spot above his left eye, and when he pulled his hand back, it was smeared with half-dried blood.

A voice said: "Easy, now. You have to take it easy."

Clark opened both eyes – and found himself lying on a cot, in the middle of a large pop-up tent. A youthful couple sat beside his sickbed on a pair of battered camp chairs. Clark groaned and ran a hand along the left side of his head and face. The hand told him what he didn't want to know: Part of his head was wrapped in wet bandages. *Blood.*

"What happened to me?"

"Your head went against a tree-trunk strainer about two hours ago, and you went out like a light. I'm Enos Mitchell, and this is my wife Joan. We were forty yards behind you – and we barely missed the strainer, ourselves.

"It was touch and go for a while, believe me," said Enos. "I jumped overboard and grabbed your boat painter. Then I tossed the lifeline to Joan. She managed to get it tied to the bow of the *Tripper* and I wrapped it around a tree. That caused the boat to swing around – so that we could get you out of it and wrap you in blankets.

"We were hoping to get you to a doctor today, so he could check you for a concussion, but it's a mighty long trip. Besides, I'm a physician's surgical assistant and Joan happens to be a third-year medical student. Anyway, the bottom line is that we think you're probably okay; you're conscious again, and your vital signs appear ok."

Jim took a deep breath, and for a moment his eyes glittered with tears. "Hey, I can't thank you two enough. You're terrific! But I don't have time for a doctor, or a hospital. The job I'm working on will pay me very little, if I arrive at my destination late. I think I'll be all right, I really do. All I've got is a headache . . . and maybe a little muscle soreness."

He tried to sit up, and felt a wave of nausea sweep over his woozy brain. "Easy," said Enos Mitchell. "Why don't you lie still for a couple of hours, and wait for your strength to return?" Jim nodded. "Enos . . . have you seen my dog?"

The man beside the cot broke into a delighted chuckle. "Oh, *him*? Why, he's been absolutely perfect. He hasn't left your side the entire time, except to go to the bathroom. And he looks so thoughtful, so intelligent – a couple of times there, Joan and I swore we could almost hear him thinking out loud!"

Clark laughed out loud, then broke into a fit of coughing.

"Look here," said Enos Mitchell. "Why don't you let us fix you a good meal? Then you can get dressed and give the canoe another try. We'll watch you warm up – and we won't let you depart until we're sure you can handle that river."

Clark looked at them; once again he was fighting back tears. "I can't believe you two guys," he said over and over again. "Where would I be without you?"

An hour later, he found himself sitting over a steaming bowl of potato chowder, beside their tent. Had any food ever tasted this good? Joan watched him carefully. She was a tall, slender woman with piercing blue eyes. The pioneer type, Jim immediately decided – and his *favorite* type, as well.

"You look much better," said Joan. "It's good to see you eating like that." He watched her cut through a huge slice of whole wheat bread, baked fresh that morning. "Your strength seems to be returning, Jim, but you worry me. You're still pretty darn pale. Are you sure you're ready to resume this . . . this *odyssey* of yours?"

Jim laughed out loud. "I better be," he told her. "Because if I stayed around you much longer, I know I'd wind up fat! Your cooking is impossible to resist, lady."

She smiled, but her mind was elsewhere. "Jim, I'm sure you know the Muddy Mo better than I do, but I'm still going to tell you the obvious. The river is about to change on you. You're gonna be looking at some treacherous gravel bars, starting in about fifty miles – and the population of rattlers, mosquitoes, flies and gnats is about to multiply.

"Once this river turns to the south, headed for the Dakotas and Nebraska, it turns *mean*. The current picks up, and the drop-offs are on you before you know it. Over the years, Enos and I have heard a lot of stories about excellent canoers who under-estimated the Mo, and never came back."

Jim paused in the middle of a bite. "I'm hearing you loud and clear, Joan. Thanks for caring enough to tell it like it is. But you can rest assured – I was scared of the Missouri when I started, and I'm just as scared right now. I'll ride that thing with my eyes wide open, you can be sure of that."

She smiled again, reassured. "All right, then. Now, on the bright side – hey, you're in for some amazing sights. Based on the odds, you're almost certain to canoe past lots of pheasants, white-tailed deer, elk, mule deer and antelope, almost non-stop."

"I can hardly wait."

"Just imagine yourself on one of those 'Wild Safari' TV shows, and you'll fit right in."

They had a good laugh, and then Jim reached for his wallet.

"Put that away," said Enos. He had returned to throw a few more sticks on the fire.

"Won't you at least let me pay you for the food?"

"Not a chance," said Joan. "Just pass the favor on to someone else, next chance you get."

A few minutes later, they stood arm in arm on the riverbank, watching him push *Tripper* and Jack into the burbling current.

"You take care!" shouted Enos.

"Go easy, and God bless!" shouted Joan.

He waved at them for a moment, then swung around a hairpin turn and vanished out of sight.

Jim took a deep breath, and dug his paddle into the current. "Okay, Jack-O, it's just you and me again. Two pals running free on the river!"

The dog was careful not to meet his eye. *Knock off the cornball stuff, or I'll be overboard before you can blink. I tell ya, I've had enough of this sentimental stuff to last me a dog's lifetime!*

Ignoring the barbed retort, Jim sank his kayak canoe paddle into the river, and the craft shot forward. Soon they were zipping along at a heady five miles an hour, racing toward wide-open spaces that stretched a thousand miles in the distance. Eyes on the flashing water, Clark paddled for all he was worth . . . while his canine companion put on a "pointing" display that would have made any hunting dog proud.

First Jack pointed an American white pelican – a slack-jawed loafer who stood lounging in the shallows beneath a mountain ash. "Look at that guy," Jim told the dog. "Talk about lazy? He's just standing around on that sand bar all day, waiting for the fish to come to *him*!"

But the vigilant pooch had already switched targets – now he was pointing a stately great blue heron . . . followed by the majestic, tawny-gold wingspan of an American eagle. In spite of himself, Jim was impressed. "Pretty good, Jack. Shoot, I thought you were shortsighted! Did they fit you out for contact lenses, before we left Baltimore, or what?"

The dog gave him a steely-eyed glance, and Jim could almost hear him thinking: *Very funny. If you don't mind, I'd like to quote Dr. Samuel Johnson in the 18th Century: Sarcasm is the last refuge of a defeated wit!*

But even as they sparred at each other, Jim was furiously paddling, paddling. He had several days to make up, and he knew it wasn't going to be easy. Fortunately, his prowess would stand him in good stead during this long, relatively calm stretch of water. The powerful "J" stroke and use of kyak paddle, also helped to prevent spills, by ensuring stability and forward momentum on the river.

As the frail craft skimmed along the surface, Clark know he was also entering a landscape famous for its history. It was right along this wild section of the Muddy Mo, in fact, that the famed explorers Lewis and Clark and been forced to camp out for nine straight days – from June 2 to 11 in the year 1805 – while they struggled to determine if this was the Marias or the Missouri River.

Feeling a little awestruck, Jim pointed with his paddle. "My goodness, Jack, where in the world does all this *water* come from? I'll tell you one thing, pardner – I sure as hell can't afford to park here for nine days! From this day forward, I'm gonna be asking both of us the same question: How fast can we get to St. Louis? We've got a deadline to make, and I do *not* intend to miss it."

Jack listened to all of this, and snorted with derision. *If you're thinking about skipping any mealtimes, you better think again. I'm not about to go hungry – just so you can win some silly blue ribbon!*

The sun rose higher in the sky, and morning turned into afternoon, as Jim's paddle rose and fell against the spring breeze. Half-hypnotized by the repetitive motion, he dreamed of a hundred different things . . . of his long-dead brother Johnny, the heroic Vietnam vet . . . and of Veronica, accompanied by little Henry, racing along the sand at Kitty Hawk, her long, blond hair snapping and billowing in the ocean wind . . . and even of his first wife Jeanne, so many years before, standing beside him in the produce department at a Washington, D.C., Safeway: "Hey, let's get one of those pumpkins for Halloween, Jim – we'll have a blast!"

Memories: what were they? And which famous writer – was it L.P. Hartley – had crafted that famous line: "The past is a foreign country; they do things differently there?" Lost in his reveries, and wandering endlessly through the pages of his mental scrapbook, Clark was startled to hear a deep male voice suddenly booming at him from an approaching inboard runabout:

"Yo! Can I help you with directions? I am John, a member of the Mandan Native American Tribe."

Amazed, Jim gazed across the stretch of open water that separated them. "John, it's a pleasure to meet you . . . even if a bit unexpected! I am James, from the American City of Baltimore."

As the runabout nosed in closer, Clark noticed a tall, dark-haired maiden sitting in the bow. She was a classic beauty: hazel-eyed, smiling, and blessed with a mass of shining, jet-black hair.

"Let me repeat my offer," said the man in the power-boat. "I always enjoy directing travelers on the Great Missouri – because my great-great-grandfather actually helped Lewis and Clark to find *their* way in the 1880s. And I must also warn you: It's easy to get lost on this part of the river!"

Jim slipped easily into a reverse "J" stroke – a deft move that held the canoe on a steady course. "Thank you, my friend," he told the new arrival. "Believe me, I'm not too proud to accept some good advice from a veteran boatman. What do I need to know, in order to get down this river as quickly as possible?"

The two of them were smiling at him now. "Okay, first piece of advice," said John. "You need to keep to starboard as you pass the tall pines, then bear hard to port until you've cleared the giant rocks. After that, you will find yourself safely in the middle of the main channel. You will be fine – but you must be careful to take your bearings often."

A moment later, he was easing the elegant watercraft in next to Jim's flashing paddle. "Here, Connie has written them down for you – since you probably set your course by compass."

Jim accepted the scrawled notes gratefully. "I can't thank you enough, John. Fortunately, I *am* competent with the compass – but I did need this information in order to get past the Marias."

The Indian in the runabout nodded cheerfully. "You're mighty welcome, my friend. If we can help you further, it would be an honor. Just drop by the general store in Mandan Village – only a couple of miles from here – and ask for assistance. Believe me, you will receive it quickly!"

Encouraged by his dialogue with the Mandan sage, Clark didn't hesitate. And within a few hours, he and Jack were gliding smoothly past the breathtaking beauty of White Cliffs – a wild and untamed section of river where majestic pines, firs and junipers stood poised like wary sentinels at the purling water's edge. It was here, Jim knew from his earlier research, that he would canoe through the very heart of the 149-mile-long Missouri stretch that had been designated as a *National, Wild and Scenic River.*

In spite of his anxiety about running late, the Clark-man couldn't resist a quick video-shoot. Accompanied by the scowling Jack – ***Are we canoeing here, or producing a Hollywood extravaganza?*** **– the big man spent nearly two hours aiming his high-tech camera at a series of unforgettable sights . . . including a trio of leaping, white-tailed deer, a riverside Native American teepee (complete with a plume of wood-smoke trickling from the chimney hole), and a straight-arrow formation of snow geese honking their way across the bright, blue sky.**

After pausing to interview several canoe-borne campers for his magazine opus, Jim whistled at his trusty first mate and then led the way back to ***Tripper.*** **Soon they were once again zooming along the waterway, flanked now by the famed White Cliffs that loomed several hundred feet above their frail craft.**

"Jack-o, I've got some very good news for you," said Clark with a delighted laugh. "I am now going to switch to my special double-bladed paddle – and ***you*** **are about to travel very fast, Dr. Fido."**

Jack thought about the concept for at least two seconds, then fired back. ***I assume you don't expect me to take a turn with that double-dipper of yours?***

But they were zipping along at better than five miles an hour, now, and Jim lacked the wind for another snappy rejoinder. During the next amazing week, ***Tripper*** **would rack up more than 40 miles per day – in spite of several thunderstorms that threatened to blast them all the way the bottom of the surging river. Somewhere on the fifth afternoon, the canoe entered the widening mouth of a**

vast, sky-blue body of water – famed Ft. Peck Lake – a vista that would highlight their passage toward the North Dakota border.

Once they reached that milestone, they could brag about having finished 600 miles of the journey – with only 1,900 miles remaining in the quest for victory!

First things first, however. At the present moment, Jim Clark had only one thought in mind: to get across the vast expanse of Ft. Peck Lake without a boating catastrophe. And this would require more than a little canoeing skill – especially if he and Jack were unlucky enough to find themselves caught up in one of the river's notoriously unpredictable, springtime squalls.

"I don't want to frighten you, Jack-o," the captain had told his glowering first mate on several occasions, "but the thunderstorms on Peck Lake will get your attention in a *hurry*. I'm talking about 80-mile-an-hour winds – hurricane-force winds, mind you – and waves that routinely reach heights of seven and eight feet.

"Trust me: You do *not* want to be noodling around in a heavily-loaded canoe under those conditions."

Jack listened calmly to all of this, but he refused to panic. *Don't worry, pal – I can smell a thunder-boomer 50 miles out . . . and the first whiff I get of approaching turbulence, I'm outta here! I'll go over the side so fast, you'll think you're watching a professional vanishing act!*

Jim opened his mouth to respond to these obnoxious thoughts – but then he closed it again. What was that tiny speck on the distant shoreline? A female wearing a bright blue kerchief? Was she waving at Jim and his passenger? Yes . . .

and she was also jumping up and down! Amazed by this odd behavior, he changed his paddling stroke again – and sent them flying across the chop all the way to the river's foaming edge.

It was Angela – Joy's landlady and the owner of the deli! And she was waving at them frantically, both hands whirling, as if she carried an extremely urgent message from one of the major river gods.

"Angela, is that you?" Hoarse from lack of use, his voice croaked in his own ears.

"Jim Clark! Get over here right now – I've got some news you need to hear, big man!"

The battered canoe grumbled against the pebbles as it came swiftly ashore. A moment later, Clark was standing beside the youthful Angela, who looked every bit as desirable and attractive as she had at the time of their parting.

"Say, you're a long way from home, aren't you, young lady? What brings you all the way out here, anyway? Did you hear something from Joy? She vanished on me two weeks ago, and I've been half-crazy, searching for her."

Angela stared at him as if he'd just arrived from Pluto. "Joy? My tenant at the deli? No, I'm sorry to tell you – I haven't heard a peep from her. I came out here to see *you*, Jim. I had a few days off, and I thought it might be fun to hang out with a canoe-riding journalist!"

She gave him her best smile, followed by a mischievous wink. "I'm also going to insist on buying you a New York strip at my favorite restaurant in town . . . along with a baked potato and a giant-sized slab of cheesecake drenched in wet strawberries.

“How’s *that* for an offer you can’t refuse?”

Clark eyeballed her for a moment, then found himself laughing out loud. “If you’re trying to tempt me away from the river, you chose the right tactic – how can I say no to a New York strip?” He turned for a moment to the dog: “How about it, Jack – should we accept this lady’s kind offer, or turn her down?”

Jack shot his partner a look of utter disgust. *Are you telling me you’d even* consider *saying “No” to a high-end steak like that? Have you lost all touch with canine reality, or what?*

Grinning widely now, the explorer threw up his hands. “You’re on, Angela. But I’m feeling pretty nervous about the canoe – every time I turn around, somebody steals it from me, or moves it to some other location. Is the restaurant you have in mind close enough that I can stash *Tripper* on the cart, and then keep it in eyeshot during dinner?”

Angela didn’t hesitate. “You betcha, wild man. The place is called the River Steak, Ale & Inn, and you’ll find it only 200 yards down this paved path. You just grab that skinny boat of yours, and I’ll help you cart-walk it all the way to the food!”

Once inside, they ordered steaks all around . . . and even made arrangements for Jack to be served an impressive beef-cut at the restaurant’s backdoor. As they ate, Jim brought Angela up to date on his end, and told her some hair-raising tales about his frequently interrupted progress. Angela listened intently, then startled her companion with some puzzling news of her own. “Jack, there was a man, a solo

canoeist, who stopped in for lunchmeat, drinks and other food supplies a few days ago. He didn't ask for you by name – but he did ask if there was another solo paddle up ahead of him."

Clark stopped chewing. Watching Angela intently, he leaned forward in the restaurant booth. "That's a very interesting development, I must say. Can you tell me what he looked like?"

Angela frowned, struggling for recall. "Well . . . he was kinda chubby, and balding in front. And he had a pair of thick black eyebrows – really wild and ragged. Not terribly handsome, I'm afraid."

Clark returned his fork to the table.

"You're kidding, Angela?"

"Not at all. That's exactly how he looked. And he also wore a pair of gold-rimmed sunglasses that he kept on an elastic cord around his neck."

Angela shook her head. "I'm afraid I can't answer that one, Jim. All I can tell you is what he said . . . although I must admit that I found his questions a little strange, myself. For one thing, I'm sure he already knew the obvious – the fact that except for kayaks, there haven't been more than a half-dozen solo paddlers through Ringling this entire year."

Clark sank his fork into a hunk of cheesecake. "I wish somebody would explain what is going on," he told his companion after a bit. "Every time I turn around, my canoe gets stolen or hidden on me. The last time, I lost Jack as well. For all I know, the CIA planted a radio-beeper inside his dog-collar!"

Angela chuckled at the image, then grew serious. "Jim, it sounds to me like somebody might be trying to put the kibosh on your expedition. Or maybe they're just trying to slow you down. But who would care enough about a canoe trip to do *that*?"

Baffled, Clark had begun to bite his lower lip. "I wish I had an answer for you, Angela – but I'm as mystified as you are."

Angela reached for her coffee cup. "Okay, let's put that problem aside, while I ask you Question No. 2."

"Fire away."

"What are you going to do if you can't find Joy?"

Clark touched flame to the business end of a Newport Light. "What are you saying, Angela? Are you predicting that she *won't* be found? Or are you suggesting that she isn't even *trying* to make her way back to me?"

Angela's eyes darted away, and she answered in a rush. "I can't speculate about her motives, Jim. Who knows what goes through a woman's head? But if you want my gut feeling . . . no, I don't think she would intentionally stay away from you." Angela smiled, then looked coyly across the restaurant table. "It seemed obvious to me that she was powerfully drawn to you – and for good reason.

"Considering you're an Easterner, you don't seem half-bad! Which reminds me that I'm single, myself. I hope you find your friend . . . but if you don't, I'm also hoping that we might spend some time together. Believe me, it gets pretty boring out here after awhile, living alone." Her eyes had gone soft and dreamy in the candlelight above the table.

"You know how it is, Jim. I'm sure you've been lonely at times in your life, haven't you?"

Embarrassed by this sudden intimacy, Clark was looking at the floor. "Well, Angela, I really don't think. . . "

She was giving him her best smile now, and he watched the light flicker along her perfect white teeth. "You know, Mr. Clark . . . I've got a really nice room, right above the restaurant. Shower *and* a bath! Why don't you bring your shaving kit upstairs, then shave and shower and change into clean clothes?

"You'll feel like a thousand dollars after you clean up." She gave him a flirtatious wave. "After that, you can set your tent up in the backyard and get a good night's sleep.

"Joy would certainly understand . . . wouldn't she?"

Jim frowned, and looked away from her. *Watch your step, Clark.* His eyes went to the restaurant window, and to the rain that fell against it. When he spoke, his words were slow and measured. "Angela, that's mighty nice of you. I could certainly use a shower – although I really would prefer to pitch a tent in your yard, as you suggest. I guess I've just gotten used to sleeping outdoors, and I don't want to lose the habit!"

They finished their meal after that, and within an hour they were stepping into Angela's neatly furnished hotel room.

But as Jim had feared, his hostess was feeling the siren call of romance. Moving gracefully toward him, she slid an arm around his neck and pulled him close. "Kiss me, you devil!"

Before he could respond, her lips were against his. And they were hot, hot, hot. Clark groaned with pleasure, even as he tried to pull away. He wanted this dark-eyed beauty, and he wanted her bad. But he knew it would be a mistake.

With superhuman effort, he managed to pull himself back from the brink. "Angela . . . hang on. Easy, now." He could smell the fragrance of her perfume, and his heart pounded deep in his chest. But their mouths had parted, and he was fighting for air.

"I'm sorry, Angie. This just isn't something I can do right now. I hope you understand. I'm running on a razor-thin schedule, and I have to be paddling again at dawn. If I spend the night with you in my arms, I might never leave again."

She was pouting at him now. "Won't you take a break from your travels – not even for a single day?"

But Jim refused to relent. "There's nothing I'd rather do, Angela, but my instincts tell me it would be the wrong move. I hope you understand."

She nodded, and then laughed. "Darn – I never thought any man on earth would be able to resist my charms!"

He was pleased to see that she wasn't too badly hurt by his refusal, and that her mood had suddenly become much lighter. After his shower and shave, he set up his tent and slept there for the night, joining her for breakfast the next morning. The two of them walked the loaded canoe back to the river and talked some more.

She nodded. "No doubt about it." She hesitated for a moment, and then added: "I met Joy's ex-husband. He came by looking for her, as well. He wasn't tall, but very handsome. I wonder why she left him. I don't think I could have done so."

Jim stared at her, and placed a hand on each of her pretty shoulders. "Angela be open with me. Why did you really come here now? What's the real story? All this time and you never mentioned seeing Joy's ex. Are you telling me you came all this way simply for a good meal and maybe a quick romp in the sack?

"Or did one of your visitors at the deli tell you I needed a little break from my travels?"

Angela didn't hesitate. "I don't know what you're talking about, Jim. I like Joy a lot and I wanted to help you in your canoeing, that's all. I knew you and Joy hadn't known each other long . . . and I just figured that if you were lonesome, you and I could have some fun." She tried to smile, but he could see the tears in her eyes.

"It's okay," he told her quietly. "Don't give it a second thought."

The fog was still heavy as he and Jack paddled away from the dock. "Take care, Angela. I'll be in touch. In the meantime, you be careful, also. Somebody's chasing me, and I don't want you to get hurt."

She nodded quietly, and watched his canoe out of sight.

At the last moment, Jim turned for a final look at Angela, who was still waving from the end of the dock. Even from a distance of 100 yards, she looked terrific! Had he just made a big mistake? Instinctively, he understood that he'd closed the door on what could have been a very comfortable relationship, both physically and emotionally.

No. He shook his head. Then he addressed his faithful companion. "I'm a horse's butt, Jack!"

The dog reflected thoughtfully on this assertion, then nodded enthusiastic agreement. *You got that right, Jimbo!*

Once again, you're right on the button. Truer words have never been spoken!

"Dumb as I am, however, I am *not* stupid enough to violate the most important principle in the War of the Sexes: `Never, ever sleep with your girlfriend's landlord!'"

Makes good sense to me, captain. Why set yourself up for disaster?

"I'm not saying I wasn't tempted, mind you. That Angela was hot enough to set my socks on fire. And how about that smile of hers? Enough voltage there to light up Yankee Stadium for a night game. That was a close call, Jack-O, you better believe it!"

You don't have to convince me. I saw the way you were slobbering all over your sports shirt. You humans . . . ugh.

But they fell silent after that. Jim was already working hard on each stroke. His destination today would be the famed Virgelle's Ferry crossing, located at least 30 more miles along this stretch of muddy, silt-laden water. At this point in its journey, the Mo was anything but pretty. Everywhere you looked the sluggish current ran heavy with leaves, feathers, cottonwood fuzz and small branches torn from the surrounding trees.

Wild and untamed, the passing countryside looked much the same as it would have looked to Lewis and Clark and their 50 adventurers, as they pushed their way upriver with the help of giant poles cut from white pine and mountain ash. Try as he might, Jim could not imagine the amount of raw courage and endurance that

would have been necessary – in a world crawling with physical dangers and hostile Native Americans. What would it be like to push forward day after day, deep into a world that was completely unknown?

Musing on these historical questions, Jim paddled steadily while Jack dozed occasionally in the bow. Six hours passed, then seven and eight . . . until at last the captain was forced to conclude the obvious: ***I must've gone right past the ferry – I'm totally lost!***

No matter how he analyzed his situation, there was no denying one basic fact: he should have arrived at Virgelle's Ferry and Missouri Canoe Company between four and seven p.m. Frustrated beyond belief, he turned to the scowling dog. "Jack, I asked you to navigate this trip so we wouldn't get off schedule, and what did you do? You napped on me, bozo! You lay there snoring like a drunken stevedore, while we went right past our target!"

That's right – blame the dog. You're really pathetic, do you know that? Every time you blunder – which is frequently – the canine takes the rap!

"We went past a ferry boat around four o'clock, but the darned thing didn't carry a name. I waved at the ferry operator, but he didn't return my greeting and he was the one who dropped us off. And where were you at that moment? Hey, you could've sniffed that out for me – instead of sawing wood up there in the bow. Talk about snoring! I'll tell you one thing – you're the first dog in recorded history to develop sleep apnea!"

Yeah, yeah, yeah. Well, at least I don't talk out loud while I'm napping. You oughta hear yourself – you sound like you've got a loudspeaker wired to your tonsils.

They went on like that for a while, jabbering fiercely and trading insults, but their verbal sparring didn't change the stark reality they now faced. With a sinking heart, Jim realized that they would soon run out of daylight. It was too late now to turn around and retrace their journey; hungry and exhausted, they would have to camp out on the riverbank until first light, and then go in search of help.

What a bummer. Instead of enjoying a good meal – followed by a hot shower – at the Canoe Company, he would be required to "rough it" from dusk to dawn. Groaning, he actually laughed out loud; somehow, the fates had conspired to give him an up-close look at exactly the kind of privation that Lewis and Clark had experienced!

It was a real shame . . . especially given the fact that the rest of the day had gone so well. The ride had begun quietly enough, that morning, with Clark successfully employing his GPS guidance system and the Mandane chief to get them safely past the Marias River mix. At that point, the current had seemed so slow as to be almost non-existent. And Jim had decided to take advantage of it. While remaining in the canoe, he had snapped off dozens of photos of wildlife: whitetail deer, bald eagles, even a frantically paddling beaver or two. Too bad that this very fine day would now end with the two of them shivering among the weeds at the edge of the river!

Around eight o'clock, the sun dipped behind the rugged Montana mountains and darkness arrived in earnest. Weary in body and spirit, Jim paddled on – but without any real hope that he would now come upon the ferry. The moon rose

slowly in the east, flooding the scene with reflected light. The breeze had turned downright chilly by now, and the big man understood that they would have to seek shelter soon.

After a few minutes of strenuous paddling, the canoe bottom was grinding against the pebbles. Still sitting in the stern, Jim reflected on the fact that the Virgille employee told him his cell phone wouldn't get a signal so he left it in the truck!" Later, another employee told him he could have reached with a cell phone by walking up to the top of the rise above the River.

Groaning with misery, he said, "Well, Jack, this is a fine mess we've gotten ourselves into, don't you think?"

Sensing that he would not be fed on this moonlit evening, the loyal canine bared an impressive set of teeth. ***What do you mean 'we,' you human disaster area? I had nothing whatsoever to do with this absurd snafu, so stop pointing that finger at me!***

But Clark was already on his feet. After some sliding and grunting, he managed to get the canoe onto the grass and a short distance up the steep bank. Soon he was unpacking the big dry bag . . . only to discover that he hadn't packed a flashlight or food. "Okay, Jack," he growled at his sidekick. "We've got probably ten minutes before the moon goes down – during which time we have to set up the tent, eat some of the peanut-butter crackers I brought along, and settle down to sleep. Are you ready to rock and roll?"

Peanut-butter crackers? You're kidding, right? I can't run that goop through my digestive track – I'll end with a major-league case of canine constipation!

"Guess what, Jack-o? No blankets. I never expected to be camping out tonight, so I didn't bring them along. And I'll bet you a dollar the temperature dips all the way down to freezing tonight."

The miffed pooch snickered loudly. *Good thing we Labs have our winter coats on and can curl in a ball and keep comfortable.*

Jim fumbled badly in unloading the dry bag and his sleeping bag, pad and tent. And then at the last moment, he decided the bank was too steep and he didn't have enough light to set up the tent at all. Later, he would regret this decision; as he explained to the searchers who found him: "If I'd known there was going to be such a heavy dew and frost, I'd have fought to get it up! Instead, I woke up with frost-burns on the back of my neck, from lying on a pile of icy tent-fabric!"

After they settled in, Jim held out a cellophane-wrapped package – about the size of a deck of cards – to his peeved roommate. "Peanut-butter crackers, Jack-o. Don't turn up your nose . . . peanuts are rich in protein, my friend."

The dog didn't even look at him. *I'd rather eat tree bark and wild thistles, you pathetic sad sack!*

It would not be an easy night. Clark lay motionless on the tent fabric and watched a billion stars glittering back at him from the infinity of space. He remembered a college course he'd taken in astronomy . . . remembered the silver-haired professor who'd pointed out Spiral Andromeda and Ursus the Great Bear and a hundred other constellations as well: "Most of the stars in the universe are so

distant that when we look at them, the light-image we see in front of our eyes is already ten or twenty or even a hundred years old.

"How big is space? Remember, class, those light-rays from stars like Alpha Centauri have been zooming along at 186,000 miles per *second* – and yet it has taken them a dozen years or more to reach us here on earth!"

It was all pretty amazing, when you thought about it. Unable to sleep, Jim yawned and turned on his side. Should he try counting sheep? Part of the problem was the cold – hard to believe that the month of June would soon be upon them. And here he was, Helpless Jim Clark, with his teeth chattering like runaway piano keys, and his entire body riddled with quarter-sized goose pimples –

Sploosh.

Clark froze in place. What the hell was *that*?

He waited. Nothing for a few seconds. And then, clearly and distinctly
Sploosh . . . burble.

Now the big man was sitting up straight on his lumpy bed of canvas. "Jack, did you hear that?"

What? Did I hear what? Can't you see I'm trying to get some shut-eye over here?

"That . . . that *splooshing* sound. There's something crawling in the water – something creeping around the canoe!"

Oh, my God. Calm down, you hysterical grandma – it's just a couple of fish breaking the surface.

"That's easy for you to say. But I heard a slapping sound, Jack – the sound of a mighty tail cracking against the water. For all I know, we're surrounded by hungry cougars!"

Cougars? Have you completely lost your grip on Basic American Reality? I hope to God you brought along some medication . . . if so, go take it!

Sploosh . . . burble.

"That's it, Jack . . . I can't stand it any longer." Jim was on his feet now, and bending over to retrieve the heavy double-bladed canoe paddle. "I'm going into battle, Jack – but I understand, if you want to just stay curled curl up in a ball like that, safe and warm.

"I'll be fine without you, I'm sure."

The dog made a groaning sound, then dragged himself to his feet. ***Somebody tell me I'm dreaming. Because I know this can't be true. I mean, we're now in the middle of a cougar-hunt – armed with our trusty canoe paddle!***

Creeping steadily forward, Jim had now reached the edge of the water, where several dark, bushy forms appeared to be swimming around the half-beached canoe. The big man raised his twin paddle blades high in the air . . . then lowered them swiftly back to the ground.

"Why, it's a family of beavers, Jack! Nothing more than a few hungry beavers!"

The black Lab snorted with sarcastic laughter. ***A platoon of dangerous beavers, is it? Oh, dear! Quick, Daniel Boone – throw them a pack of peanut-butter crackers, before they tear your head off!***

He settled back in, right after the beaver-attack, but he knew sleep would not come easily. For one thing, the night had already grown cold – so cold that he could see his breath frosting against the damp tent fabric beneath his cheek. Twisting and turning, he could feel the gelid river air creeping into his bones and sinews. With his feet stuck in the dry bag and his head wrapped in an extra sweatshirt, he was as miserable as any riverman had ever been!

Yet he could also laugh at his plight. That had always been a strength – Jim Clark's ability to laugh at himself. "Well, Jack, I hope you're comfortable over there. Nice night for a campout, don't you think?"

Right. Just peachy, Mr. Clark. I haven't had a scrap of dinner, and my right leg is covered with frostbite. I feel like a cross between White Fang and Nikki, Dog of the North! And I blame you for this mess. Why didn't you keep an eye out for that ferry? No excuse! If brains were dynamite . . . you couldn't blow your nose!

But Jim was snoring loudly. His head rose and fell on the sweatshirt, and his face was a mask of pain. Because Johnny was back. Johnny had returned. In Jim's dream, Johnny paddled through the shallows toward his younger brother's feet – paddled right up the canoe, right through the area where the beavers had cavorted so happily. Now he was pulling himself across the grass . . . pulling himself toward his horrified brother, who stared and stared at the place where Johnny's legs should have been. "Johnny, what happened . . . what have you done . . . where are your legs?"

But his wonderful brother only smiled. That sweet, sweet smile. And with those freckles, scattered all around his nose. "My legs, Jim? They're fine.

Everything is fine, my brother. Why can't you understand? What can't you understand that everything is just fine?"

But Jim stared harder at the blood-soaked pants, torn to shreds at the knee, where his brother's legs had been torn away. "Johnny, I wanted to save you. I know I could have saved you. I think about it night after night, year after year. How could I save you?" In the dream, Jim's mouth was opening and closing – but the words made no sound. Only silence. Nothing but silence.

Johnny said: "You don't understand. Everything is fine. Everything is what it is. Why can't you grasp that, Little Brother?"

And Jim woke. He was lying on a collapsed tent beside a river, shivering with cold, nearly frost-bitten toes. And, shivering with fear.

The next morning at first light, Jim pulled on his soaked shoes, took a deep breath . . . and then set out on foot downstream with the dry bag on his back in search of a route that would lead him back to civilization. He remembered that Judith Rapids were somewhere further and hoped to get there if not the ferry.

After an hour or so, he realized that wasn't going to work and retraced his steps back to ***Tripper, where he spotted*** **two fishermen in a large jet-ski boat. He thought it was a mirage at first.**

One called: "Are you Jim? When he responded yes, he was informed the Search and Rescue Team were just upstream headed our way thinking Jim had drowned or been eaten by a bear or cougar.

After sitting in the fishing boat for an hour, they went back to Jim's canoe they had missed coming down. Loaded it and his gear and headed upstream at 30 miles per hour. The boat could run in water only three-inches deep.

"We have him," they informed the Search and Rescue Team. The young men were laughing and happy that Jim was ok.

Apparently the S&R Team called the sheriff, because he was waiting, arms crossed for Jim at Virgille's Crossing 1-1/2 hours later.

"Do you realize what we have to go through when people such as you don't think?" he asked.

Don, the owner of Virgille's was even angrier and demanded Jim pay $250 to reimburse the Sheriff and him for an extra meal and day with the canoe. "Guess I won't come back through here soon, again," Jim thought. He would have described himself as being "in shock."

*****

Jim was snoring in his tent, a few nights after leaving the Inn where Angela had treated him to dinner. Beside the big man lay a sprawling dog, also snoring loudly. They almost didn't hear the female voice at first.

"Jim? Are you in there? Yoo-hoo! Calling Jim Clark! Say, are you still looking for a paddling partner on your marathon voyage to St. Louis?"

Clark came back to himself slowly, like a swimmer who rises from great depths. When he was awake enough to see, his eyes widened to amazed saucers and the breath rushed out of his body. "Joy? My God . . . Joy Price, is that really *you*?"

Moving in a blur, he had somehow managed to gain his feet. And then a moment later she was in his arms – the slender, dark-eyed, raven-haired lady of his burning dreams. "Joy . . . Joy . . . it's a miracle. How can this be? It's a gift from out of the blue!"

Wonderful kisses. Total happiness! He took a deep breath and got a whiff of her frangipani perfume – that faint, mysterious fragrance he knew so well. She buried her head in his chest, nuzzled contentedly there. "It's so good to be back, Jim, so good to be back."

They swayed together in the doorway of the tent, and Jim's world shrank down to the size of her embrace. And it was at least ten minutes before they could begin to catch up.

"Three weeks, Joy. My God, it's been three weeks!"

"I know, I know. And yet seemed more like three *years*. I was abducted from the river, Jim, actually led away at knife-point by a man named Joe. I never did learn his last name. But he broke down after awhile and told me that he'd been paid to carry me off – by a fellow he refused to identify." Now the young woman's almond-shaped eyes glistened with tears. "But he also told me that he wouldn't harm me physically, and he kept his word.

"I have no idea why somebody would want risk prison for kidnapping a woman in a canoe. But I did my best to placate him – and then the first time he turned his back, I slipped away."

Clark laughed out loud, then hugged her fiercely. "You're the most self-reliant human being I've ever encountered, male *or* female."

She planted a soft kiss on the point of his chin. "I knew that escaping from that thug was the only way I could ever get back to you. I'm just sorry it took me so long."

Jim hugged her for at least the 15th time. "I'd have waited for you until 2000 and beyond, babe."

"My heavens, you *are* loyal, Jim."

"That's me. If only Jack, here, could be so faithful! But seriously, did Angela tell you she met me at the Inn a couple of days ago?"

Joyce shook her head. "I didn't see Angela, Jim. She was gone by the time I escaped from Joe."

Jim nodded, and changed the subject; the less said on the subject of Angela, the better! After an hour of coffee punctuated by more kisses, the two lovebirds headed out to visit the local outfitters – where they arranged for transport of Joy's canoe from the location where Jim had stored it three weeks ago. The battered watercraft arrived the next morning. They also purchased a replacement double-bladed paddle.

She listened carefully while he made an important point: the double-blader would be an essential tool for them in the days up ahead, because the river was now widening to lake-size, and they would be able to move much faster by taking advantage of that fact. And indeed, Jim had already begun using the double-bladed paddle he kept lashed to his own vessel.

"Okay, geography lesson," said Jim. "We should reach the beginning of Fort Peck Lake in about two days. At that point, we'll take off on a 90-mile run that

could include high winds and waves – to say nothing of the potential dangers posed by water-skiers and motorboats. The lake is about five miles wide.

"Joy, I'm thinking that our best move is to have your canoe transported to the end of Fort Peck. I'll meet you about halfway – or about two days after we get on the lake. That would be at about the 40-mile point, according to the map."

She nodded calmly at him. "Ten-four, commander."

"Now, listen: I don't you to worry if I don't make it in two days. That's just an estimate. My actual travel-time will depend on the wind, the waves and possible rain squalls."

Jim knew what he was talking about. More than once, he'd watched all hell break loose, as a squall line thundered across open water, kicking up white caps and boat-swamping waves that could easily capsize a average-sized canoe. It was no joking matter, and hundreds of canoers had paid with their lives because of their failure to respect the power of wind on water.

"The river can be tricky during a storm, Joy, and *Tripper* runs with her nose too low in the troughs as it is. The captain of a 40-foot commercial fishing boat would probably scoff at the storm-waves on Ft. Peck Lake – but you gotta remember that we're riding in a 17-foot, 35-inch-wide canoe with a 600-pound load!"

Joy was smiling at him. "Do you think it's possible that we might be out of our minds, Jim?"

The dog made a growling sound deep in his throat, and both humans could hear him thinking: ***Possible? I can tell you for an absolute fact – you're both mad as March hares! But at least you've got an excuse: you're human.***

What I can't figure out is why I'm riding along with you!

Jim did his best to ignore this canine salvo, however. "Joy, I've come up with a plan that could make my life a bit easier, out there on the water. I'm going to try and rig up a custom-made sail – provided the wind is steady and at my back. Wouldn't it be great to be able to hitch a ride on the breeze, babe?"

Joy hugged him hard, but Jack wasn't buying any. ***Well, shiver me timbers – a sailor in command of a 17-foot canoe! How weird will this river odyssey become? There's no telling, folks . . . you better stay tuned!***

"Joy, the charts I brought along look pretty promising. They confirm that a prevailing wind out of the southwest will usually give me a tail wind. But there's a problem: ***Tripper's*** **carrying a mighty heavy load, remember – and if she ever gets hit by water falling from the crest of a wave when the canoe topples into a trough, I could easily end up taking an unexpected bath.**

"But here's my solution: I think I can cross the waves at about a `quarter' of the crest. As long as those boomers don't get too strong or deep . . . and as long as I keep us nose-first into the waves, I don't think I'll get swamped."

You don't THINK you'll get swamped? Hey, fella – if I'm gonna be aboard, you better be darn certain!

Jim pretended not to have heard this. Instead of whirling on the smart-aleck lab, he patiently explained to Joy how a ranger had warned him to hug the shoreline

on the north side, so that he could quickly get off the water in the event of a squall. But it was a tricky assignment – because if he "hugged" too closely, he'd end up being blasted by reverse-action waves from the shore.

The key calculation, according to the ranger, was this: Jim had to avoid taking on any crests and troughs deeper than twice the width of *Tripper's* waterline. "The danger is real simple," the ranger had said in a laconic drawl. "If you can't adjust to the roll of the water and you allow waves to break over the side of the watercraft, you'll find yourself doing pushups in Davy Jones' Locker."

Clark had taken careful notes. He was ready for the challenge that lay ahead. "Joy, I may have to set up camp a couple of times before I reach you, and I may not show up before the end of three days. But you'll be able to reach me on my cell phone a lot of the time – or you can leave me a message that you called.

"It's do-able, babe, but it won't be pretty. Why, even tandem canoeists are advised to have their canoes shuttled the full length of Peck! But if the wind and waves cooperate, I may be there early on the 2nd day. Jack will stay with you, of course – so I'll be far less concerned about your safety than my own."

Suddenly, the ebullient black Lab was wreathed with happy smiles. *Hallelujah, and let freedom ring! I'll be staying with the lady – and I'll be staying dry as toast! GOOD PLAN! Say, Joy, what's on the menu at your place?*

*

It was raining when Jim and Joy reached Kohler's Landing – a fine, cold drizzle that licked against their necks and sent icy shivers along their spines. The battered

landing – dominated by a weathered billboard that sagged from the roof of Grandma Kohler's Groceries, "Welcome To The Muddy Mo" – marked the end of the scenic section of the *Missouri*, and the beginning of the Charles Russell National Wildlife Refuge. Another few miles of riverway, and they would enter the deep-water environs of Fort Peck Lake.

The operator, a chubby young woman who wore a *Smile!* Button pinned to her sweater, listened to their plans and then frowned. "No hard feelings, sir, but I strongly advise against a solo paddler with a loaded canoe attempting the length of Russell and Peck.

"The Peck area is so remote, there might not be help if you run into a problem. You don't want to get stuck out there in an emergency, do you?"

But Jim only smiled – and Joy could tell that he regarded her warning as a challenge, and that he was determined to continue. After all, he had a "wild river" movie to make! Armed with his tiny video camera – he'd strapped on a short pole through the carry-handle – he intended to nail down some good footage, at whatever the cost. (Still pictures were out of the question, though, if Joy wouldn't there to manage them with her amazing talent for photography.)

*****

An immense sheet of cobalt-blue water, Fort Peck Lake stretches to the horizon as if yearning to become an ocean. Created by the great concrete slab that is the Fort Peck Dam, this vast segment of the *Missouri* runs about 90 miles to the west and nearly as far south. Standing on the boat ramp, they held each other tight.

Like most visitors to Peck, they were suddenly very aware of their puny stature, their insignificance on the face of the teeming earth.

Embracing for half a minute, they whispered encouragement to each other. "My darling Jim, won't you please be careful? I'll think of you every minute of every day!"

Jim tightened the collar of her jacket against the rain, which was falling harder now. "I'll keep you in my thoughts the whole way, babe. You'll probably be in more danger than I am, to tell you the truth. That's why I'm leaving Jack with you. Of course, he's also a very good listener!"

That's right, pal, and I've been listening to you for way too long. Good riddance! When do we eat?

But the humans ignored Jack's sardonic badinage. They both understood that the next few days would be full of peril. Jim, for his part, would be going up against some of the most potentially violent water in the entire *Missouri* system. Joy, meanwhile, knew that the assailants who had masterminded her abduction might very well attempt it again.

They'd been careful to alert both the Natural Resources Police and the Montana State Police to their situation, but the lawmen hadn't taken their concerns seriously. These water-borne cops spent their lives rescuing people and boats – but they didn't know a thing about crimes like abduction and kidnapping.

Jim wiped a fat drop of rain from Joy's eyebrow. "You take care, sweetheart."

Then he pulled his cream-colored Tilly hat down over his own eyes, so she couldn't read his emotion. A moment later, he was seated in the stern, already brandishing the double-bladed paddle. The canoe slid easily into the water, headed due east.

"Jim Clark, I want you to watch out for the wind and the waves – and don't let any strangers creep up on your camp this time!

"I love you, Jim!"

Me, too, big guy! Will you please try to keep yourself INSIDE the canoe for a change?

The canoe hadn't gone 50 yards before Jim abruptly made a hard sweep and u-turned straight back to Joy. "Babe, I can't leave you without giving you the lowdown. I didn't want to scare you . . . but this needs to be said."

Joy stood on the riverbank, blinking slowly at him. "What, Jim? What is it? Just say the words – I can handle them!"

Jim had clenched his jaw. "Joy, the fact is, you may be in greater danger than I am – from forces I don't completely understand. That's why I left Jack behind. But I'll also have 50 pounds less to move with my paddle. This is an endurance race, and I'm going to need every bit of help I can get."

"I understand, sweetheart, I really do."

Jim smiled at her. "Good. Now, do you remember the key commands I taught you for Jack? Just a few one- or two-word phrases are all you'll need. 'Stay! Get

him, or her! Hold him, or her. Easy! Stop! Fetch!' Keep it simple, and he'll always understand."

Joy nodded, then looked at the dog. He was not pleased to hear himself described in this fashion. *Keep it simple, huh? Listen, pal – I'll match my canine I.Q. against your human smarts any day of the week!*

"He's one hell of a watchdog, Joy. I know Jack well – and he'd sacrifice his life in an instant, in order to protect yours."

Now that's more like it. Gosh, I really do sound wonderful, don't I?"

"Joy, all I ask of you, regarding Jack, is that you make sure he always has water available. He can go a couple of days without eating, if he has to, but he needs water daily."

Wait a minute – a couple of days without chow? What kind of outrageous bullshit is that?

The canoe was sliding away from her again, and this time Jim's departure would be for real.

Joy stood on the bank and smiled until he was completely out of sight. Then she turned quickly away. "Come on, Jack. There's no sense standing around here moping – we've got a ton of work to do!"

The dog's features quickly sagged. *Work, Joy? Actually, I had something else in mind – maybe a couple of T-bones, medium-rare?*

But Joy was already hurrying toward her pickup truck, eager to prepare for the next leg of the journey.

He paddled. The hours passed one by one, and he paddled. He watched the wind ruffle the sky-blue water of Fort Peck Lake. He watched the birds in their ceaseless wheeling and turning – the eagles, the ospreys, the loons, the ducks and the geese. Welcome to the Kingdom of the Birds!

Head down, he paddled for all he was worth.

He'd been on the water for about four hours, when the mosquitoes arrived. They came at him dark, boiling clouds, and they were without mercy. Half crazed with distraction, he stuffed a foot of mosquito netting under his hat. But they kept coming, and the sound of their feeding was a drunken siren in his struggling ear. Ah, well. He was free of the biting flies, at least; they couldn't survive on these vast stretches of open water. He paddled, and he was grateful for the cooling wind against his skin – a gale of at least 20 miles per hour, running at him from behind. The sun was bright, but not scalding.

Somewhere in the early afternoon, he put up his makeshift sail – and was pleased to see that his tiny watercraft maintained the same speed, but without the need for paddling. His skin was growing red from the sun, but he didn't worry; he knew it would change into a dark, burnished brown within a few days.

He sat in the stern, breathing slowly, meditating on his progress so far. "Let's see where I am on this trip. Okay . . . I've done about 500 miles, and I'm

beginning to settle into the rhythm of the journey. I'm actually starting to believe I can make it."

Calm now, and very thoughtful, he took stock of his supplies. He had an excellent first-aid kit designed specifically for long trips on the water, and he had two durable flashlights. And it was very nice to be able to sit on the seat with the wind at his back. He could rest for a while, and that was important because he would be facing some very fast river currents in the days ahead.

He had studied his maps carefully; he knew that dangerous Lake Sakakawea in North Dakota, would be coming up in a week or so – and he knew it would be very windy and very hazardous.

"All right," he told himself after eight hours on the water. "I am not going to overdo this. I am going to call it a day, set up my tent and have a bite to eat. Then I'll hit the hay. If the lake is as cooperative tomorrow as it was today, I will be joining Joy and Jack by tomorrow night!"

But that was a very big "if," and deep down, Jim Clark knew it.

*

Clark opened one eye and then struggled to focus it.

But he didn't like what it told him. Sure enough, the big sky-blue lake at his feet had decided to turn cranky overnight. Climbing to his feet, the big man groaned at the sight of the gun-metal clouds that now boiled in the stormy sky. Beneath them, the great expanse of water rose and fell beneath the giant hand of the

wind, while three-foot waves battered themselves to pieces on the broken rocks that littered the shore.

It was ugly, and it was only going to get uglier in the hours ahead.

By the time he pushed off from the lakeshore, a cold rain was already falling. To make matters even worse, the wind had shifted around and was now roaring in from the northwest – making it extremely difficult to keep *Tripper's* nose pointed into the waves. Clark was taking on water with every swell, and he knew he wouldn't be able to stay afloat much longer.

After covering less than 10 miles, he was forced to concede defeat.

Muttering with frustration, he beached the canoe and unloaded it so that he could pour the water out. Still wearing his protective mosquito netting, he ate a cold supper without tasting a bite. By now the flies and mosquitoes were swarming so hard that he decided to duck into the tent to wait for his coffee to boil. Bugs or no bugs, he wasn't going to miss his cup of java!

But then a stray thought crossed his mind . . . and sent a chill through his bones: What if the strong scent of the coffee attracted one of the region's famous bears? It was no joking matter – as more than a few campers had learned to their sorrow. Because he knew that a hungry bear represented a serious threat, Clark did his best to protect his campsite – first by loading everything that carried the scent of food into his metal storage box.

Tying the box securely in a tree, several feet above the ground, he found himself suddenly missing both Joy and Jack. How he yearned for Joy's gentle laughter, and her soothing hands. Even Jack's nasty sarcasm seemed appealing now – so lost and lonely did the Clark-man feel!

After a while, he crawled out of the tent and watched the last flickers of twilight fade out into the deep porcelain sky. The great lake was silent now, as darkness approached; even the ducks, geese, herons and pelicans had fallen silent. The vast sheet of water was devoid of movement – it was as if Jim Clark had fallen off the edge of the earth, into a world of silence and sleep.

Having spotted some bear "scat" and tracks earlier, he wondered if he would be able to sleep. What would happen if a six-foot bear decided he wanted to join the big man in the tent? "Jack," he groaned as he settled down on his lumpy mattress, "where are you when I need you most, big fella?"

For a moment, Clark imagined the response: "I'm digging into a bucket of chopped sirloin, pal – you're on your own!"

He laughed out loud. Good old Jack!

He fell asleep, then, but for only a few minutes. Jerking back awake with a start, he gradually became aware of a scratching, rustling sound in the distance. A night owl, tearing at a felled log in order to feed on termites? Or maybe a coyote, slashing at some small, furred animal in the depth of the forest?

Probably nothing to worry about. But what if that crackling and rustling was actually coming from the paws of a marauding bear?

He shuddered, then second-guessed himself: Why the hell hadn't he hung that bear-bucket in the tree before darkness fell? What if one of those huge, iron-clawed predators had gotten a whiff of his foodstuffs, before he'd wrapped them and stashed them so carefully away? Crawling with anxiety, he began to imagine all of the things that could go wrong out here on the river – perhaps with life-threatening results. What if a rattlesnake nailed him as he collected firewood? He'd have no way to get help – the poison would kill him long before assistance arrived! And what about the dangers out there on the water? What kind of fool would take a fragile, 17-foot boat into the violent and storm-wracked waters of Ft. Peck Lake?

All at once, he wanted to quit. Give it up – and hurry on back to dear old Baltimore! But then his heart sank – as he realized that Veronica and little Henry would not be waiting to greet him. There would be no balloons tied to their front door, and no yellow ribbon dangling from the big oak tree in Veronica's front yard.

If he did quit, he'd have nothing to return to. And how would Joy react – after discovering that Big Jim Clark didn't have the guts to complete this difficult journey? She'd see him as a failure – a timid "wuss" who threw in the towel whenever a challenge became difficult.

No, sir, he would *not* quit! Better to be eaten by a bear, if it came to that, than to hang his head and retreat from the challenge he'd set for himself! "All right," he muttered fiercely at himself. "Let's take a deep breath, and let's get back on task. What do you need to take care of that bear problem?"

He was on his feet now. *I need a rock weighing about a pound to tie to the bear-bucket rope – and then I can just toss it over a tree limb. I'll just step a few feet into the woods and grab the first big rock I come across. And if there's a bear already waiting for me in the undergrowth, so be it!*

A few moments later, he was out of the tent and striding purposefully toward the spot where the scratching and rustling had taken place. Laughing, he fought through the fear by announcing in a triumphant shout: "If you're waiting for me, here I come!"

How could have known that two dark, whispering shadows heard his shouted challenge – and then leaned toward each other in the hazy darkness of the forest?

"Here he comes," growled Kip.

"Too bad for him," said Sam.

*

Jim moved forward slowly, almost tip-toeing. The rain had stopped falling now, and the distant stars flashed here and there through the shaggy branches of oak and beech and cedar. So far, so good . . .

Swoosh! – a black shadow lunged past his ear – but it was gone before he could react: a harmless bat!

He began to hum a little song to himself, in order to defend against the fear: *L.A. is a great big freeway; put a hundred down and buy a car.*

He took another step forward. He could hear his boots crunching into the leaves and twigs that carpeted the forest floor. Why be afraid? He was tired of living with fear. Fear was the enemy, and it would not be conquered until he found a way to overcome it.

In a week, maybe two, they'll make you a star. . . .

There! Gleaming softly in the moonlight, a large white rock invited his hand. Bending at the waist, he prepared to wrestle it free from the earth – it would be perfect for his bucket –

He heard a brief hissing sound – a snake?

No . . . a net! Stunned, he gaped at the loops of rope that now surrounded his startled body –

Panic rose in his throat – *a strong animal net*!

He thrashed violently, uselessly, against the cords that now bound him. A moment later, he heard a voice shouting above the sounds of his own desperate breathing: "That's it – grab him – hold him good – where's the straight-jacket? Come on, come on – knock him out, if you have to. Knock him out!"

Fascinated, horrified, he watched an arm lift a camp shovel high in the air . . . watched the heavy iron whistle downwards toward his head. Watched the pale vanilla moonlight gleam on the edge of the shovel-blade. . . .

Do you know the way to San Jose? I'm headed home to find

Some peace of mind . . .

The air lit up with strings of fiery red Chinese firecrackers – ***bap, bap, bap*** **– and then he was watching a sparkler throw gems of flickering blue light into the mouth of the dark. He shouted something . . . a single word . . . "Joy!" and a moment later, the world went dark and airless, and he imagined that he was lying beneath the big white rock in the heart of the forest, and his eyes were as dead as the stone above them, and his heart was frozen like a hunk of glacier ice on the Arctic tundra, and if this was dying, it seemed quieter, softer, slower than he had ever imagined it would be. . . .**

*

When Jim came to, he found himself bound with heavy rope and reinforced fish netting. It was daylight. He was seated on the ground with his back against a black oak tree. His body hurt all over – and he could feel where the blood from his head wound had congealed on his face. For a moment, he almost laughed at the absurdity of his situation.

Try as he might, Jim Clark couldn't seem to overcome the forces that were arrayed against him. For the first time, a sinister thought crept into his fevered brain: ***Somebody is trying to prevent me from beating the St. Charles deadline.*** **But who? And why? It didn't make any sense! What did anybody have to gain from preventing a lone canoeist from successfully completing –**

Then it hit him.

Holy cow!

All at once, he was remembering the furtive, darting look in Jack Spader's eye. Remembering the way the publisher kept staring at the floor, while they discussed the contest that was about take Jim Clark down the Muddy Mo. "This story will draw readers like flies!" the publisher had said. "People love stories where an underdog struggles to succeed against overwhelming odds. And when they find out that you stand to collect a cool one-hundred thou by getting to St. Charles on time, they'll start rooting for you, bigtime.

"If we get lucky, you'll end up on the network news, telling Dan Rather and Peter Jennings why you're so intent on paddling 2,500 miles in three months. It's a natural, Jim!"

But then his eyes had darted away again, as he took a long pull on his Hav-a-Tampa.

Remembering that moment in Spader's mahogany-paneled office, Clark took a deep breath. All at once, he was thinking the unthinkable: ***Spader doesn't want to pay me the damn prize-money, and he's hired some thugs to make sure I don't complete the journey in time.***

His theory made sense – ugly sense. And now he was obviously the prisoner of Spader's goons. If there was any good news in his situation, it consisted of a single

fact: His assailants didn't have to kill him, in order to accomplish their mission and earn their paychecks from the magazine publisher.

All they had to do was keep him incommunicado for a week or so, and the deadline would be out of reach.

Groaning with pain from the shovel-blow he'd taken, Clark braced his aching head against the tree trunk. Suddenly he found himself praying that Joy hadn't listened to his last, off-hand remark: "Listen, honey, don't worry if I'm a day or two late!"

His only hope now was that she'd become alarmed – and beg the authorities to send out a search party for him. But would the State Police and the DNR cops even listen to her? Moaning with frustration, he could almost hear them telling the frantic woman: "Don't you worry, little lady. This kind of thing happens all the time on the Muddy Mo – and experience shows that sooner or later, the missing canoe turns up on its own. We'll keep an eye out for him – why don't you check back with us in two or three days?"

While the big man sat helplessly bound to the tree, a frantic Joy was engaged in precisely the kind of conversation that Jim had been hoping for. Fighting back tears, she had nearly driven off the road a couple of times in a frantic dash to the offices of the Department of Natural Resources – where a highly skeptical lawman (his silver badge identified him as "Ranger Carter") listened calmly to her torrent of frightened words.

"Ranger Carter, I'm desperate and I need your help. I'm a Forest Ranger, myself – here, take a look at my I.D." She thrust the pale green card under his nose.

The tall, lanky ranger examined the photo I.D. for a moment, then offered her a toothy smile. "It's good to meet you, ma'am. What seems to be the difficulty?"

She frowned. Struggled for the right words. "My canoeing partner – a guy named Jim Clark – he was crossing Ft. Peck, and he's way overdue. I'm convinced that he's in danger."

The ranger squinted thoughtfully at her. "Yes, ma'am. Ahh . . . what do you think might be wrong?"

She took a deep breath. "I have reason to believe some people might be chasing him. Trying to . . . trying to injure him, maybe even kill him."

Ranger Carter blinked slowly. "I see. How long has your friend been missing?"

"Only a couple of days."

"Uh-huh. Well, maybe the weather drove him off the lake. We've been getting reports that the wind and rain have reduced visibility to less than 50 yards, in many areas."

She shook her head in frustration. "No, I'm sure he didn't give up because of the weather. I think he's been attacked!"

The ranger nodded. "Okay. Attacked by whom, exactly?"

"By the . . . the *people* I mentioned. They're trying to stop him for some reason, shut down his canoe trip!"

The tall ranger had begun to chew at his lower lip. "I see. Did these . . . these people threaten your friend, Miz Price?"

She thought about it for a moment. "Well, not exactly. But somebody attacked him before, higher up the river, at Canyon Ferry Lake. And they also stole his canoe at one point – even stole his dog! It's clear that he's being followed – these things didn't happen by chance! And I was abducted, myself, only a few days later!"

The ranger's blue eyes widened considerably. "How's that again, Miz Price? Are you saying you've *also* been attacked by these . . . these bad folks?"

She shook her head violently. "No, no. My situation was different – it was my former husband who abducted me. He kept me locked up in a cabin for days on end – but I'm convinced he was working for the same people who are after Jim!"

The ranger took a long, slow breath. "Miz Price, I'm afraid I'm going to need more evidence, before I can send out a Missing Persons Alert. How do you know your friend didn't simply decide to get off the water and wait out the storm?"

Joy had begun to shake her head violently. "Ranger Carter, you need to understand: Clark should have been here 48 hours ago! Call it a woman's intuition – but I'm positive somebody's trying to hurt him, probably in order to keep him from a historic accomplishment: solo-canoeing the entire Missouri in 90 days. I've

got this ominous feeling in the pit of my stomach that he's been badly injured, somewhere between the western entry to Ft. Peck Lake and here. "

The ranger nodded. "No offense, but that's pretty speculative and huge country, Miz Price. How can I assist?"

"Just help me find somebody with a motorboat – and let me leave my dog here – I'll search for him, myself!"

The tall ranger smiled calmly – and then surprised Joy Price. "I tell you what. I'm off duty in an hour – and I've got one of the fastest, safest runabouts on this section of the water. If you like, I'll take you on a quick run down the river, and we'll see if we can find any sign of your friend."

Amazed, Joy clapped her hands together. "Ranger Carter, you're a gift from heaven above – I can't thank you enough! Let's do it!"

Ranger Carter proved to be as good as his word.

Within 90 minutes of their high-adrenalin powwow, the tall man in the jade-green DNR uniform was speeding both of them toward Ft. Peck Lake in his four-wheel-drive Jeep. At the last moment, Joy had suddenly changed her mind about Clark's loyal canine – which meant that an eager-eye Lab Retriever named Jack now reigned supreme in the back seat.

Ranger Carter drove with his eyes glued to the winding road. But he didn't remain silent; there were too many things that needed explaining. "Joy, you're a park ranger, yourself – so I'm sure I don't have to warn you that we're heading into

some pretty wild country. We've had several grizzlies on the move around Ft. Peck in recent months – along with a platoon of cougars and some pretty aggressive timber wolves. That pal of yours in the back seat should give you some protection . . . but we need to take some additional precautions.

"I'll stay in the general area while you patrol the lakeshore in your canoe. That way, I can respond quickly, if you suddenly decide you need some help."

Joy turned to face him, and her warm smile could have heated an igloo in January. "Ranger Carter, I can't thank you enough for all you're doing. Just give me time to slip on my backpack – I'm carrying a small tent and some food in metal containers – and I'll be ready to go. I'm all set . . . got my outdoor clothing and my compass – to say nothing of my mosquito repellant and a hat with a bug-net."

"I hear you, Joy." The ranger broke into his drawling chuckle. "I've been caught out there on the water a couple of times without repellant, and it was rough, lemme tell you."

"Okay," said Carter. "Let's get down to business. How about if I take you and Jack about 20-25 miles west before I let you out? It'll take me at least an hour to start hunting for the type of cove where an exhausted canoer would pull into – and where a couple of *banditos* might also be hiding."

He went on to explain how a series of well-worn trails flanked the lake throughout much of its length. "Maybe you and Jack could pick one of those trails, and give it a run," he said. "Keep your cell phone humming, just in case. Maybe you'll get a signal."

After Ranger Carter selected a good spot and landed the boat, Joy and Jack quickly climbed out and waded ashore, then moved away from the lake. The dog had begun to growl by now, and his neck hairs were standing up straight.

"That's it," said Joy. "Now we're talking! Jack, where is Jim? Go find Jim, Jack!" Joy swung her arm in a parallel arc to indicate to Jack that he should do what he was born for – finding things that had gotten lost. Jack responded with a thunderous bark, and for once his sarcasm had evaporated: *You can count on me, Miss Joy. My best friend may be in trouble – but not for long, if I can help it!*

Suddenly, the growling dog vaulted away into the undergrowth and vanished without a trace. The two rangers paced back and forth beneath the jack pine . . . waiting anxiously for his return. And they weren't disappointed: Within ten minutes, a triumphant-looking Jack stood in front of them, barking furiously.

"Come on," hollered Joy. She was already running. "He wants us to follow him back into the woods!" The two of them raced through the undergrowth, with the dog leading the way. They couldn't keep up, and Joy kept calling, "Wait up, Jack! Whoa! Stop!" But the excited dog only seemed to run faster.

Stumbling and staggering, they moved as fast as they could along the rocky trail. Jack's bark was louder than ever over the next five minutes. And then it happened.

The frantic dog lurched around a twisting turn . . . and skidded to a stop in front of a large object that appeared to be tied to a tree! The object was wrapped in canvas . . . no, a closer look showed that it was entangled in a heavy net.

Joy felt the wind rushing out of her body.

It *was a man*!

It was Jim Clark. Would she find him dead . . . or still breathing?

Holding her breath and praying silently, the terrified young woman bent over the man beneath the net. "My God," she told Ranger Carter with a gasp, "he's pale as a sheet!" For a moment she was afraid to touch him . . . but then a blast of sheer terror surged through her and she reached out to caress his blood-streaked forehead. "Jim, are you there? Can you hear me? For God's sake, say something!"

For a heart-stopping moment, he remained motionless, while her hand lay against his cold, white face.

Then he made a groaning sound. One eye fell open, and it stared at her for a few seconds without recognition. Joy could feel her heart beating, pulse by agonizing pulse. "Jim . . . it's me. Joy! I've been so worried; I've been half-crazy with fear. Can you speak?"

He struggled for a moment, and then she saw his lips moving. But the words came out in a whisper. "Hey, babe. It's me, all right. The Clark-man. Never felt better in my life."

"Oh, my God." She had begun to stroke his right cheek, where the coagulated blood lay thickest. "Who did this to you, Jim? Who?"

He smiled, or tried to – his mouth twitched a couple of times, and then went still again. "I never got a look at them, Joy. One minute I was wandering through the

underbrush, hunting for a rock – and the next minute, a piano fell on my head. A baby grand. I haven't been hit that hard since I tried to block the middle linebacker in the Oklahoma game!"

Joy breathed a huge sigh of relief; if the big man had started making jokes, it meant he would probably survive.

"Jim, you sit tight – Ranger Carter – he's been a lifesaver, believe me!"

Jim nodded, then winced with the pain it caused. "Many thanks to you, officer. Duty above and beyond the call!"

"No problem," said Carter with a smile. "Looks to me like you're grappling with Excedrin Headache Number 1, Jim. Hang on a minute – I've got some aspirin in my first-aid kit, back in the Jeep."

As soon as the tall ranger was out of sight, Joy bent over the blood-smeared man on the ground. "I'll cut you free in a second Jim . . . but while you're my prisoner, I'm going to take full advantage of you."

She put her mouth against his, and the world dissolved into a smear of wet cotton candy. They stayed like that for half a minute – lost to the great lake beside them, and to the quiet dog who had kept a respectful distance, waiting to see if his master was alive or dead. Their kiss was a world unto itself, a special place in which nothing else existed . . . only the faint, steady, rhythmical sound of two hearts beating as one.

They awoke to the sound of Ranger Carter clearing his throat.

"Okay, I brought you three aspirin, Jim. Whaddaya say we cut you out of this spider web and get you moving toward some serious first aid?"

"Go for it," said Jim Clark.

While the ranger slashed away at the thick netting, Joy fired off a series of flash photos that would document this part of the adventure for *Wild Rivers*. Within five minutes the injured boatman was free of his bonds, and Joy had begun washing the crusted blood from his forehead and around his eyes, nose and mouth. He smiled at her through blistered lips. He was thoroughly embarrassed by the odor that rose from his abused body; the call of nature had reduced him to soiling himself during his 48-hour stretch as a prisoner.

Still, he hadn't lost his ability to make fun of himself. "My head feels like Omaha Beach, about 15 minutes after the invasion," he joked after a bit. "Are my eyes crossed, Joy?"

She hugged him. "No more than usual, Jim."

"I love you, babe."

She echoed his phrase, then kissed him gently, with the tears still streaming down her face. The ropes and the netting had fallen away completely now, and Joy untied the straight jacket and removed it. She allowed him a few swallows from her canteen . . . but then made him sip and wait a few minutes before attempting more.

Ranger Carter watched all of this for a few minutes, then decided to get busy. "Jim, do you know how to reach your campsite from here? If we can get you there,

you'll be able to clean up and change your clothes." Jim nodded, and the two of them helped him to his feet. Together they limped toward the campsite. The big man would have fallen two or three times along the way – but they kept a firm grasp on him from one step to the next.

After ten minutes of strenuous effort, they reached the campsite. The tent and its contents were a shambles. The boat contents, including the dry bags, had also been tossed and emptied. Animals had been clawing through Jim's meager belongings, it appeared. Nonetheless, Joy and Ranger Carter were able to assemble a change of clothing for Jim, along with a towel and washcloth. With Joy's help, Jim limped down to the lakeshore, removed his soiled clothing, and began to wash his lacerated body. Joy helped him dress himself in fresh new clothes.

"Hey, I'm starting to feel halfway human again – even though I've been whipped with an ugly-stick!"

"Thank God we reached you in time," said Joy. "I don't want to think about what would have happened without Jack!" She smiled in the direction of the beaming canine, who sat nearby. "That dog was amazing, darling. The moment I told him to start looking for you, he took off like a shot."

Jim laughed. "I'm not surprised, Joy. As soon as we get back to civilization, I'm going to buy him a month's supply of ground chuck!"

The dog shifted his hindquarters, then scowled. *Ground chuck? Hey, pal – I just saved the Clark-man from certain disaster . . . so let's not waste time talking about*

mere hamburger! Tell me, Jim: Do you remember those two French words I love to hear: filet and mignon?

*

By now, Ranger Carter had returned from a brief inspection tour along the waterline. "Jim, you're in luck. As far as I can tell, your boat has weathered the storm. She looks to be intact, and she's perfectly seaworthy. You're one lucky boatman, fella.

"I've gone ahead and repacked your dry bags. I righted the canoe, as well – but I only came up with one paddle. Looks like you lost a regular paddle and your double-bladed kayak paddle."

Jim nodded. Meanwhile, Joy had her hand up, like a kid in a classroom. "Ranger Carter," she said in a rush, "the wind has calmed and there isn't much wave action. Perhaps I could paddle the canoe up to my campsite now? Under these mild conditions, we won't need but the one paddle."

Jim smiled at her. "I wish you could do that, hon. But unfortunately, the contest rules won't allow it! As bad as I feel, I'll have to do the paddling, according to my contract with *Rivers*. But, it would be wonderful if you could make the run with me to your camp. I've still got a lot of pain in my ribcage and my back from the beatings – but we should be able to make it in three or four hours, nonetheless."

He took a long look at her face, and his eyes glistened with unexpected tears: "Joy . . . damn it, I've missed you like crazy! To be honest, I never thought I'd see you again."

They said goodbye to Ranger Carter after that, and Joy vowed to write his supervisor a glowing thank-you letter within the next few days. "Ranger Carter," she said with a mile-wide smile, "you and the other guys in your unit are what made this country great. Talk about going above and beyond the call of duty – wow! I'm proud to know that you're part of the Park Service!"

Thoroughly embarrassed, Ranger Carter simply saluted in military fashion: "Just doing my job, ma'am. No big deal, huh?" He paused to give them a quick wink: "You two stay safe on the water now, you hear, so we don't have to come find you again!"

A few seconds later, they were listening to the sound of his runabout rumbling away to the east.

It was time to go. They loaded the canoe with the last of their belongings and prepared to set sail.

But where was their canine hero, now that departure time had finally arrived? Jim found him sitting on his haunches, ten yards deep in the underbrush. "Come on, Jack, it's time to go! What's the matter, Jack-o? Why the long face?"

The dog refused to budge, and his long-muzzled face was a mask of sullen outrage. ***Whaddya mean, What's the matter? Have you completely forgotten the two***

little French words we talked about? I saved your hindquarters – and I expect to be paid!

It took Jim a lot of coaxing – along with several outlandish promises involving future filets and rib-cuts – before the miffed Retriever finally agreed to climb into the wobbly canoe.

But at last they were off. The race to St. Louis was back underway!

They skimmed the river like a pair of intoxicated water bugs – and why not? They were together again, and nothing else mattered. And now, because they had found each other once again, they took pleasure in the smallest things. They marveled at a stilt-legged great blue heron, his silver beak flashing like a dagger against the mid-day sun. . . .

They applauded a family of turtles – papa, mama, and four little tortoise-shells trailing behind, as they waddled along the top of a bumpy, mud-smeared log. . . .

Joy cried out – "Look, there!" – and they caught their breaths together – a majestic bald eagle wheeled against the blue horizon like a fortress outfitted with wings, and his black shadow swept over their tiny canoe like the shade from a bomber crossing the sun.

The world was fascinating again, and mysterious, and full of life – because *they* were full of the energy that flared each time their eyes met, the vibrations that began each time their hands and feet touched.

What was time? What was space? For Jim and Joy, alone together on the vastness of Ft. Peck Lake, five hours zoomed past in what seemed like 15 minutes, so unconscious were they of their relentlessly ticking watches. They took turns oohing and aaahing over scenery that grew more breathtaking with each and every minute. Gravel bars, sandstone cliffs, foaming rapids . . . and everywhere they looked, they witnessed the burgeoning wildlife of the river, the creatures in their teeming millions flashing and soaring against the porcelain-blue sky.

"My God," Joy kept saying, "how beautiful, how beautiful it all is!"

But at last they reached Joy's camp, and unloaded the gear. For the next day or so, Joy would nurse the big man slowly back to health. His joints were still rusty, and his poor face looked as if it had been whipped with a tangle of fishhooks – but the adventurer was still breathing, still kicking – as she quickly discovered when he pulled her down onto his sleeping bag and covered her trembling body with his own!

"Go easy . . . slow down . . . be *careful*, Jim," she gasped as he tore at her clothing and thrust himself deep into the space between her heaving thighs. "My God, you'll have a *heart* attack if you keep this up!"

He lifted his head for a moment: "What a terrific way to go, Joy! If it does happen, will you tell Jack that I died with a smile on my face?"

When calm finally returned, Joy set about building their campfire and cooking their chicken and broccoli and scalloped potatoes. Meanwhile, Jim went to work on

the phone. He wasn't looking forward to this conversation – but he knew it was time to have a hard-nosed conversation with a gentleman named Jay Spader.

It was time to demand a few *answers.*

"Hello, Jay? This is Jim Clark, calling you from the Missouri River!"

"Oh . . . ah . . . yeah! How you doing, Jim? And where *are* you?"

"I'm nearly across Ft. Peck Lake, Jay. I've run into some problems, though, and I wanted to touch base with you."

There was a long silence, during which Clark could hear the wheels turning in his publisher's head. Then: "Jim, if you're still crossing Ft. Peck, you're way off the pace. Doesn't look to me like you'll be able to make it. Have you decided to throw in the towel?"

Clark didn't hesitate. "I'm facing an uphill battle, I know that – but all I need is a few five or six 12-hour days, and I'll be right back on schedule."

"Uh-huh. I see. Fine, then."

Jim frowned. "You don't sound terribly enthused, Jay."

There was another lengthy pause, during which Jim could hear the metallic snap of a lighter: Spader was torching up another Hav-a-Tampa. It was easy to picture him sitting at the big mahogany desk in St. Louis, with the stogy jutting from his triple chin.

"Jim, you know we're rooting for you to make that deadline! Everybody at this magazine is behind you, believe me. But the fact remains: You're *way* behind schedule, and things don't look good.

"Did you say you've encountered some 'problems' on the water? What kind of problems, Jim? Did you spring a leak, or something?"

Clark snorted impatiently. "I can *fix* a leak, Jay. I'm talking about the kinds of problems you can't fix – such as getting hit in the head and tied to a tree for 48 hours."

"Hit in the head? You're kidding!" Spader's voice was full of empathy, but it came off exaggerated and overdone – at least to Clark.

"Actually, I've been attacked several times on the river, Jay. On one occasion, somebody even took my canoe – along with my dog. I'm having a lot of trouble figuring out why anybody would want to stop me from reaching St. Louis on time."

More silences. He could hear Spader pulling on his cigar, while the wheels turned and turned. "Jim, it sounds to me like you're suffering from fatigue, that's all. Okay . . . so you ran into a few hooligans out there on the Muddy Mo. The same thing could have happened to you in downtown St. Louis!"

Clark shook his head. "In St. Louis, I'd have been robbed. Just another mugging. But that didn't happen here. Jay, I've been knocked around several times since I left Three Forks – but nobody's taken as much as a dime from me.

The way it looks right now, the real purpose was to slow me down, prevent me from beating your deadline."

"Uh-huh. Okay, Jim, Tell you what -- I'll check it out. I've got dozens of sources all along the river – I'll ask 'em to eyeball the neighborhood and find out if anybody's mad at you."

"Right. Thanks a lot, Jay."

"You bet, pal. And good luck! Remember – we're all pulling for you to make it, here at *Wild Rivers*."

"Uh-huh. I hear you, Jay. And thanks."

But the phone had already gone dead in Clark's hand.

He hit the "Off" button, then stood motionless for half a minute, while his gaze wandered across the royal-blue waters of Ft. Peck Lake.

For the first time since the long journey had begun, he was forced to acknowledge a sinister fact: By gosh, *I can't trust my own publisher. From here on, I've got to watch everything that moves on the water.*

*

The thought wasn't pretty, but it would have to be confronted. Increasingly, it seemed clear that Jay Spader didn't want to pay him the $100K – and that the fat man with the Hav-a-Tampa would do anything to stop him! His high-paying and high-status job probably was in the balance.

Spader had told him he "couldn't imagine why anyone would hinder his progress but that he would look into it. Perhaps you angered some landowners along the *Missouri.*"

"Jim, I will paddle alongside you until we pass the *Yellowstone* River and cross the North Dakota border heading to Lake *Sakakawea.* I will continue gathering information for my report. Then, I will return to my work location in Montana. I will drive or fly to join you later as you continue to St. Louis. Let's plan on Bismarck, ND." Joy had now been away from her work assignment for 5 weeks.

In spite of worry of flooding, they had been camping on gravel bars because much less time and labor and due to Jim's health. It would have required a lot of strenuous work to move the canoes and their contents. "It is so beautiful, Jim, I am going to have difficulty in tearing myself away from here. You and this trip have become such a part of me. I can't bear to think of not experiencing this beautiful country from a canoe and seeing you everyday and night."

Even better, he now felt closer to Joy than ever.

"I'm the luckiest dude on the planet, babe!"

Smiling, she looked back at him from the bow of the racing canoe. "Thanks, Jim . . . but what brought *that* on?"

It was eight o'clock in the morning – a balmy spring day with the temperature set to reach 75 – and the big man wanted to sing out loud: *June, June, June is busting out all over!*

He restrained himself, however. Instead, he pointed his double-bladed paddle at her. "Okay, why do I feel like Mr. Lucky today? It's simple, Joy. For

starters, I'm riding in a canoe paddling next to the most beautiful woman in the entire Missouri River drainage area."

She grinned in spite of herself. "Yeah . . . *right.*"

The dog turned slightly, so that he could eyeball the paddler directly. *You're also privileged to be sailing with a Blue Chip, World-Class Retriever, pal. No wonder you're on Cloud Number 9!*

Jim chose to ignore this powerful insight, however. "But you're not just beautiful, Joy – you're also an extremely gifted photographer . . . and a woman blessed with a Super V-8 intellect. In short: You're the finest female canoe passenger in all of North America – and you can quote me on that!"

Jack made a spluttering sound. *My God, Clark, are you without shame? That's the most sickening speech ever uttered by a male member of homo sapiens!*

"Thank you very much, sir," said Joy. "You're not so bad, yourself."

Oh yes, he is. The guy's a walking disaster area, Miss Joy. Wake up!

"*Muchas gracias,*" said Jim. "Of course, I *also* like the fact that you're half Lakota Sioux – especially given the fact that we're about to visit one of their largest enclaves, known as the Ft. Peck Indian Reservation!"

The visit began three hours later – after some vigorous paddling on Joy and Jim's parts – when the heavily laden canoes nosed into the Reservation Dock. Within a few minutes, several Sioux officials had arrived to greet the Missouri River adventurers, and to offer them as much help as they needed in accomplishing their mission.

Soon they were talking strategy with a youthful, thoughtful tribal leader named Running Bear – the chief of this particular family of Lakota, as it turned out. "It's good to meet both of you," said the slender Indian, who wore a trim sport coat and freshly pressed slacks. "Jim, I want you to know that the Lakota Sioux respect the name 'Clark' very much – and for reasons that you probably understand."

The big man nodded. The three of them were sitting over coffee in the crowded Ft. Peck Trading Store Café. "That respect cuts both ways, Running Bear. Every history ever written about the Lewis and Clark expedition tells us that the explorers couldn't have gotten twenty miles down the trail without the enormous help they received from the Native Americans along the way!"

Both men blinked, then – as Joy's flash camera lit up their corner of the café with a sudden flash of light. "Don't mind her," said Jim with a smile. "Joy's one of the best photographers in the Midwest – and if we're not careful, she'll put us both on the cover of *People* Magazine!"

After thanking their Native American hosts profusely, Jim and Joy huddled for a brief strategy session.

"From here on, it's nose to the grindstone," said the big man. "Joy, the window of opportunity is about to slam shut on me. I've got to spend some long days on the water – or give up my hope of reaching St. Louis on time."

"Never!" snapped Joy. "I'll tell you what – how about if I paddle alongside you until we pass the *Yellowstone* River and cross the North Dakota border heading to

Lake *Sakakawea?* I'll continue gathering information for my report – but right after we hit the lake, I'll return to my work location in Montana.

"After a couple of weeks or so, depending on your progress, I can join you at Bismarck, ND."

"I hear you, babe. Sounds like a good plan – especially given the fact that you've been away from your own work assignment for five weeks."

Within an hour of their impromptu powwow, the two voyagers were paddling for all they were worth. They skimmed past Wolf Point and Culbertson . . . then flashed through the confluence of the *Yellowstone* and the Muddy Mo. The great state of Montana was history now; they'd entered North Dakota, and they wouldn't be here long.

They reached a stretch of dappled, blue-green water overhung by forests of weeping willow. Bright shadows played on the surface, and the warming breeze was alive with turquoise-hued butterflies. Like an illustration in a children's storybook, the landscape vibrated with warmth, color, mystery.

Joy pulled her canoe up beside her partner's. "Is this unbelievable, or what, Jim? How in the world am I going to leave this river behind tomorrow? I feel like we've wandered into another dimension, entirely – the kind of unspoiled paradise Adam and Eve must have known, at the very beginning!"

Clark laughed out loud. "I wish you didn't have to go, babe – but I know you don't have a choice. Just remember that the river will always be here; we can pick up our paddles and go, whenever we want, throughout all the years that lie ahead!"

Jack's eyes opened. The big dog had been napping in the middle of Joy's canoe, with both paws hanging lazily over the water. *Oh my God, has he started giving speeches again?*

"I hear you," said Joy, "loud and clear! In a way, just knowing the river is *here* will keep me feeling strong and hopeful. After all these days out on the water with you, I feel like the Muddy Mo has become my friend."

Jim nodded. "Makes sense to me, Joy. If you think about it, the Mo is actually a living creature. Just like a person, she changes from second to second! She's smooth as glass one instant, and roaring with turbulence the next. Just like a woman I know! Have you heard that famous Chinese saying: 'Try as you might, you cannot step in the same river twice?'"

Jack's eyes widened. *You're kidding me, right? Now he's doing Chinese philosophy – and we're nearly an hour past lunchtime! Hello? Can we get back to terra firma here? Where is the CHOW?*

A moment later, however, the ticked-off retriever was relieved to see that they were easing into port. And the sign above the outfitter's station – Welcome to Ely, N.D. – told them what they most wanted to hear: They'd finished the first and toughest leg of the journey.

Okay, welcome to North Dakota, Jack growled at himself. *You humans never cease to amaze me. You think you deserve a medal – for sitting in your little boat while a river carried you across Montana!*

Instead of standing around bragging about how great we all are, do we think we could stop by the Meat Counter and get serious about some prime rib?

They spent their last night together at the River Outlook, a Victorian-style inn that featured 19th-Century Chippendale oak-wood furniture and a graceful balcony extending from each room. After their torrid lovemaking finally concluded, they sat on a wicker banquette beneath the stars, holding hands and dreaming of the future that might someday be theirs.

Above their nodding heads, a billion stars glittered like some fabulous jewelry that had been flung against the vast ocean of the dark.

"Look, there's Gemini," Joy told him, "just below the handle in the Big Dipper. Can you see it? The Twins! They say it's good luck to spot them on a clear night – it means you and the ones you love will be together again soon."

Jim smiled. "I'm glad to know I'll see you again soon, Joy. We're going to be facing some fearful days up ahead, you know that. You don't canoe the Big Mo risk-free, for one thing. And I'm also a little bit concerned about the human factor – those nasty guys who seem to have been following me all the way from Montana."

"Jim, I'm counting on you to be cautious." She snuggled against his warm shoulder. "What good is the prize money if you never get to spend it? I'd rather

have you sitting at the dinner table with me, safe and sound, than all the wealth of Persia!"

He chuckled. "My sentiments, exactly, babe. If things start to go south out there on the water, you can bet that I'll high-tail it home in a hurry. I'm not too worried about the dangers, though – shoot, I've got Big Jack to protect me."

The well-fed canine – he'd been dozing at their feet, while digesting four pounds of Grade A rump steak – opened one eye and rolled it. ***Jeez, has he started the soap opera speeches again? Why can't this guy just contemplate the stars in silence, like I do – instead of blabbing his darn head off?***

"I'll be thinking of you every night at bedtime," said Joy with a long, drawn-out sigh.

Jim winked at her. "Didn't they teach you that 'lustful thoughts' are a sin, Joy?"

She gave his leg a playful slap. "I didn't say it would be ***lustful*** **thinking!"**

But a moment later, their lips were together again, and the balcony-temperature was rising fast.

Jack came to his feet quickly, and had soon departed the balcony.

Are these guys without shame, or what? Talk about embarrassing yourself in front of company!

But the loyal dog was soon asleep again. The two lovers remained on the balcony, while the great constellations wheeled and flared above them, and the night breeze riffled the branches of oak and beech and cedar. They clung to each other as hard as they could, and they did their best to fend off their growing sense of melancholy. This would be their last night together for several weeks, and they both knew it.

Williston had an international airport, so Joy decided she would like to leave for her work in Great Falls from there. They stayed in a very clean hotel and enjoyed each other being clean and smelling fresh for a change. "Lounging and making love with you in a tent is a wonderful pleasure, Jim, but stretching out and doing it on a king-sized bed is even more wonderful!" They shipped her canoe back to Great falls.

They toured Ft. Union and Ft. Buford, taking photographs and videos. Interviews and photographs of some of the locals helped round out their stay there. The residents and visitors were very cordial and made this part of the journey especially enjoyable. ***Of course, I had to stay in a kennel, but do they feed good steaks!***

Joy called for a limo to the Williston airport. "I will be on the 180-mile Lake Sakakawea for about six days before the river cuts south and then perhaps four more paddling days to Bismarck, about 225 miles downstream. Plan on flying in and spending a weekend with me. After that, I expect another 60-70 miles on Lake Oahe will bring Jack and me into South Dakota. Goodbye for a while, my sweet, until you fly into Bismarck. My ardor of our rendezvous will motivate my paddling speed."

I plan to stop at some of the reconstructed forts and perhaps see and film some of the Indian dances that are classic. It should take me about two weeks to get to Bismarck. I will keep in touch with you by cell, e-mail or land phone every day that I can." They kissed and held each other tightly for several long seconds. Questions in Jim's and Joy's minds were unexpressed for fear of raising more concern and stress.

Jim and Jack were back on Lake *Sakakawea* within a half hour to get in as many daylight hours as possible on a non-windy day. They camped and Jim fixed beautiful steaks for both he and Jack. "Wonderful. I don't even hear a comment about my cooking from you, Jack. *If I could express it in human terms, you would SURELY hear some partner!*

Not that Joy complained, but I could tell she'd rather grill them herself. The scenery was breathtaking, although there were high winds with plenty of flies and mosquitoes. Uniform of the day included mosquito netting, plenty of bug dope and sun block. Also very appealing were the historic sites where North Dakota had gone all out to reconstruct earth lodges and the forts. Jim stopped to take still pictures and also videos of some of the colorful tribal dances and a rodeo. He recorded some interesting interviews with the Mandan Indian Natives. The Mandans were magnificient people!

For some strange meteorological reason, the weather cooperated and Lake Sakakawea was as calm as a bathtub. In fact, four days later, Jim and Jack camped

at Lake Sakakawea State Park. They were approaching Garrison Dam, which created the 180-mile long *Lake Sakakawea.* They would have to portage around it.

*

In two days they were off the Lake and back on the *Missouri* proper. There were so many beautiful sandbars that choices of routes were required. "For some unknown reason, Jim seemed to be able to pick out a canoe-able route around sand bars, miss floating trees and stumps. Although most of the sandbars look easy to maneuver around at eye level, not so at water level Jim and Jack camped on a couple of sandbars even though the State brochure said there was a possibility we would get flooded by rains upstream. Time didn't allow time to struggle into the rough shores.

About a day off of Lake Sakakawea, Jim was almost certain they passed "Kip" and another person around a smoky campfire. They had a huge dog with them that appeared to be a mix of German Shepherd and wolf. One of the men gave a friendly wave. If it was them, they probably brought the dog to hold off Jack. "My gosh! They're stalking us?"

"Jack, let's put in here at Fort Mandan. Lewis and Clark wintered here in 1804-1805 and met Sakakawea after hiring her husband Toussaint Charbonneau who was a trader with ties to North West Company. Charbonneau was hired as an interpreter. They had been living in a Hidatsa village. Jack had a pained look.

"The Mandans treated the Corps of Discovery very well. If you're lucky, maybe you can find a female Indian dog to sidle up to." Jim requested interviews

with the local Chief and his staff, who were most cooperative and informative and posed for pictures and videos.

Back in the canoe, Jim continued practicing his story on Jack. "I sure don't know how Lewis and Clark and crew survived the river, mountains, rains, snows, the unfriendly Indians and being away from home for so long. According to George Catlin, writer, disease almost wiped out the Mandans at one point in time.

"Jack, most of the land bordering on the *Missouri* is private and we must have prior land manager permission. However, Joy has arranged for us to camp at several places, with the understanding that I may or may not arrive as scheduled." Jack just nodded and closed one eye. *When will he ever stop?*

*****

The phone rang on Jay Spader's desk. He picked it up and upon answering, received a reply from a familiar voice. "Don't use names on the phone. How are you doing out in the great State of Montana? I have a conference in a few minutes so we'll have to speak quickly. I heard from Jim Clark that someone is attacking him and has even stolen his canoe for a short while. You wouldn't have any knowledge of such, have you?"

"No. I have just been trying to keep up with Mr. Clark---the man can surely paddle."

"I would hope you haven't been using violence against Jim Clark. My CFO will be upset enough with my expenditures. If some negative publicity turns up, I can't promise to keep paying you."

"No, no! I am like John Wayne, 'I'm a peaceable man. However, I will admit I have been aware of some people from this area who think Clark might be a good target to get some money. "

"I got an e-mail from Clark saying he had been attacked, his boat stolen and he was attacked again later and tied up for 2 days along Ft. Peck Lake."

"I did hear that Clark now has a beautiful girl friend paddling with him. Had you heard about that?"

"Hey, he's supposed to be going solo. Is she paddling with him or alongside?"

"I understand that she is in her own boat, *but* he certainly isn't hurting for company, from what I've heard."

"Don't give me gossip! I am having second thoughts about what we're doing as it is. I had intended the race be fair and square. No monkey business. You're both outstanding athletes and should be able to paddle a great race without getting into any side issues. If I am to pay you $5,000 if you beat Clark to St. Louis, I expect a better job. I've got to get back to work now. Just remember our conversation as you continue your quiet float down the *Missouri.* How do you like paddling solo?"

"You can count on me. I really have the hang of solo paddling now." As he hung up, the unidentified person said, "Dang it! I don't want to paddle like crazy

every day, and I didn't mean to lie about going solo. There are some beautiful women out here and I get lonesome. But, there are beauties in St. Louis also. board." He had begun to realize if he was going to win this competition, he might have to do it on skill, strength and focusing on his paddling.

*****

The next morning dawned crisp and clear, as if the heavy rains of recent days had washed the earth clean. For the first time in weeks, Jim felt truly hopeful of completing his journey on time---in spite of his suspicions that his own publisher might be trying to doublecross him.

*****

From Jim Clark's *Mighty Mo Notebook:*

Loved this line from Jerry Dennis' book, *From A Wooden Canoe*, quoting a fellow named Bill Mason as follows: "Portaging a canoe is like hitting yourself on the head with a hammer (because it feels so good when you stop)!"

Mason sure got it right.

Explaining his logic, the very perceptive Mr. Dennis goes on to note: "Humping a 75-pound canoe and a 60-pound pack over a winding, uneven, hilly, rock-strewn, log-obstructed, mud-sucking, mosquito-laced backwoods trail is nobody's idea of fun."

Talk to me, Jerry! Sounds like this hard-nosed raconteur has gone up against some of the many dams and locks that require portaging on the Missouri River.

Yeah, the Mo is a real challenge, in this regard. But that's why I like it. It's like the ancient philosopher once said: "Nothing worth having comes easy." I've spent the last few days breaking my back on the Missouri portages, and yet I've never felt better in my life! Never had to work so hard, either. The heat, the bugs, the snakes underfoot . . . and every time I turn around, Mother Nature dumps another bucket of rain all over my head. What glorious fun! For the first time in years, I feel like I'm worth a darn.

Sleeping pretty good, too. You don't need to be "rocked to sleep" after 35 miles of dodging floating trees, fighting high winds, fending off the rain squalls and running on an adrenalin-high hour after hour.

Wonder if I'll get any more visitors like Kip and Sam? Had to laugh, last night in camp. I was sitting beside the fire, half-asleep, digesting my franks and beans – big shadow leaps at me from the underbrush! I damn near crapped myself! Jumped to my feet, ready to fight to the death – Jack's roaring and ripping, with his bared fangs slashing the air – and guess what?

It was a sheet of old newspaper some deer hunter had left behind the previous autumn – must've caught a gust of wind off the lake, and the shadow it threw came at me like a bloodthirsty cougar!

As usual, Jack had a good laugh at my expense.

After so many weeks alone with that dog, I swear I've learned how to read his mind. He thinks I'm the biggest bozo in the State of North Dakota – and most of the time, I have to agree with him.

*

And so it began – a long stretch of exhausting days during which he paddled, and then he paddled, and then he paddled some more.

Arising each morning at dawn, he would begin an unvarying ritual. First he rebuilt the campfire . . . by patiently adding an armload of dry sticks to the coals left over from the night before. Once the flames were leaping, he would spend a few precious minutes brewing a canteen cup of Taster's Choice, then sit on his haunches while he sipped the strong brew and watched the dawn unfold over the awakening river.

This was the hour he liked best – the hour of singing birds and scurrying chipmunks and pale mist rising from the surface of the flat, silent water. At dawn the forest world looked fresh and unspoiled . . . it was a great, leafy cathedral gently illuminated by the newborn sun. At this mild hour, the mosquitoes and stinging gnats were in full retreat before the advancing light, and the distant horizon swirled with pearl-gray clouds and salmon-tinged light. Clark was not a praying man . . . but these dawns brought him very close to what most people would have called "prayer." Finishing the last of his coffee, and watching a distant heron stalk the shallows in an age-old quest for the sustenance that would carry him through another day, the canoe-borne explorer would bow his head in reverent homage to the majestic beauty he saw all around him.

And then he would begin to paddle.

Accompanied only by the dog, he would spend nine or ten hours of hard paddling and J-stroking his slender craft through the purling shallows, the deep pools and the drifting logs and floating tree branches of the river's passage through North Dakota.

Only once during this marathon run to Bismarck did he catch a glimpse of the pursuit he feared. It happened somewhere in the middle of the state, as he slogged his way past a series of weathered, limestone cliffs near the village of Settlers Run. Looking up from his work, he was startled to find himself looking directly into the eyes of an unshaven, scowling man in a ragged sweatshirt. He couldn't be sure – but the scruffy guy beside the smoky campfire closely resembled the attacker who'd been called "Kip," way back near the start of his journey.

Hunched above the fire, the man in the sweatshirt ducked his head away the moment Jim spotted him. Another camper – tall and powerfully built – stood nearby but with his back to the river, making it impossible to read his features. The two roughnecks had a huge dog with them – a snarling brute that appeared to be a mix of German Shepherd and wolf.

Was this sinister-looking threesome a real threat to Jim's safety?

Or was the big man simply giving in to the paranoia that had dogged him, ever since the last attack?

Before he could answer the question, *Tripper* had rounded the next bend, and the smoky campfire had vanished from sight.

All at once, Jim was glad to know that the Smith & Wesson – still neatly wrapped in blankets – lay nestled at the front of the canoe in the dry bag he'd packed before setting out.

Clark had the weapon he needed, if another struggle broke out.

But he hoped to God that he would never have to use it.

Then he took a long, thoughtful look at Jack, slumbering on his perch in the middle of the canoe. When he spoke, his voice was low and indistinct, almost a whisper: "Jack-o, I also pray that you never have to go up against that wolf-dog.

"Let's just hope they're drifters – and that we never see them again."

*

He paused only once during the two-week jaunt across North Dakota, in order to take a quick side-trip to Ft. Mandan, where the famed explorers Lewis and Clark had wintered in 1804-1805. The tiny settlement had earned a permanent name for itself in the history books, and for good reason: It was here, after all, that the bold adventurers had hired on the well-known Toussaint Charbonneau, a trader with ties to the fabled North West Company. That step, as every school child could now tell you, had led to the discovery of the Indian woman Sakakawea, who would play such a key role in the journey toward the Pacific. Charbonneau was hired as an interpreter, and was thoroughly conversant with the ways of the Native Americans, having lived in a Hidatsa village before encountering Lewis and Clark.

During his brief stay, Jim requested interviews with the local Chief and his staff – all of whom proved to be cooperative, informative . . . and quite willing to pose for pictures and videos.

Apparently, nothing had changed over the centuries . . . since the Indians once again seemed more than willing to help a man named Clark accomplish a marathon huge canoe-journey along their great muddy river.

Back on the water, Jim paddled with furious determination for several hours, while lecturing his canine companion in friendly fashion: "Jack-o, have you heard that famous Greek saying: 'The more things change, the more they stay the same?'"

The dog made a dry, snickering sound . . . was it derision? ***You're full of these little sayings, aren't you, Mr. Jim? Why don't you just man your paddle for awhile, and let me enjoy my nap?***

But Jim was just getting started. "If you haven't heard that epigram, Jack-o, I'll be glad to explain it to you. The phrase refers to the fact that many basic human situations recur again and over again in history, and they always seem to turn out the same. In this particular scenario, the man from the so-called 'civilized world' travels deep into the wilderness – and discovers that his survival depends almost entirely on the so-called 'savages' that he once scorned.

"It's called 'A Lesson In Humility 101,' Jack, and I've become a very good student in recent weeks!"

But the dog did not respond. He was snoring – like a drunken stevedore at the height of an all-night binge.

Jim looked at him, and grinned. "That's right, Jack-o – you sleep on, and leave the thinking to me!"

A moment later, with a peal of self-mocking laughter, the big man took a long, hard stroke with his double-bladed paddle . . . and the sleek canoe shot across the border into South Dakota.

When a woman has fallen in love . . .

Standing beside the check-in counter at the Bismarck Holiday Inn, Joy Price could not stop smiling. And why not? Within the next few hours, a gentleman by the name of Clark would be arriving at the dock behind the hotel in his very own battered canoe! After more than two weeks of separation, the two lovers were desperate to be together again. Was it any wonder that the slender young woman in the beige-and-gold slacks pants suit kept grinning at everyone around her?

The clerk watched her sign her name to the charge-slip, then handed her a plastic key. "You're in Number 212," he said cheerfully, "and you're also in luck – that's a balcony room, with a terrific view of the river."

Joy wanted to hug him. "Why, that fabulous! Jim will be so pleased – "

The clerk's eyes widened with surprise . . . but before he could ask her any questions (hadn't she just said she was "traveling alone?"), Joy was already hurrying toward the high-speed elevator in the middle of the lobby.

Once in her room, she set to work preparing for the romantic festivities that surely lay ahead. She expected him to arrive within the next two or three hours . . . and when he did, she would be *ready* --- meaning that she intended to be rested, sweet-smelling and looking *good.*

After filling the tub with steaming water, she stirred in the most luxurious and sexy bath salts to be found at the upscale Bed & Bath. A moment later, she was doing a strip-tease act in front of the gilt-framed, full-length mirror. Like wandering butterflies, her hands darted across her taut breasts, then traced a series of graceful loops along the length of her slender, sun-browned body. Was she beautiful? Really beautiful?

She laughed out loud then: "If *he* says I'm a beauty, then it must be true!"

Climbing into the tub, she felt herself beginning to shiver with delight. How hungry she was for Jim's kisses, and for the touch of his hard, hard body! With a long, happy sigh, she lay back and soaked up the perfumed warmth of her bubble bath. And she stayed that way just long enough to feel relaxed and sexy – but not long enough to develop a case of major-league wrinkles!

Toweling off at the end of her invigorating bath, she could almost feel Jim's strong arms surrounding her and his sweet, sweet kisses. . . .

"Where are you, Jim?" Gazing out onto the great river, she asked the question in a reverent whisper. And then . . . incredibly enough, she was suddenly watching the bright red canoe skim toward her window!

Could it be? Yes! For a moment, she debated running onto the balcony and shouting his name. But she wasn't dressed yet, and he was probably too far away to hear her. Intent on beating him to the Holiday Inn lobby, she flew into her clingy, milk-colored silk blouse (no bra for *her* tonight) and the tight beige skirt that so

nicely accentuated her statuesque hips and buttocks. On this night of nights, her high heels would tighten her buns perfectly.

Ready for action! Whistling happily, she hurried down the marble stairs and nestled deep inside the telephone alcove that flanked the Main Lobby. From this hidden perch, she could leap out to surprise him in a flashing instant, as he headed for the check-in counter.

She didn't have long to wait.

She heard his voice before she saw him: "Come on, Jack-oh, pick up the pace, fella!"

Loaded down with bags, he held the excited dog on a leash as he came barreling through the revolving doors of the hotel. Eyes flashing with delight, Joy prepared to spring upon her man and smother him with kisses. . . .

But it never happened.

At the last possible moment, *another* woman – beautiful, blond, stylishly-dressed and also youthful – stepped from the shadows directly into the big man's path!

The newcomer wore diamonds on her wrist, and her shoes were by Gucci. And she wasn't alone, either. At her side walked a handsome young boy – maybe six or seven – who was obviously her son.

Could this be happening? Stunned and disbelieving, Joy watched the photogenic mother-and-son duo fall on Jim Clark and begin hugging and kissing

him frantically! With his arms full, Jim could only stand there while the outpouring of affection continued.

"Veronica! Henry! Where did *you* two come from?"

But what Clark really wanted to say was, "Why in the name of heaven did you two decide to come *here* – to the same hotel where I'm about to meet the woman I love!"

Staggered to the teeth, the big man fought for self-composure . . . while his frantic eyes searched the lobby for Joy. Where *was* she – and what in the world could he say to her, if she *did* show up?

In an agony of indecision, he turned back to the new arrivals. "I . . . ah . . . well . . . " Half-strangled, he fought to compose a sentence, then blurted: "Welcome to North Dakota!"

Veronica stared at him for a moment. "Thanks, Jim. Henry and I thought this would be a wonderful surprise for you – and we also needed a vacation! This is truly beautiful country."

"You bet," said Clark. His tormented voice cracked wide open on the word "bet," however, and he groaned like a man twisting on a medieval rack. "Beautiful landscape, Veronica! River, the Muddy Mo – birds everywhere. Too many mosquitoes, though – eat you alive. Hah-hah!"

Veronica blinked slowly at him, and it was easy to see that she suspected brain damage.

"Say, I hope we haven't messed up your plans, Jim? Henry and I certainly miss you and Jack – and we were hoping this would be a nice surprise for you."

Jim's face contorted in pain. Once again, his distracted eyes were searching the lobby in a fruitless quest for Joy. Had he died and gone to Hell, just as Sister Margaret Mary had once predicted? How could this be happening to him? "Veronica . . . I wonder. Do you think – ah, could I speak to you alone for a moment?" He turned to the little boy. "Would you please excuse us, Henry? Would you like to take Jack for a short walk out in front of the hotel?"

"I sure would, Mr. Jim!" Henry was already grabbing for the leash, and he didn't notice how the dog's expression changed: ***Can you believe this? 'Mr. Jim' gets his tit caught in the wringer – and right away, I gotta be put through a workout!***

A moment later, Henry was hustling the pooch through the revolving door.

Jim turned to Veronica, blurted: "Listen, I am so sorry! I've been . . . well, you see . . . canoe – I got locked up in Montana, and I met this – look, Veronica, I thought from your letter – didn't you tell me you were engaged? I thought you were married by now! You told me to get on with my life . . . well, ah, I ***did*** **meet this young lady, and we're tight – "**

Veronica listened to the babbling for a while, then cut him off. "Tight, you say?"

Purple-faced, Jim fought for air. "Ahhhhh . . . well, we've gotten very close, yes. Marriage could be in the works!"

"Marriage?" Veronica made a small, gasping sound.

"Well, you know – provided she'll have me, that is. Hah-hah!"

"Have you?"

"Joy!"

"Joy?"

"Joy Price – the young woman I'm referring to! You see, she was supposed to meet me here today. Are you . . . are you staying here, too?"

Veronica nodded. She was crying softly. "Oh, my God. Jim, I don't know what got into me. Yes, I'd been dating without letting you know – and I had no right to `dump' you the way I did. I'm so sorry! Can you give me another chance?" The words were flooding out now in a chaotic rush. "Please, Jim! Henry and I both care so much for you, and I now know you're the only one for me."

Jim stared at her as if she'd just arrived from the planet Neptune. Buffalo Snake had predicted this back at the beginning of the Missouri. What should he do? He couldn't hug her, couldn't comfort her – what if Joy was somewhere in the lobby, watching like a murderous hawk?

Moaning inwardly, Clark forced himself to take a deep breath. "Veronica, listen to me, please. What you have to understand . . . it's been only a couple of months since I left you and Henry in Baltimore – but for me, it seems as if a lifetime has passed. I'm in a survival struggle out here! I spend ten hours a day paddling, and I've been attacked twice by some really nasty folks who don't want me to complete my canoe trip in time to win the prize money."

"Attacked, Jim? My Gosh! Did you call the police?"

The big man shook his head wearily. "It doesn't work that way on the river, hon. There are no police, really, except for the DNR – although they've been very good to me. On the water, you have to take care of yourself."

Veronica had begun wringing her hands. "Well . . . did they hurt you?"

Clark groaned. "Not really. I got knocked around some, and they left me with a pretty bad headache, on one occasion. The toughest part is, I don't really know who they are – but I do have my suspicions."

"I see." Veronica stared blankly at him.

"Anyway, the good news is, I met this really terrific young woman in Montana. She's part-Indian, and she loves the outdoors as much as I do. We've gotten pretty close, and . . . "'

Veronica was studying him. "And . . . what?"

"Well, we've . . . that is . . . "

"Do you intend to marry her?"

Jim coughed. Shrugged. He was turning purple again. "Ah . . . stranger things have happened, Veronica!"

"I see." Her voice had gone flat. Cold.

"But nothing final has been decided yet."

"Yet?"

Writhing beneath her steady gaze, Clark waved helplessly at the air, as if trying to drive off a crowd of pesky gnats. "Veronica . . . I want you to know – even if we *do* marry, I intend to remain friends with you and Henry. If you'll *have* me, that is. But I . . . if I can be up front with you – I really don't want to return to our previous relationship."

He watched a glittering tear slide along Veronica's cheek. Watched her wipe her eyes and then force a painful smile. "Jim, I think you know that you and I will always be friends, regardless. But will you please spend a few minutes with Henry, and do your best to let him down gently? The kid idolizes you!"

She tried out another quivering, tremulous smile. "Maybe you could promise to send him a videotape of your voyage, once you've completed it?"

"You bet! I'll talk to him right now, Veronica, and I'll ask him if wants to ride with me for a few miles on the Muddy Mo!" He reached out to pat her shoulder. "I can't thank you enough for your understanding. This is really very kind of you."

She smiled, but it was a sad kind of smile, and fleeting. "I think Henry would love that, Jim. But let's wait and see how this situation with Joy shakes out, before we make any plans, okay?"

*

While the Baltimore reunion unfolded in the middle of the hotel lobby, Joy Price stood frozen in her hiding place beside the pay telephones. Was this nightmare really happening? Who was the gorgeous, blond, beautifully-dressed woman in the Gucci footwear? And the boy – was he her son? Her nephew? A family friend? Half-crazed with anxiety, Joy was also beginning to smolder with jealousy. How *dare* he complicate their lives with these new, obviously intimate arrivals?

And then she remembered.

Veronica and Henry! The girlfriend from Baltimore and her son! But that chapter in Jim's life had ended, hadn't it? According to her lover, Veronica had sent Clark a brutal "Dear John" letter terminating their relationship forever. Had the good-looking woman in the high-fashion leisure-wear suddenly changed her mind?

Leaning against the plastic-glass wall of the phone alcove, Joy struggled to control her breathing. Would she burst into tears? Would she run screaming through the lobby, then throw herself on the woman who seemed to have taken her place? "No . . . somehow, I will find a way to control my feelings. I am one-half Blackfoot Indian! I have to get out of here!" Frantic, she scanned the complex of lobby elevators, then darted a look in the direction of a back stairway marked "EXIT."

"Yes! There is my escape route." Easing out of the phone alcove she pressed against the green-painted, stucco wall of the lobby. Head down, eyes on the floor,

she crept along the wall until she stood beneath the EXIT sign. She put her hand on the doorknob, turned it.

Climbing the stairs toward her room, she felt the tears beginning. "Crybaby!" She would give Jim and the others a few minutes to finish their business in the lobby, then check out and head for home. What a disaster. What a cruel twist of fate – and to think of how much time she'd spent dreaming of what this night would bring! *My God*, she told herself, *I wish I'd never met him!*

Within a minute, she found herself back in her room . . . and standing once again in front of the mirror where she'd done the "striptease" only an hour before. What a stupid fool she was! Talk about deluding yourself! For a moment she felt a wave of hatred against men – all of them. How could he have made her so many promises, when all along he was waiting for the return of that attractive duo she'd just spotted in the lobby.

With the tears rolling down her face, she began to pack her suitcase.

She had no way of knowing that Jim – at that very moment – was begging the desk clerk to tell him of her whereabouts.

"I'm sorry, sir," said the clerk. "Our policy at the Holiday Inn does not allow us to identify guests of the hotel, or to give out their room numbers."

No sooner had the big man turned away in anguish and departed the lobby, than Joy was creeping down the same back stairs toward the check-out counter. Handing the clerk her charge card, she felt a wave of desolation roll over her soul.

She swore him to secrecy that she was checking out. At that moment, it seemed crystal-clear that she would never see Jim Clark again!

Half-crazed with anxiety and frustration, Clark struggled to restore order to his scrambled world.

First step: "I'll secure lodging for myself and my canine sidekick, and pronto."

Moving quickly, he nailed down a room equipped with double beds, just in case Joy turned up and he managed to convince her to rejoin him. At the same time, he arranged for a luxury-kennel for Jack, who would *not* be pleased with this arrangement, for certain.

As he turned the key in his door, a terrible question preyed on his mind: Had Joy witnessed the debacle in the lobby? Clark didn't put much stock in intuition – but his gut told him that the woman he loved had been nearby during the agonizing exchange with Veronica and little Henry.

If only he could explain himself! If only he could take her in his arms and tell her in a frantic rush: "Joy, hang on – you need to understand – Veronica is *old* business, she belongs to the past. And the first thing I did this afternoon was tell her all about you. Don't you understand – I'm hoping to marry you, the moment this canoe marathon ends?"

Groaning, he sat down on the bed and put his head in his hands. If Joy *had* witnessed the hugging and kissing with Veronica, Clark was in deep trouble, and he knew it. How could she *not* assume that he was still deeply involved with the

Baltimore contingent, after watching the effusive outpouring in the hotel lobby? How in the world had he gotten himself into this state of swarming, stuttering confusion, anyway?

Utterly miserable, he stood up and walked over to the full-length mirror that flanked the bathroom door. For at least a minute, he stared at the disheveled face in the glass. It was the face of a man whose life had turned to dust, almost overnight. Clark was lost, and he knew it. He hadn't managed his relationship with Veronica – hell, he hadn't even gotten over the loss of his brother, years before! Why couldn't he handle his relationships better?

Now he shook his head and gritted his teeth. "Listen up, pal," he told the flickering image in the mirror, "it's time you started *taking care of business*. It's time you got a grip on your life and on your relationships."

If the big man hoped to put his life back together and complete this marathon on the Muddy Mo, he would have to start taking things one day at a time. Maybe even one hour at a time!

In this hour of supreme crisis, only one thing seemed certain. Clark had to find Joy, had to explain the situation fully. And if he couldn't find her – if she refused to return his phone calls – then he had no choice.

An hour later, when he learned that she'd checked out of her room without leaving any messages for him, his worst suspicions were confirmed. She knew. She had witnessed the confrontation in the lobby.

So be it. He would make excuses to Veronica and Henry, and he would depart at dawn. Another 20 miles on the water, and he'd be in South Dakota – and headed for the homestretch in the endurance test his life had now become. "I will talk to her soon."

*

It sounded like a good plan – but once again, fate intervened. Instead of escaping cleanly at first light, Jim made the mistake of answering the phone in his room, and soon wound up in yet another painful *tete-a-tete* with the incredibly tenacious Veronica over coffee.

Interestingly enough, however, Clark's Baltimore friend seemed more interested in repairing the damage done to Joy than in patching up her own relationship with the big man. "Jim, please let me talk to her, won't you? I just know she'll believe another woman – and especially a woman who has been so close to you in recent years."

Veronica sent him a sad, sad smile. "This woman must be very much in love with you, if she fled the scene and checked out early. I have no doubt that you two will make things right again, and soon." Brightening a little, she squinted at him over her cup of English Breakfast tea. "But if she does refuse you at the end of your journey – will you give me a call?"

Clark stared into his cup of Mocha Java.

"Honey, I've missed you something terrible, you know that. Your absence taught me a painful lesson. I never realized how few 'real men' there are out there in the world."

He blinked slowly at her. "*Real* men, Veronica? I'm afraid I don't know what you mean."

"Yes, you do. I'm talking about men with the steadiness – and the courage – to raise children, while remaining faithful to their mates. You offered me that, Jim, and I foolishly tossed it away. Never again! And if our relationship somehow works out, in spite of my silliness, I'll consider myself the luckiest woman on earth."

Jim thought about her offer, but ultimately decided against it. "I'm sorry, Veronica, but I think this is probably Joy's call. If she truly loves me, she'll find a way to get in touch. She's got to trust me enough to understand that I would never deceive her, and that I really do want to make her mine.

"Unfortunately, both of us have been through failed marriages, which doesn't make this situation any easier. I'm just hoping we can work through this mess and find a way to resume our closeness."

He shook his head and heaved a weary sigh. "Honest to God, what I'd like most right now is just to climb in that canoe with Jack and set sail on the Muddy Mo, headed toward St. Louis. We've got a schedule to keep, and all of this melodrama isn't helping us a bit."

And he was as good as his word. Within an hour, the big man had reloaded the canoe and he and Jack were pushing off into the river. Groaning audibly, he crawled aboard and fell into his seat at the stern. Slumped there, he wondered if he would ever again find the strength to lift his paddle. "I just can't face anyone right now, Jack; I feel so empty inside, I can hardly breathe."

The dog remained unimpressed, however. Blinking calmly, he looked his master straight in the eye. *Can't breathe, and can't even lift your poor paddle? Over what? Over a mere woman? A homo sapiens female, who's 72 percent water? Hey, you've still got ME! Get serious and get your butts in gear!*

Amazingly enough, the dog's strategy worked. Within 30 seconds, Jim Clark was paddling hard.

The canoe shot through the water with tremendous force, as if the big man in the stern had decided to vent all his misery on the Muddy Mo. Hour after hour, as the sunlight rose around him and the river came alive with birds and leaping fish, he bent his tousled head to the task.

But when he finally did look up, he got a shock.

The Missouri had been transformed into a lake – Lake Oahe, according to his maps – and the landscape had altered dramatically. As far as the eye could see, a vista of electric-blue water and soaring gulls stretched to the horizon. Along the banks, picturesque villages alternated with long stretches of prairie grassland and great hummocks of fertile, chestnut-brown earth. He was crossing the heartland of American now – the center of the vast breadbasket that stretched across the

midsection of the nation – and the landscape was enough to take your breath away. The first 59 miles of the South Dakota portion of the Mo had been designated a *National Recreation River,* and it was easy to see why: In many ways, this primitive landscape remained unchanged from the one Lewis and Clark had journeyed across in the early *1880s.*

Astonished and delighted by the panorama, Jim turned to his companion for some uplifting discussion. His spirits had brightened a little – a few hard hours with a canoe paddle can do that – and he chuckled out loud as he addressed his shipmate. "Pretty as a postcard, don't you think, Jack? What a shame that we have to hurry through it so fast!"

The dog ruminated for half a minute, then shrugged his bushy eyebrows. *You're the one who set up the crazy schedule, Mr. Jim.*

The big man pushed himself through a dozen J-strokes, frowning all the while. "Has it ever occurred to you, Jack-O, that the best way to live might be right out here on the water? Permanently, I mean? Get yourself a big old houseboat and just spend your days drifting back and forth between Montana and Nebrask and Missouri – all at the daredevil speed of three or four miles an hour?"

Jack thought about it. *Well, maybe . . . provided, of course, that we could go ashore whenever we wanted for a double cheeseburger or a pound of thin-sliced sirloin!*

Nodding cheerful agreement, Clark paused to lay out his Global Positioning System gear, in order to begin navigating through the tangled labyrinth of islands

and inlets that honeycombed this section of the river. "Thank heavens for the good old GPS," he told the loyal Lab. "Most of the time I just confuse myself with the math involved – but sooner or later, if I keep after it, I can make the damn thing tell me where I am!"

Jack released a long, exaggerated sigh. Oh, *you humans and your marvelous technology. I could track a gnat down from six miles out with my nose – and you're bragging because you know where you ARE?*

But Jim missed this keen observation; he was too busy watching a diamondback snapping turtle scramble across a floating tree stump. "Tell you what, Jack – what say we camp out tonight at Fort Abraham Lincoln State Park? I'll interview a few of the Mandan tribal elders, and maybe get some nifty photos, as well. Whaddya think?"

The dog yawned thoughtfully. *Sounds okay with me, big man – provided my dinner arrives on schedule!*

But Jim didn't catch his canine pal's internal remark – he was laughing too hard. "Jack, I hate to tell you this, but the Mandans were friendly to Lewis and Clark for only one reason, according to their medicine man. As it turned out, they dearly loved the taste of the White Man's dogs!"

Jack recoiled, and his jumbo-sized yap fell wide open. Stark fear!

"You better stay near me, when we call on the Mandans," said Jim.

The dog elevated one eyebrow, a la Groucho Marx. Then he drawled: *You bet yer sweet life I will, Jimbo! I'm gonna be all OVER you at that reservation. I'll be like white on rice, big man! I'll be your second skin, pardner!*

Fortunately for Groucho, the Mandans actually turned out to be quite hospitable. Their graying spokesman – a white-haired and wrinkle-eyed Native American named Assistant Chief Horse Speed – welcomed Jim to the Tribal Council Building with open arms, and quickly invited both man and dog to an early supper.

Alarmed by the invitation for a moment, Jack relaxed noticeably when the Indian leader boomed: "We've got baked chicken on the menu tonight!"

Moments later, while Jack sighed with relief, Chief Speed was describing how his tribe had been "very friendly to Lewis and Clark, and also to George Catlin, the famous writer who followed in their footsteps.

"About that time," noted the Indian administrator, "a series of smallpox and cholera epidemics almost wiped us out, along with a nearby Arikara Village. I'm not saying the White Man brought us the illnesses – although I suppose it was possible. No, the real problem was that our people hadn't been exposed to such diseases, and we had no natural antibody-protection against them."

He shook his head a bit sadly, recalling the immense suffering that had accompanied the plagues. But then he gradually brightened. "These days, of course, everything has changed. As you can see, we're as modern and up-to-date as any small city in this area. We're equipped with modern schools, gymnasiums and

stadiums, housing, parks and playgrounds, movies and all sorts of other entertainment.

"Our Council and Chief serve as governor or mayor, depending upon the jurisdiction. Oh, we've got our share of problems – just like any other small city, county or state in the U.S. But we work pretty hard at keeping ourselves on an even keel. As you know, money is always short for Native American settlements, but we make do.

"I want you to meet my talented granddaughter, Mr. Clark. I'm very proud of Minnie Dove. She's majoring in newspaper journalism in college – and I know she'd love to interview you. If you'll follow me, I'll introduce you."

The big man sent the Indian his brightest smile. "You bet, Chief Speed. I don't know what I can add to her education, but I'll be glad to try!"

Jim liked the Chief right away. He and Jack jumped into their host's Lincoln Continental and set sail for his modern brick home. Huge cottonwoods surrounded the circle drive, and the hedges were neatly trimmed. Jack settled back and refrained from passing gas, for once in his life.

He figured it was the least he could do – in return for NOT being featured as the main course at suppertime!

A few minutes later, a dark-haired and dimpled young beauty appeared before them. She wore attractive shorts and a colorful halter, and her tawny eyes radiated enthusiasm. The Chief introduced her as Minnie Dove Speed, then

departed – after pointing out that he'd return later to take Jim and Jack back to their trusty canoe.

Minnie Dove didn't waste any time.

"Mr. Clark, I'm impressed!" sang the 20-year-old student. "My father told me some of the background on your unbelievable trip down the *Missouri,* paddling solo."

Jim chuckled out loud. "Did he tell you I was crazy to try it?"

Minnie Dove's eyes widened. "No, not at all. He did say you were pretty darn brave, however – and also pretty enterprising." She was studying his face carefully. "I understand that you're a professional journalist – and that you've been interviewing, photographing and video-taping interesting people all along the way for *Wild Rivers Magazine."*

Jim nodded. "That's right, Minnie Dove. But a lot of them have also been interviewing and photographing me and Jack. They're too polite to say so – but I suspect they think we're freaks of nature, or something."

The two of them laughed heartily. Then Minnie Dove sighed. "Gosh, I really envy you, do you know that? I'll be a junior at the University of Chicago in September – and so far, the only reporting I've been allowed to do has been based entirely on exercises from textbooks. I can't tell you how much I yearn to get out there on the street and start interviewing some bold, courageous *people*!"

Clark gave her a bright smile. He liked this feisty kid. "Minnie Dove, I really don't know if I can qualify as bold or courageous. Actually, I suspect my dog might have some opinions on that – especially after watching me run away in terror from a couple of splashing beavers on the riverbank one night!

"Really, I don't think I'm any braver than anyone else along the Missouri. I'm just too hard-headed to give up when I should!"

Minnie Dove waggled a finger at him. "I doubt that, Mr. Clark, I really do. What interests me about your story is the word 'Why.' What is it that drives you to push yourself so hard, anyway?"

Clark winked at her. "Is this an interview, Ms. Dove?"

She laughed. "I guess it is, Mr. Clark!"

"Okay, fine. Why don't we sit down and get ourselves a root beer and you go ahead and ask all the questions you want?"

"Really?"

"Really!"

And that's exactly what they did. For the next 45 minutes, the big man regaled the college kid with tales of his thrill-a-minute journey from Three Forks, Montana, starting on May 15, all the way to the Mandan Reservation in central South Dakota. The kid hung on every word, pausing only to scribble choice phrases on paper from time to time.

"So there you have it," he said at last. "I'm in a race against the clock, Minnie Dove, and my goal is to reach St. Charles, Missouri, before the first of October. If I make it, I'm a big winner – to the tune of $100,000. If I don't get there by the first, I'm just another also-ran, and all I'll collect are my expenses.

"But you know what? I wouldn't trade this experience for anything, win or lose! I've already learned more about the river, and the country – and *myself* – than I ever thought possible." He paused for a moment, then reached down and patted the loyal Jack's furry head. "I've also gotten to know *this* guy pretty well – and I can tell you that he's one of the finest canine specimens now running loose on Planet Earth!"

The dog did not respond. His face remained utterly expressionless, while his eyeballs swiveled from the student to the professor. And both could hear him thinking, loudly: *So now I'm a 'canine specimen,' am I? Why won't this human hot air bag talk plain English, for once in his life?*

I'm a dog, for goodness sakes! I'm an ordinary, walking-around-on-four-paws American mutt – and I want my dinner!

As always, Jim pretended not to hear the wisecrack. Instead of responding, he invited Minnie Dove to pet the pooch. She did. As she scratched at the back of his hairy ears, the pampered canine lit up like a 1,000-watt bulb. *Verrrrrrry cool, Minnie Dove. I guess I'm a big media celebrity now . . . and to think I was afraid I might end up as an entrée at dinner!*

Thirty minutes later, Chief Speed reappeared and Jim bid Minnie Dove a fond farewell. Along with a fatherly hug, he gave her one of his business cards. "Call me whenever you want, my friend. Maybe I can put in a good word for you after you graduate and start job-hunting!"

Minnie Dove replied with a giant smile. "Oh, I didn't tell you, did I? I'm going to open my own newspaper, right here on the reservation. The Mandan *Tribune* will be a state-of-the-art daily – complete with savvy reporters and editors who know how to dig out a breaking news story!

"I hope our journalistic paths will cross again somewhere down the road, Mr. Clark – and I want to thank both you and Jack for your extremely helpful insights."

"No problem," said Jim. "I know we'll be great friends!"

Ditto*, thought Jack. *Anytime you want a pal to throw a stick to, just holler, Miss Minnie!

Chief Speed looked on, smiling from ear to ear. "As you can see, Mr. Clark, my daughter speaks with wisdom far beyond her young life. If you care to take some more photographs and videos, please feel free. I've written out a permit for you to show our law enforcement or other citizens, should they question you. Perhaps Dove would like a photo of you and Jack in your canoe, if you could find time to send one?"

The big man nodded enthusiastically. "You bet, Chief. I would indeed like to take some photos and interview some of your successful business people, if you don't

mind. I'll send copies back to you as soon as I can after my arrival in St. Louis." He gave the Chief's hand a friendly shake. "You know, I really do appreciate your hospitality – and I'm mighty impressed with your daughter. You must be very proud of her, and for good reason."

After spending two hours interviewing – while also shooting stills and video -- Jim and Jack said their goodbyes. Jim offered brisk handshakes all around, and Jack wagged his tail frantically, then did a high-stepping version of the *cha-cha* up and down Main Street. And why not? Wasn't it perfectly clear by now that these Indians had no intention, whatsoever, of eating him for lunch?

The Chief roared with laughter at the sight of the pirouetting Lab. "Come back for a visit whenever you can, Jim, and don't forget to bring that dog! We'd love to have you stay in our village – might even let you spend a night or two in a tepee!"

After another round of hugs and handshakes, and after a few quick pictures of local businesses, Jim and Jack returned to *Tripper* and prepared to leave. In less than five minutes, they were once again navigating the Muddy Mo.

Jim paddled furiously for several minutes, then suddenly stopped.

"Uh-oh, Jack. I don't like the looks of that sky. Take a look over to the west, and you'll see what I mean."

Jack looked. And froze! The western horizon radiated a pale, greenish light, while gunmetal-colored clouds lumbered along the skyline. Then they heard a faint rumbling, like giant rigs thundering along some distant highway. Fascinated by

nature's violent drama, the big man watched a dozen tongues of lightning snake toward them, then just as suddenly retreat. Soon the thunder grew louder, until it roared in their ears like a squadron of bronze cannons firing for all they were worth.

Jim sank his paddle into the roiling water and dug frantically through the chop. "It's a cold front, Jack – and she's probably packing 60-mile-an-hour winds. If we don't get off the river – and I mean pronto – we're gonna wind up electrocuted or drowned, or both!"

Jack thought it over. But he didn't seem terribly afraid. ***Jim, at this point, I'd like to remind you that I'm a Labrador Retriever, okay? Definition: "A natural swimmer who enjoys splashing around in turbulent waters." Sorry, but I'm just not all that concerned about the minor tempest that seems to lie ahead!***

Jim lifted his paddle threateningly – but then decided against delivering the blow. He needed to focus all of his energies on making a safe landfall, and quickly. The problem he faced at the moment was the steepness of the riverbank to his right. It was too late to try and cross the river now – but the banks on the port side of the canoe were so steeply angled that he knew it would be impossible to get ashore.

But then he got a break.

Paddling frantically, the wave-drenched pilot shot into a 100-yard run along a sheer cliff face . . . and then discovered a sudden break in the towering wall of limestone shale. Moving on instinct, he barreled through a series of vicious double-ended paddles and J-strokes that delivered just enough torque to send them curling

away into the muddy passage. Grunting with exhaustion, Clark slid the battered canoe onto the crumbling bank and skidded to a stop. Jack immediately jumped ashore, then looked back at his partner: ***Thanks for the outstanding paddle-work, Mr. Jim; I barely got my feet wet!***

Clark quickly rolled out the dry bags and the rest of the floatable equipment. Then he turned the canoe over. Next he uncoiled one of the painter ropes and tied it to a cottonwood sapling, in order to keep the craft securely anchored during the approaching storm. Pulling his tarp from the large dry bag, he called for Jack to follow him to a small cutout near the top of the hillside. There he tied the tarp down in two places, then crawled beneath it in order to hide from the oncoming deluge.

Jack watched all of this activity without comment. Then he stepped into the nifty shelter – exactly two seconds before the hurricane exploded all around them.

Suddenly the air was full of slashing, golf-sized hail. Lashed by howling winds from the river, the rain fell horizontally and the nearby cottonwoods bent like fragile harps in the grip of a merciless giant. The air color became yellow-green, and the lightning flashed repeatedly, as if the earth were taking its own strobe-lighted photo again and again.

But Clark had done his work well, and the two of them remained almost entirely dry throughout the raging squall. The temperature plummeted at least 15 degrees, and when the sun finally popped back out, both man and dog found themselves shivering.

In spite of the sudden chill, however, Clark found himself delighted and amazed by the meteorological pyrotechnics he'd just witnessed. Moving quickly, he managed to photograph the gorgeous rainbow that followed the deluge. He also nailed down some nifty images of the ping pong ball-sized hailstones that had plunged to earth during the downpour.

But there was no more time to waste on sight-seeing – and within 20 minutes of the storm's departure, both man and dog were back on the water and racing once again toward St. Louis.

All too soon, however, they found themselves confronting yet another major challenge. Everywhere they looked, smoke-belching tugboats appeared to be hard at work, pushing coal barges upriver. Like giant water-beetles dragging their prey behind them, the squat boats labored furiously to move the mountains of raw coal on the crawling barges. As their powerful engines fought for traction on the sluggish water, surging waves boiled out of the propeller-wash, then rushed toward the tiny canoe. Each time the two-foot-high waves slammed against *Tripper*, Clark found himself in a life-and-death struggle to avoid capsizing. It was a thrill a minute, here in Wild Barge Country – and the tons of floating debris didn't help much, either.

As he battled to stay afloat, the big man noticed that the weary captains and crews of the tugs paid no attention whatsoever to the dangerous wakes that were hammering his fragile canoe. Meanwhile, dozens of jumbo-sized motorboats from

Mandan and Bismarck were leaping into and over the tugs' waves – in a reckless and thoughtless sport that only served to create more turmoil on the water.

The minutes passed with agonizing slowness, and for good reason: Jim knew that his and Jack's lives absolutely depended on keeping their small, skittish craft away from the barges, in order to avoid being sucked under their giant maws. Somehow, he managed to get the job done . . . and the barge traffic gradually thinned away, as they put more and more miles between them and the Muddy Mo traffic jam that had nearly ended their odyssey for good.

Encouraged by their success, they pressed onward – and the next few days passed in a blur of paddling, then bailing water from the bottom of the canoe, followed by more paddling. The weather had turned nasty and unpredictable at times, with high winds and blasts of frigid air at night, followed by scorching sunlight, breathless afternoons and clouds of swarming flies and mosquitoes at twilight. From time to time, the barges also returned to threaten their safety, as they crawled southward along the wave-slashed river.

Through all the daily, grinding struggle that now consumed Jim Clark, one bright beacon burned steadily: his love for Joy.

How long would it be – before he held her in his arms once again?

And what if the answer to that question was . . . "Never?"

Had he lost her forever? Was the best thing he'd ever found in his life already receding into the distance . . . fading like one of those distant barges now vanishing into the twilight mist of the Muddy Mo?

*****

While Jim Clark paddled through the last few miles of South Dakota, a young woman sat gazing into a gilt-edged mirror attached to her dressing table. Her name was "Joy" – but her somber features reflected only a deep and growing melancholy. How could he have forgotten her so quickly? How could he have thrown it all away? Gold-flecked and luminous, her tear-streaked eyes stared back at her from the glass. They were full of questions that couldn't be answered.

Sighing wearily – another pointless day was about to begin – she made her way down the spiral staircase and greeted her mother. But there was a surprise waiting for her, downstairs. Mrs. Price, a slender woman with silver-streaked hair, set down her steaming cup of Irish Breakfast tea. "Well, good morning, Joy! Listen, I didn't want to wake you – but you got a phone call late last night from a woman in Baltimore. She said her name was Veronica . . . I didn't catch the last name."

Joy blinked slowly at her mother, while the words slowly registered.

"Baltimore, *Maryland*?"

The older woman chuckled out loud. "Well, the last time I checked, Baltimore *was* still located in Maryland!"

Joy was holding onto the banister, while her face went white and her heart lurched violently. "My God, mother! That was Veronica!"

Mrs. Price squinted at her daughter. "I know, dear. I just *told* you that. Are you all right, honey?"

Joy nodded slowly. "I . . . I guess so."

"Anyway, her name and number are on the caller-ID. She said she was a friend of that man you mentioned, that Jim Clark?"

But Joy was already walking away. Head down, she had begun to grind her teeth in suspense. What could this amazing phone call mean? "I'll phone her from the porch swing, Mom!"

Mrs. Price set down her tea cup. "You don't think it's too early, dear? Why, it's not even eight o'clock yet!"

Joy didn't answer. She was already struggling to make the call, and her hand shook so badly it took her three tries to correctly dial the number. But at last the signal went through, and she found herself listening to the ringing tones in Baltimore. Without realizing knowing it, she had begun to hold her breath.

"Hello?"

Joy frowned. It was the voice of a child – and young boy whose voice hadn't changed yet. He said his name was Henry, and that Jim Clark and Jack were "best friends" of his.

Joy smiled on her end of the line. "I'm his friend, too," she said. "My name is Joy. Could I please speak with your mother?"

"She's already gone to work," said little Henry. "But she told me to go ahead and give you the number there. Do you really live in Montana?"

This time Joy laughed out loud. "I sure do."

"Golly gee! Are you a rodeo cowgirl?"

Once again, Joy found herself dissolving into helpless laughter. "Not really, Henry. But I've often wished I could run away and join the rodeo, believe me!"

"Me, too!" the youngster roared in her ear. "Say, have you ever been canoeing with Mr. Jim? He used to take me all the time, on the Gunpowder River."

She smiled sadly. "Oh, yes. Yes, indeed. Mr. Jim and I have spent a lot of time in his canoe. He taught me how to solo on the river – and he also told me some really neat things about you and Jack."

"He's cool, isn't he, Miss Joy?"

She was dabbing at her eyes now. "Yes, he certainly is. And so are you, Henry!"

They hung up, and a moment later she was struggling to dial the number the child had given her. After a couple of rings, she heard a gentle but business-like voice come on the line. "Good morning. This is Veronica. How may I help you?"

"Ah . . . yes. This is Joy? Joy Price? In Montana?" Her voice broke suddenly from the tension, and the word "Montana" came dangerously close to being a sob.

"Oh, of course," said the gentle voice. "Hello, Joy."

"I believe you called my mother's home last evening, after I'd gone to bed? Sorry I missed you. I decided I'd better ring you right away – hope it's not too early!"

"No, no. Not at all."

"Henry gave me the number."

“Of course. Listen, Joy, I'm very glad you called, but I have to work – so if you don’t mind, I'll get right to the point.”

“Sure enough. No problem.” But her voice broke again, this time on “problem.” She looked at the knuckles on her left hand, the ones holding the phone: all five had gone white and bloodless.

“Joy, I already know all about you. We have a mutual friend . . . well, he's much more than that, actually. Jim Clark? I asked him to have you phone me, right after our mix-up in Bismarck, but he refused. I . . . I need to tell you something personal about Jim and me, if you don't mind? This won’t be easy for me – but Henry and I care so much for Jim that I just made up my mind I was going to do it.”

Joy had stopped breathing again.

“Jim told me that evening in Bismarck that he is very much in love with you and that he planned to ask you to marry him, if you will have him,” Veronica blurted. “Of course, you understand that I’d already asked him to return to Henry and me, and I’d told him I was sorry for breaking off our relationship. My son, Henry, is very fond of Jim . . . but the truth is that seems to be deeply in love with you. That hurts, to be honest – but I will not stand in the way of his happiness. And if you're part of that happiness, then so be it.”

There was a pause on the line; now Veronica was the one perilously close to tears.

“Perhaps you and I can become friends, Joy? I certainly hope so – for my son’s sake, and also for Jim's sake. I was wrong to surprise him by showing up on

the scene so unexpectedly – especially after dropping him like I did, only two months before."

Joy was struggling for air. The room had begun to revolve slowly on her, as if she were riding the Ferris Wheel at the County Fair. Frowning deeply, she struggled to find the right words. "I don't know what to say, Veronica. When I saw you and your son hugging Jim . . . . well, the truth is you looked so beautiful, and so elegantly dressed – to be honest, I just didn't see how I could possibly compete for him."

Joy had bounced up from the swing, by now; she was smiling happily as she paced back and forth across the wrap-around porch. All at once, her heart was singing!

Veronica also seemed pleased, in spite of her sadness. "You must really be quite a gal, Joy."

"Why do you say that?"

"Because when Jim Clark commits himself to something it takes an earthquake to jar loose! I know he wanted to make Henry and me happy. I also know he loved the feeling of being needed so much. The truth is, he would have stayed with the two of us forever – but then I was dumb enough to give him the boot, and he fell in love with you. Honestly, I suspect that you're the type of person he needs – an outdoorswoman who's also beautiful. But also a woman with love in her heart and a sense of humor, which I lack at times.

But Joy's knuckles had just gone white again. "Veronica, you're very sweet – but the truth is, I've probably hurt him so badly that he'll reject any attempts to

renew our relationship." She hesitated. "Do you think if I called or maybe e-mailed him that we could patch things up?"

Veronica laughed. "Without a doubt. He's clearly deeply in love with you. Call him on his cell phone or send him an e-mail or both. I'm sure he'll be thrilled, and I don't blame him a bit. But I gotta run now, Joy – I have an important business meeting in 10 minutes, and I need to pull my papers together and get down to the conference room."

"Veronica, I can't thank you enough."

"I want you to promise me that after you contact Jim, you'll call me and let me know if he wants to see you again. Fair enough? Joy, I'll be bluntly honest with you; if you two don't manage to get together, I plan to make one more attempt at keeping him with me and Henry."

She was crying now, and Joy felt her heart go out to this woman who, only hours before, had seemed like a merciless competitor.

"I understand, Veronica, and I don't blame you a bit. I'm so thankful to you for calling me, and for your heartfelt advice. I'm sure you understand just how much it means to me. I've been too upset to eat or sleep or even work! I promise to let you know what happens next. It's all very exciting, but also scary, don't you think? My stomach is in knots, because I love him so much.

"It's amazing, when you think about it: Both of us want the same man to be happy and I obviously made a mistake by running away in Bismarck. Thank you so much for sharing your deep feelings with me."

The two women hung up. They were both weeping openly now. But they were friends now, and both of them knew it. Veronica cried softly for a couple of minutes, and then hurried into the restroom to wash her face and apply fresh makeup.

She arrived at the meeting with her head held high and a bright smile on her lips.

*

Within half a minute, Joy was sharing the phone call with her mother. Mrs. Price liked what she was hearing. "According to my tribe, dear, both the heart *and* the head know what's best for us. And it sounds to me as if both are speaking to you, loud and clear! They're letting you know that Jim still loves you and will return to you." She paused to run a hand through her daughter's gleaming hair.

"I suspect the river spoke to you as well, my beauty. I feel sure this Jim is your soul mate! I can't wait to meet him and welcome him into our family."

Joy frowned. She wanted to believe her mother, but it was hard, hard. "Oh, how I hope you and Veronica are right, mother! But that lady is so beautiful . . . and she seems so elegant, so self-assured. And her manners! Just watching her walk across a hotel lobby, that first day, I felt certain she was exactly what Jim needed in a life partner."

Now the younger woman closed her eyes. Sighed deeply. "My heart is heavy tonight, mother, so heavy. I can't stand the waiting – can't endure the hours that will have to pass before we're together again. Sometimes it seems like I was just a port in a storm for him, and nothing more."

"Nonsense, my dear. You're a beautiful woman; you know that. Even more important, your heart is bursting with love for Jim Clark, for his dog, for the outdoors and for the work that man so dearly loves. Trust me – you're perfectly suited to one another." She fell silent for a moment, and her eyes took on a soft, gleaming light. "I dreamed of you and him last night, and in the dream I felt certain that the mighty river and our majestic Rocky Mountains are both on your side.

"Follow your heart, my sweet, my honest and caring Joy! Happiness is within your reach, if only you can be brave enough to reach out and take it. Grab hold of the magic ring of life, and grip it tightly. And never forget: Nothing worth having ever comes easily!"

*

A man and his dog! Is there any joy like it?

"Jack, I want your full attention now!" boomed Jim Clark. "Why? Because I have something very important to tell you, that's why?"

The lab stared up at his master: *Would you mind lowering your voice a few decibels? I'm gonna end up deaf!*

"Jack, I'm pleased to report that we are now approaching Mobridge, South Dakota, where Captain Clark of Lewis and Clark saw his first grizzly bear tracks. This is such a great adventure, don't you think? And poetic, too. Why, the river seems to be speaking directly to us about her history, while encouraging us to witness her power and beauty – in spite of all the mud you see everywhere."

Jack yawned. ***Please save the poetry for somebody else, pal.***

"Hey, don't look so smug – and stop raising those eyebrows at me, Jack. I'm telling you, this area is positively crawling with history! Somewhere in this very area, Private John Newman with Lewis and Clark was 'punished with lashes and disbanded from the expedition for mutinous expression.'"

Clearly unimpressed, the dog sent his owner another jumbo-sized yawn.

"Look here," said Jim. "I don't want to seem unpleasant – but *you* might want to think about what happened to poor John Newman. He was mutinous, Jack, and he paid the ultimate price. Do you know what it means to be 'disbanded,' Jack? To be left helpless and unarmed, without food, among a pack of bloodthirsty savages?

"Avoid mutiny, Jack. At all costs, avoid mutiny!"

The canine showed no fear, however. His head sank onto his paws; ten seconds later, he was snoring loudly.

"Besides, if you're nice to me, and if you show a bit of respect – well, I might be persuaded to cut you a piece of my steak tonight, instead of serving you up another bowl of that dry, stale, desiccated dog food you always seem to prefer."

Jack opened one eye. Focused it. ***When does chow-time begin, bozo? And stop lecturing me. Haven't you read about Seaman, the bold-hearted Newfoundland dog who guided the Lewis and Clark Expedition to glory, just as I am guiding your butt to international stardom?***

They paddled on, man and dog, through the rising heat of noontime. Jack did all the work, as usual, and the dog dozed fitfully, as usual. From time to time,

Jack suppressed the urge to crack his canine buddy's skull with the paddle. "He's sleeping and I'm busting my hump," Jack told himself again and again. "Which one of us has this thing figured out?"

But at least they were together. Man and dog. No joy like it!

*****

THE RIVER: A Thumbnail Sketch from Jim Clark's "Mighty Mo Notebook:"

Aug. 10: Writer George Catlin in 1841 called the 1000 miles of the Missouri between here and the Mississippi River the "River Styx." Why? Because almost every sandbar and island was covered with huge piles of floating trees, driftwood and floating rafts that threatened keel-boats and steamers on their way up the river. I'm seeing a lot of floating stuff right now. And the trees and drift wood are threatening us today.

I began taking notes on wildlife along the banks and in the water to pass the time. A couple of days ago I spotted a regal bald eagle perched in a tree and an osprey circling, apparently fishing; a great blue heron was fishing in the shallows and came up with a blue gill and proudly showed us his catch – from a distance, of course. A little farther downstream, a small heron picked up smaller fish, minnows and some bugs he'd found along the edge of the river. We passed a turtle as big as my Tilly hat riding a huge log.

Jack barked, "Hello, slow poke!" but received only a sarcastic look in return. Jack was quite chagrinned – he's convinced that he has unlimited friends in the animal kingdom as well as among humankind. Two hours later a mule deer doe and her fawn lifted their heads from drinking to investigate our strange-looking

craft – but since we didn't tarry, she returned to gathering what will be the largest part of her milk from the river. That fawn will be forever grateful to the river for its life, just like the other creatures all around us.

Next an osprey circled, glided and then dove into the river, coming up with lunch for the young birds in the nest built in a metal stand the Game Commission had provided. A red-tailed hawk was pursued relentlessly by crows; earlier, blackbirds had pursued a crow! It was all part of the pecking order. I watched a muskrat cutting reeds along one of the numerous sandbars – and I was amused to see that he didn't seem to "give a darn" about our important trip past his home.

Next we noticed a fair-sized herd of horses. Many of them had foals lingering by their sides, and most were enjoying breakfast, lunch or dinner. They milled around the edge of the river for their "morning milk break" . . . and gave me a light-hearted break, as well. They were Hereford, Angus, Charlaigh and also some mixed-breed cattle that drank from the river and ignored the mud they stirred up.

I figure we should reach Pierre, South Dakota, the state capitol, in two to three more days. I will visit the Cheyenne Indian Reservation near Highway 212. The Cheyenne have a reputation for being warlike, but it all depends on who's writing the history, doesn't it? We'll visit the town nearest our campsite tonight, and I'll buy a steak for Jack and me. Hopefully, the campground supervisor will keep an eye on the canoe. I'll set up the tent before we leave. End of notes for today.

After gorging themselves on two Montana-sized steaks, Jim and Jack were taking turns belching. They were both smiling, as well. Could things get any better than this? Yes, they could – but only in the presence of gorgeous, thinly clad females who were starved for sex. As they strolled back toward their campsite, Jim was musing aloud: "Isn't it amazing what a good steak can do for your morale, Jack? I feel like a million bucks!" But then he frowned. "Well, maybe $700,000. If only Joy were here to join me in a cup of post-sirloin coffee. . . ."

But he broke his speech off here – much to the dog's relief – in order to visit the all-important spot-a-pot located at the south end of the campsite.

Moments later, perched on his throne, Jim sighed the deep, profound sigh of the just – and cut loose with a volley of internal explosions so violent that it threatened to bring down the tent and sink the canoe at its mooring. The eruption was followed by a deep silence, through which the big man could hear his four-legged pal thinking: ***Does that guy have no shame? That was at least a nine on the Richter Scale, and he's only getting started!***

But Jack's next thoughts were cut short.

And a moment later, Jim heard a deafening racket begin. Snarls, vicious snappings, clashing teeth and howls of pain – all at once the campsite had roared into what sounded like a battle to death among giant wolves. What the hell was going ***on*** **out there? Frantic with anxiety now, the big man was struggling to get his pants up and buckle his belt. It took him at least ten seconds . . . and when he finally came crashing out of the mobile outhouse, the first thing he spotted was the loyal Jack going nose to nose with an enormous wolf-dog!**

Paralyzed with shock for a moment, Jim watched helplessly while the wolf-dog leaped onto the Jack's back and clamped his huge fangs on an unprotected shoulder. Without mercy, the huge intruder tore at the valiant Lab's back, while keeping his own throat protected from assault. Gaping, Jim whistled with surprise – the attacker was easily half-again as large as his domestic opponent, whose blood was now dripping from the wolf-dog's jaws. But Jack hung on, undaunted. He was limping desperately now, while spouting geysers of blood . . . yet he gave no ground at all. Instead, he continued to circle the campfire site, growling furiously and guarding his stomach and throat.

For a few seconds, the amazed Jim Clark stood motionless, utterly fascinated by this display of naked savagery. It was as if Jack London's classic fighting dog "Buck" – the hero of the unforgettable *Call of the Wild* – had suddenly been reborn in this forest clearing beside the Muddy Mo, and was fighting once again for his own glorious life.

How could Jim help? For a few frantic moments, he looked around desperately for other campers, or maybe another canoeist. *Nada.* In a flash he realized: There would be help from any other quarter. It was as though this huge, ghost-like animal – probably a mix of wolf and Malamute, or maybe German Shepherd – had frightened off the entire population of the river landing.

And things were getting worse by the minute. When Jack shook his head to sling the blood from his eyes, he lost his focus on the brute . . . and paid for it, a moment later, when he was knocked completely off his feet. Within a micro-second,

the bigger dog was at his throat. But Jack still had a few tricks in his bag. *Not so fast, King Kong – you ain't seen nothing yet!*

A moment later, the underdog was rolling away from the favorite, while reaching up with his powerful black jaws and sinking his sharp white fangs deep into Kong's soft underbelly. Maintaining his deadly grip for several seconds, he kept his sharp-edged teeth buried in the monster-dog's flesh. The invader's blood was also flowing freely now, as he screamed repeatedly with pain and anger. And a moment later Jack was back on his feet – as the wolf-dog lunged for him again and slammed with brutal power into his torn and bleeding shoulders.

The contest was nip-and-tuck now, with scarlet blood flying throughout the campsite, but Jack was determined to remain on his feet. The Lab had tasted hot blood, and he seemed to enjoy the taste . . . because he suddenly clamped his jaws down on the wolf-dog's left ear and hung on for all he was worth. Stunned and horrified, Jim heard the larger canine moan with hideous pain as the ear tore cleanly away from his skull, leaving only a ragged stump behind.

What to do? Half crazed with fear and rage himself, Jim finally shook off his trance and raced to the river's edge, where he quickly located a rusted fishing net. Without hesitating, he grabbed the device and zoomed back to confront the two snarling and slashing beasts. With the heavy net fully opened, he managed to fling it over the wolf-dog – triggering an insane burst of howling and snarling from the deranged animal. But Jim would not be frightened off. Displaying the kind of strength he hadn't needed since his football days, he forced the net down over the big dog's massive and bloody head. At the same time, the big man dug his heels into

the soft turf of the campsite and struggled to lift part of the wolf-dog from the ground. Deprived of leverage and traction, the vicious intruder wound up clawing helplessly at the cords in the net, while his blood-laced spittle soaked into the shirt of the man who was holding him.

Hanging on for dear life, Jim shouted at his ally: "Whoa, Jack! Back off, fella! I've got him . . . keep away!" For few long seconds, however, Jack simply refused to give up the fight, and kept lunging frantically and snapping at the brute caught in the net. This went on for a bit longer . . . before Jack finally seemed to understand that his opponent had been captured. Once that fact was clear, Jack's police training kicked in, and he began to calm down and return to his senses. At last, with his fangs bared and his eyes on his huge foe, the Lab retreated a few paces and sat down on his haunches.

It was over. Trapped inside the strait jacket provided by the thickly corded net, the wolf-dog couldn't use his teeth against them anymore. "You monster!" growled Clark, whose own blood was also running hot by now, "you're lucky I don't shoot you! And the only reason I didn't was . . . I might have hit Jack!"

Within a short time, the wolf-dog had stopped struggling. Still, Jim had to be very careful as he climbed off the animal, in order to avoid a sudden confrontation with those razor-sharp teeth. But he got it done, and then managed to wrap a painter rope around the net and tie both dog and cage to the nearest tree. "I'll have to wait before I put a collar on him," he told Jack. The Lab looked calmly at his master: *Good plan. But how about letting me rip his other ear off, first?*

Jim opened his mouth to reply, but no words came out. And for good reason: The air was suddenly full of flying, sizzling lead.

"What the . . . "

Somebody was shooting at them! No . . . make it *two* somebodys. Amazed all over again, Jim went airborne, even as he screamed at the startled pooch beside him: "Hit the deck, Jack, we're under fire!"

Incredibly, amazingly, they were taking rounds from a pair of rifles located about 100 yards back in the tree line. Stretched out flat on his belly, Clark struggled to make sense of a world that seemed to have gone mad. Who could be shooting at them, and why? But this was no time for pointless questions. Somehow, he had to find a way to get down to the canoe and retrieve his own weapon, before he or the dog (or *both* of them) caught a stray round or the ricochet from one of these scarred tree trunks.

"Stay down, Jack." Face pressed against the leaves, Jim tried to estimate the location of the two gunmen who were firing at them. But he was also counting the rounds as they emerged . . . and when his assailants paused to reload, he made his move. Rolling across the muddy earth, he crawled to his feet and dashed for the canoe. Groaning with fear, he struggled to pull the rifle from its holder beneath the gunwale, then dove face-first back into the mud as the enemy firing resumed.

A moment later he was crawling back up the slope toward his waiting comrade. The Winchester was loaded by now, and he walked on his knees and elbows across the clearing to the edge of a massive granite boulder. There he

quickly planted his Tilly hat atop the stone, making sure that its silhouette could be seen easily from at least a hundred yards away.

But then the firing stopped. Jim waited a few minutes . . . and nothing else happened. He frowned. "Stay here, Jack – don't move." A moment later he was sprinting from one tree to the next, moving quickly through the dark line of trees that flanked the river. Investigating carefully, he found six ejected cartridges lying in the muck, then studied the boot prints of what must have been a pair of assailants. And he groaned with frustration when he saw how the prints gradually petered out in the rocky soil. "Dang it," he snapped furiously at himself, "I can't tell which fork they took in the trail!"

After another five minutes of futile searching, he hurried back to the canoe. Had his attackers doubled back to wipe out Jack and sink their frail craft at the river's edge? No . . . everything seemed to be the same as he'd left it – except that poor Jack was now stretched out on the floor of the forest, while his blood trickled soundlessly into the leaves.

Jim stood over his old friend, worried sick. "Jack, I'm sorry – but I can't let you sleep. You've lost too much blood, and I have to make sure you don't lose any more." Now he bent over the half-conscious warrior, who opened one eye and moaned weakly in pain. "Easy, boy," said Jim in a low, soothing voice. "I'm going to examine you for wounds now, but I'll do it as gently as I can."

Then he went to work. Concentrating intently on his injured comrade, Clark didn't see the two men who suddenly materialized at the far edge of the tree line. They were tall, shabby figures in faded bib overalls and mud-spattered boots, and

they walked with the lurching, disorderly gait of small-town losers who spend half their lives in the local tavern. For at least half a minute, the two marauders stood watching Clark tend to the wounded Jack. Then one of them spat. "Come on, Jed – we'll come back for them later." They turned away, then, and began to lope back toward the fork in the trail from whence they'd come a few minutes earlier.

Meanwhile, Jim was doing his best to stanch the blood that still dribbled from half a dozen slashes on his pal's flanks and ribcage.

"Okay, buddy, it looks like most of these cuts are clotting up pretty well," he said calmly, as he patted the dog's torn hide with a wet towel. "Do you think you can walk okay? You don't seem to have lost as much blood as I thought – but those cuts sure aren't pretty to look at. Hang on a minute while I grab the first-aid kit – I'm gonna have to sew you up in some spots, and also rub on some antibiotic. We don't want any germs – or any of these pesky black flies – to start chowing down on your wounds."

Jim was no veterinarian, but necessity required that he develop some doctoring skills fast. And he did. After retrieving the first-aid kit from the canoe, he went to work washing the cuts with alcohol, then sewing them up with needle and thread. The antibiotic went on smoothly enough – although the suffering dog snapped at the doctor out of pure instinct, each time he grazed a sensitive nerve.

The last step was to spray the wound areas with insect repellent in order to stave off the hungry flies. Then he fed the courageous mutt four Tylenol wrapped in a slab of salami from the canoe. After a quick hug: "Okay, my friend, I think you're all set. I want you to lie here quietly for a while. Got it?"

The dog rolled his eyes. *Lie here for a while, Jim? How hard is that concept to understand?*

Jim studied him for a bit. "Well, I'm glad to see that your sense of humor is still intact. I want you to close your eyes and sleep for a few hours."

Will do, commander.

"It's okay to dream, if you must, but I don't want any other activity for the rest of the day."

Sounds like a plan, pardner. Will you fetch my pillow from the canoe?

Jim ignored this request, however. "Luckily for both of us, you're young and strong, and you should be fully recovered in a couple of days. Until then, I don't want you doing anything more strenuous than eating and sleeping."

Now you're talking! Got any more of that sirloin left? Hey, seriously, I do want to thank you for saving my life. If it hadn't been for you and your net, that big bruiser would've eaten my lunch for sure. . . .

Before Jim could reply to this, however, the Hero of the Hour was snoring raggedly and dreaming of the chocolate Lab – a winsome creature named Shadow – who lived down the block from Veronica and Henry's house.

Clark smiled, and then turned immediately to the problem posed by the wolf-dog. "What the hell am I supposed to *do* with this fanged colossus?" he asked himself as he eyeballed the groaning behemoth in the net. But a moment later, he realized the obvious: He was equipped with a cell phone! Why not leave the

predator tangled in his web and simply dial 911 for the nearest law enforcement agents?

Sixty seconds later – after some very hurried conversation – the feds had dispatched a ranger to the campsite, while explaining that they would retrieve the animal, test him for rabies . . . and then probably put him up for adoption. Clark thanked the dispatcher, then clanked the green "Call" button on his Kyocera.

It was time to check in with magazine publisher Jay Spader and file a quick report on these latest – and thoroughly amazing – developments.

After punching the numbers into the phone, Clark found himself predictably irritated – once again, he would have to deliver his report to a mere machine. "Hey, this is Jim Clark again," he told the publisher's voice mail, "and I'm still in one piece. But it hasn't been easy – my dog just got attacked by some kind of wild wolf-dog, and two guys started taking pot shots at me with rifles. I managed to drop a fish net over the wolf, and the gunmen ran off after I fired a few rounds at them, myself.

"Other than that, things have been going quite smoothly out here."

He paused for a moment to reflect on his situation – and suddenly burst out laughing. All at once, the absurdity of what he was doing seemed overwhelming. Was he really standing here on the edge of the Missouri River, using a hand-held machine to tell *another* machine that he was "doing just fine" – only minutes after two men had done their very best to kill him? And what did "just fine" mean, exactly? That he was still breathing? That he still had a pulse?

Unreal! "I tracked them for a while," he told the tape recorder in St. Louis after a bit, "but I lost the trail at a fork, and I had to give up the chase. It's just as well, because Jack needs me – he got pretty cut up during the fight and lost a lot of blood. But don't fret about that, either – this dog doesn't have an ounce of quit in him, believe me. It's like my old football coach used to say in the middle of the fourth quarter: 'When the going gets tough, the tough get going!' That's Jack, all right – and if there's a gutsier canine on Planet Earth, I've yet to meet him!

"Anyway, I'm back in the saddle and getting ready to put the canoe back in the water. But first I want to visit the Wounded Knee National Memorial over at Pine Ridge Reservation. That's one heck of a story, as you know – 300 Native American men, women and children get slaughtered in an 1890 ambush sponsored by our good old pal, Uncle Sam. Revenge for Custer's Last Stand, they say.

"I'm hoping to nail down some dynamite interviews over there, and then I'll resume the battle with the Muddy Mo. Don't worry about the Wolf-Dog Incident . . . I've already called in law enforcement and they'll be here shortly, I'm told."

He said his farewells, after that – and got a major surprise a few minutes later when the cell phone suddenly lit up again.

It was Spader. "Thank God you're okay, Jim. Jeez, when it rains it pours, huh? I can't imagine why those two maniacs would want to shoot at a lone guy in a canoe. Is this a crazy country, or what?"

"Beats me," said Clark.

"Listen, Jim, I'm concerned about your safety. That's the only thing that really matters here. Believe me, I respect what you've already accomplished, and I want you to know that if the risks seem too high on this project, I think you should drop it. Get out while you can. We'll double reimburse for your expenses and give you a decent payday. Why take a chance on being sent home in a body bag?"

Clark didn't hesitate. "No way, Mr. Spader. I told you I was in this thing to stay, and I meant it. This is one hell of a story, and I intend to finish it. They're not going to scare me off with a couple of rifle shots. And I sure as hell know they aren't going to scare Jack."

"I hear you, Jim. And you're right – it *is* one hell of a story. I just hope you can fight your way through to the place where it says 'The End.'"

Clark nodded. "Jack and I will be all right, don't worry. Right now, I'm more pissed off than scared. And I'm convinced that these two guys today were the same two who've been following us for the last several hundred miles. For some reason, they don't want me to reach St. Louis in time, and they don't want me to win that prize."

There was a slight pause on the other end. "That makes sense to me, Jim. But whoever they are, you gotta watch yourself. Safety first, always. Will you promise me you'll be careful?"

"You bet I will."

The two men hung up, and Clark quickly returned to check on his companion. Jack was sound asleep now, with no signs of distress; apparently, he was going to be no worse the wear for having gone ten rounds with the canine version of Godzilla. Bending over the dozing Lab, Jim carefully evaluated his wounds again. So far, so good. But then he got another surprise, when the phone suddenly rang once again. Had Spader called him with more instructions? No . . . it was a female voice . . . *Joy!*

Clark's heart flip-flopped like an Olympic gymnast at the top of his game.

"You're kidding! Is this Joy? I can't believe it! What a fabulous surprise – and where on earth have you *been*?"

"Jim, I'm so sorry. It was all a huge misunderstanding. . . ."

"Oh, don't worry about that. I'm just glad you're okay, honey, and I'm thrilled that you're on the telephone. Somebody better pinch me; I must be dreaming!" Brain whirling, Clark reached out to grab the nearest tree branch for support. His vision had gone all swirly, and his heart was beating like a high-speed bongo drum.

"Joy, we've b-b-b-been in a scrape," he stuttered like an idiot. "We're fine, but a monster-dog attacked J-J-J-Jack, and then two guys started blasting away at us with hunting rifles. I can't tell you how comforting it is to hear your voice right now."

"My God, Jim. Are you and Jack okay?"

"Yes, we're fine, babe. Jack got ripped up a little, but I'm nursing him back to health as we speak. Nothing to worry about."

She gasped loudly in his ear. "Nothing to *worry* about? A wild animal attacks Jack, and you're being shot at – and I'm not supposed to *worry*? Have you called the police?"

Now he found himself chuckling into the phone. "Joy, there are no police out here along the river. I did notify the federal park rangers who manage our campsite, and they've got an investigator headed here right now."

Joy listened to all of this in amazement. Then she astonished herself by suddenly blurting into the phone: "Jim, I have to ask you a very important question. Is it true that you told Veronica you wanted to marry me?"

Jim didn't hesitate. "Of course it is, Joy. You name the church and the day, and I'll get there two hours early!"

"Are you serious?"

"I've never been more serious in my entire life, babe."

"Oh, Jim, I can hardly believe it. And I feel so foolish – really, I behaved so stupidly in Bismarck, rushing away like that and then vanishing right off the radar screen. That was totally childish, and I don't know what got into me. It's like . . . at the moment when I spotted you and Veronica and Henry walking across that hotel lobby – it was like I just snapped, or something. My whole life flashed before my

eyes, and it just seemed so clear that you preferred her to me. I couldn't stand the thought, and I had to get away. It was as simple as that – but it was absurd of me.

"I should have walked right up to you and told you how I felt. And what happened next? I asked the manager to lie to you . . . to tell you I'd left the city, when in fact I remained behind for another full day. I sat around my hotel room, praying that something would happen – something magical, an earthquake, anything – that would somehow throw us back together again.

"I guess I won the top prize for Immature Behavior in an American Hotel Lobby that night, whaddya think?"

Jim was laughing out loud now. He felt like he'd just discovered $22,569 lying in the street, underneath a sign that read: "Whoever finds this dough can keep it – congratulations!" In the space of four hours, he'd gone from being shot at and nearly killed to being reunited with the woman he loved most in the world.

"Joy, I think I must be the happiest man on earth right now. You didn't act immaturely, not at all. You acted like a woman in *love* – and everything you've been telling me boils down to a single fact: You and I were meant for each other! How fast can I get to where you are and put my arms around you?"

"You're reading my mind again, Jim. Do you want to meet me in a city near the river, so I can fly there ASAP?"

"You bet I do. How about Pierre? The only problem is, it will take me two or three days to get there. Poor Jack really took a licking, and I've got to nurse him

for a day or two while I do all the paddling. I also need to put in a few hours on the water, before I forget how to hold a canoe paddle. But I'm sure I could get to Pierre in three days. Do you think you can find an airline that will take you there by Friday?"

But before she could answer, he cut her off: "Wait, I've got a better idea. How about Rapid City? We can rent a car and visit the Little Bighorn National Forest – the setting for Custer's Last Stand, if you remember your American History 101. And we can also take a drive through the Black Hills Park in South Dakota and eyeball the Wounded Knee Memorial on the Pine Ridge Reservation. After that, it will be easy to circle back to Rapid City and put you on a plane headed for home."

Delighted with the prospect, Joy was laughing out loud. "Jim, it sounds like an absolute winner. But don't forget that I'm half-Blackfoot – you and I may come away from Wounded Knee with some very different impressions."

"Oh, really? Why so, do you think?"

She smiled. "Well, for starters, most of my Native American ancestors were convinced that the massacre of Big Foot's band at Wounded Knee in 1890 was simply a needless – and vicious – retaliation for the deaths of those killed by Chief Sitting Bull at Custer's Last Stand, 14 years earlier."

Jim nodded. "I hear you loud and clear, babe. We might not agree on this topic – but who cares? Trust me, we'll be fine! Why, after what we've been through, a mild historical disagreement now and then will seem like a walk in the park."

After a few more minutes of joyful badinage, the two lovers promised to meet at the airport, rent a car and then head for the nearest Best Western Motel.

Then they hung up. Jim stood beneath a windblown pine, amazed at his sudden good fortune. She was his again! Thrilled and exalted by the news, he felt like doing a couple of exuberant cartwheels along the riverbank. And yet he couldn't help feeling an occasional flicker of anxiety, along with the euphoria. Joy seemed to be deeply, totally in love with him . . . but hadn't Veronica once sworn the same eternal kinship, only to change her mind months later and virtually lose interest in a gentleman named Jim Clark?

While he fretted and debated with himself, his restless eyes were sweeping back and forth across the mighty river. What a vista! As far as the eye could see, the muddy current swirled and rolled like a living animal, like a breathing and dreaming presence. The Mighty Mo! And all at once Jim Clark was laughing out loud: "You idiot, why can't you *learn from the river*? Does the river whine and blubber and complain each time the current changes, or a new log falls into the water from the forest? No! Because the river knows that the more it changes, the more it stays the same!"

Dimly at first, he was beginning to understand the first great lesson of the Mo: *Don't sweat the day to day changes that affect you and your world; focus, instead,*

on what is timeless and true and eternal in your life – things like your love for a good woman named Joy!

Maybe his luck was finally beginning to change? After less than an hour of looking, Jim Clark located the perfect kennel for Jack – a bright, cheery layout near the waterfront that featured an important attraction for the hero of the Wolf-Dog Saga: a black female Lab named Suzy-Q.

Operated by a smiling, upbeat couple from Canada, the canine hotel also included the services of a professional veterinarian . . . no small matter, in Jack's case, after the terrible beating he'd endured. As they strolled into the brightly illuminated area of the dog run, Jack sprang to attention. *Hey, I'm on vacation, folks; don't expect anything except snoozes and snack-times from this pampered mutt!*

A moment later, he was gazing deep into the dreamy eyes of Suzy-Q, while bragging unashamedly: *Yo, babe, I just went ten rounds with Sugar Ray, and I'll soon be wearing the World Heavyweight Championship ring on my right paw. Do you believe that diamonds are a girl's best friend?*

Simpering sweetly and batting her great black lashes at him, Suzy-Q winked at the valiant warrior, then crooned: *Why don't you drop by my kennel sometime and show me your trophies, big boy?*

In a flash, the love-struck Jack had whirled to his master: *Holy-moly, did you see that action? She's hot for me, big man!* He paused for a moment and cocked one eye. *Ah . . . excuse me, but why are you still here? Don't you have somebody to pick up at the airport?*

It didn't take Jim more than three or four seconds to understand that he was no longer needed. "Have a blast, Jack!" And a moment later, he was out the door and hurrying off to wrap up several chores . . . starting with the canoe. After arranging for an outfitter to watch over Tripper and her cargo, Jim scrambled toward the airport – where he quickly lined up his flight to Rapid City and rented the room they'd need.

For their comfort – since they faced a drive of several hundred miles – he requested a snow-white Lincoln Continental. With each passing minute, he was growing more excited and more impatient. What a treat it would be, to unwind from his hundreds of miles of paddling by kicking back and ordering a shrimp cocktail from room service! And how long had it been since the two of them had last embraced? My God, was it really way back there on the Montana-North Dakota border that they'd last enjoyed the comfort of each other's arms?

Northwest Airlines would be on time for a change, he was told, and the weather would be smooth, all the way to Rapid City. But the flight was full, with every seat taken, so once again he'd have to cram his double-wide body into a jam-packed airplane fuselage and hope for the best. Oh, well: Into every life, a bit of rain must fall! He would put up with the inconvenience – and he didn't complain, either, when the flight actually turned out to be an hour late, in spite of all the airline's reassurances to the contrary.

Joy would be coming in from Great Falls, Montana, about 30 minutes after Jim's arrival . . . which would give him plenty of time to duck in the men's room

and powder his nose. He'd brought his razor along, as well, so he was good to go. He trudged out to the boarding gate with the other passengers, then stashed his day pack under the seat in front of him. A quick snap of the seat belt buckle and he was ready to roll.

Twenty minutes later he was sipping Jack Daniels and gazing out on the vast American grasslands of the prairie. How easy it was to imagine the great herds of lowing buffalo that had once grazed these wide-open vistas. How easy, also, to envision the flowing Indian ponies and their riders, arrows at the ready, zooming among the majestic animals and taking them down one by one – but for food, not sport. In a grove of nodding cottonwoods, the hunting party watches eagle-eyed while the bison drift into a natural trap provided by a narrowing, funnel-like canyon. . . .

Go! Whooping frantically, the painted braves thunder across the meadow, spooking and scattering the herd into the draw, where the killing can begin in earnest. This was the dance of life – the dance of death – and it was a symphony so beautiful that the heart stood still, watching it.

The vision faded slowly, and his consciousness along with it. And he never saw the stewardess remove his half-empty glass from the tray table, or slide the bright blue pillow under his slumbering head.

*

The jetliner touched down without incident, although the tarmac looked hot enough to melt the tires and fry eggs at the same time. But so what? After spending

so many hours beneath the sun, the big man wasn't afraid of a little heat. Without hesitating, he hustled into the Main Terminal and headed for the nearest Men's Room to scrape his whiskers off and apply some strong deodorant. After signing on the dotted line for the Lincoln (not white, but pale gold, as it turned out) and purchasing maps for the Wounded Knee Memorial on the Pine Ridge Reservation and the Little Bighorn, Jim had just 5 minutes to spare.

By the time he reached Joy's gate, he was actually running – after having taken a few moments to pick up a bouquet of pretty jonquils and violets. The door to the boarding ramp swung open, and he watched the passengers like a greedy hawk. *There she is!* All at once he was gazing upon Joy's large, almond-shaped eyes and her slender, curvaceous figure. Her jet-black hair swung enticingly behind her, as she hurried toward him. Then she caught his eye and was overjoyed at seeing him. She could read his gaze as well, and quickly understood that he was thrilled to see her.

The line of passengers was moving too slowly, damn it! But at last he was able to push his way to her side and sweep her up in his big arms. His lips claimed hers in a deep kiss. All at once, they were home, and their passion was so great that it actually triggered a burst of applause.

Within 15 minutes they had loaded their gear in the car and glided through the well-designed city to the 4-Star Great Western Hotel. Their car was parked for them and their few bags were carried away. Jim signed them in. They were quickly shown to their room by a most cordial and dapper clerk. "Please leave your request for your favorite courtesy steak dinner with all the trimmings," he intoned as he

pulled back the curtains. "We'll have your courtesy meal served right in the room, and I can tell you that we've got the best beefsteaks in a state which is famous for them!" And he laughed out loud. "The beef in this city is so fresh that some of it's still walking around!

"We're also proud of our service, and you can expect to be eating within 30 minutes of placing your order. Would you like me to bring you some appetizers?"

"That won't be necessary, thank you." Jim wanted to scream with impatience: ***Will this fellow never leave us alone?*** **But Jim gave him a generous tip. And then they were alone at last, reaching out for each other.**

The next morning, Jim and Joy enjoyed a huge breakfast of pancakes, eggs, potatoes, sausage and bacon. Laughing and hugging and carrying armloads of maps and brochures, they climbed into the Lincoln. Without pausing, they zoomed toward into the Black Hills, called "He Sapa" by the Lakota Nation and considered sacred for thousands of years. Working her maps cheerfully, Joy directed him to the Bear Butte (or "Mato Paha"). "Bear Butte is the core of a volcano and also a sacred prayer site for the Lakota and Cheyenne people," she read from a brochure.

They also spent the best part of an hour watching mountain-carving in progress for the memorial to Oglala Chief Crazy Horse, the revered Lakota Sioux who had led the battle against Custer at the Little Bighorn. Then they toured the Badlands National Park. It was so awesome! They crept on their hands to look over the edge, and it seemed they might fall into the abyss at any moment. Jim was able to get some great photos that showed him and Joy gazing thoughtfully into the

great canyons. After setting the timer on the camera, they clicked off several pictures of the two of them peering out over the Badlands.

Next they interviewed a security employee for the State and learned about some excellent sources for more information on the Wounded Knee and Little Bighorn battles. Then they drove to the interpretative center nearby and gathered more data. Continuing southeast, they headed for the Wounded Knee Memorial. As Jim and Joy had hoped, they were blessed with enough time really get acquainted with each other, while discussing their hopes and desires for their lives.

At Wounded Knee, they solemnly surveyed the mass grave where Big Foot and more than 250 other American Indians had died. Fascinated, they listened to the story of how Black Elk and 20 Lakota horsemen arrived to drive off the Calvary and counted more than140 butchered women and children in piles, or spread out along the crooked gulch.

The massacre took place on December 29, 1890 – and the story still told about it is that Big Foot and his warriors had given up their religious dance and were being escorted to an Army encampment on the Pine Ridge Reservation. Sitting Bull had been killed on December 15, 1890. Apparently, the shooting started when Sitting Bull refused to join in the group, and was pushed in the back by an Indian policeman. One of the Indians shot the policeman, who then shot Sitting Bull in the chest. Another lawman shot him in the head, killing him instantly.

The massacre ended with the virtual elimination of Big Foot's band, including all the women and children. Listening hard to the grisly tale, Joy was overcome with grief and her tears flowed down her beautiful cheeks. With tears

streaming down his own face, Jim held her tightly in his arms and spoke of his dream that men and women everywhere would stop the senseless killing of the innocents. She smiled up at him and said, "Jim, although I'm one-half Blackfoot Lakota, my heart goes out to those of the Lakota Sioux Tribe – the Cheyenne, the Minniconjou, the Oglala, the Brule,' the Hunkpapa, the Blackfeet, the Two Kettle and the Sens Arc. They were not only forced off their lands; they also had their food supply destroyed and their gold stolen, and even the women and children were exterminated like animals."

It was obvious that Joy was well versed in her own ancestry and that of other Indian tribes. Holding hands or walking with their arms around each other, Jim and Joy tearfully viewed the Memorial. Jim was reminded of his brother's senseless death in Vietnam, although many generations and miles separated the two events. He could understand the grief of survivors of the Indian wars, whether White or Native Americans. The South and North Vietnamese suffered at each other's hands, along with the U.S. armed forces. The US Civil War and the Korean War also pitted neighbor against neighbor and family members. It was senseless!

After driving back to their hotel in Rapid City, they went out for dinner and dancing. Joy discovered that Jim was a wonderful dancer, as they melded together like they'd been born for each other. They could hardly wait until they could get back to their room, where they made passionate but gentle love. And when the long evening finally ended, they slept the sleep of the innocents.

After another hearty breakfast the next morning, they pulled a few things together for their day's sojourn into North Dakota. Then they drove the 100 or so

miles to the Little Bighorn Battlefield, commonly known as Custer's Last Stand, in what is now Montana.

Jim Clark's notes from Mighty Mo: **According to John Robert McNally, the Battle of Little Bighorn, commonly known as Custer's Last Stand, was fought on June 25, 1876, in what is now known as Montana, between a regiment of the Seventh United States Calvary led by Lieutenant Colonel George Armstrong Custer and a force of Sioux and Northern Cheyenne warriors. The discovery of gold in the nearby Black Hills in 1874 had led to an influx of white prospectors into that sacred territory and to attacks on the prospectors by the Sioux, under Chiefs Sitting Bull, Crazy Horse, and Gall.**

The Wounded Knee massacre occurred nearly 14 years later. In a copyrighted article by Wanbli Sapa and William Cooper, entitled "Wounded Knee: Are We About To Do It Again," they said "Historians like to say that the massacre of December 29, 1890, at Wounded Knee was the last major clash between federal troops and the Red Nation of this continent. This is blatantly untrue, though, and does an injustice to all those of the Red Nation who fought with or were massacred by the U.S. Army after 1890."

I will be able to see more about this when we visit Wounded Knee Memorial.

Some of the stories Jim and Joy reviewed had been written by Earl Rice, Jr., while others seemed to indicate that the acclaimed Indian Fighter Custer had bumbled into losing the lives of all his men, along with his own, on June 25, 1876. Unknowingly, with only 260 of his 655 men, he attacked 2500 to 4000 Cheyenne and Hunkpapa Sioux. In addition, he split his 260 men into three groups in order to

squeeze the enemy. But he then chose to ignore or misinterpret orders to wait to coordinate efforts with two other columns under General Alfred Howe Terry. Instead, he attacked at once. Custer did not realize there were so many warriors or that there was a maze of bluffs and ravines to attack, leaving him and his men with little way out.

Jim and Joy envisioned the soldiers having to kill their fine horses and then lie behind their carcasses to gain some protection from the warriors for a few minutes. Within an hour, though, all of Custer's men and he, himself, were dead. All except Custer were scalped, stripped of their clothing and had their bodies mutilated, with many beheaded.

Yet it must also be remembered that the Army scouts and others often scalped the Indians after killing them.

John Mac's *USA Travel Info and Images* describes Glacier National Park and the Little Bighorn Battle as follows: "Although the Indians won the battle of the Little Big Horn, it was not a major event in Sioux history. Knowing that there would be severe punishment for their victory, the Indians immediately split up and traveled on, living a hunted life so that the U.S. Calvary would have a difficult time trying to find them. Eventually, they would be forced to live on reservations as their land went into the hands of the US government."

Some of the information he and Joy studied was contained in two books: *The Battle of the Little Bighorn,* by Earl Rice, Jr., and *Wounded Knee* by Neil Waldman. Jim sadly recalled the death and burial of his brother, Johnny, as he thought about the hundreds of Indian and US soldier deaths in battle and approximately 60,000

deaths in Vietnam. Certainly, all of the warriors and soldiers wouldn't have been considered "innocent" victims of the gun, knife or arrow. But many who died had indeed been innocent. And what about their grieving kin? And what about the financial hardships that many of the survivors would face for generations to come?

For a couple of hours, there was little conversation between the lovers. However, after a wonderful meal and a chance to touch and hold each other again, the passion was re-ignited and their conversation returned to normal. "After the passing of more than a hundred years, it is time to look ahead, not back," Joy said.

Jim replied, as usual, with a joke: "It's a good thing *both* of us aren't canoeing – we wouldn't have the strength to lift a paddle after our love-making every night!"

Joy laughed out loud, then smacked him on one brawny shoulder: "I've been hinting that you should try and control your animal urges, Mr. Clark! After all, you're not getting any younger!" Dodging her elbow, he managed to capture her face for another sweet kiss.

But soon it was time to get down to business. "We're both scheduled to fly out of here today, said Jim. Let's plan on meeting when I reach Omaha, and then again in St. Louis at the wrap-up. How does that sound to you? I'll probably be rested up by Omaha – if we stay apart, that is."

Joy chuckled for a moment, but then became serious: "I'll be there, my darling. Just name the date and time and I'll be waiting with open arms and a ride to nice hotel and good steaks!"

The jet plane ride back to Pierre went off without incident. And when Jim arrived to pick up Jack, the big dog did his best to hide his joy at seeing him again. But his wide-open eyes and wagging tail gave him away. Jim shook his paw gravely – "It's good to be with the warrior again, Jack!" – but quickly noticed something different about his friend. For some reason, the hero of the Wolf-Saga had taken on a cocky, swaggering attitude.

Then Jim remembered the cute little Lab named Suzy-Q.

That's right,* Jack was thinking out loud again, *you're looking at a major-league stud, my man.

Jim stared at him. "Jack, am I imagining things – or does that silly grin mean you've just spent three straight days in the sack with a charmer named Suzy-Q?"

Jack was poker-faced. *Easy, pal. Back off. Do I grill you about the intimate details of your sex life?*

"Hey, no offense – I just wanted to compliment you on your good taste, that's all. That Lab was a real sweetheart – if you don't mind my saying so."

No problem, Jimbo. She's a looker all right, and you should have seen the tricks she could do. The action got so hot heavy after a while, I darn near suffered a stroke!

Jack roared. "Sounds like the lady had some very loose morals, my friend. Aren't you a little bit ashamed of yourself?"

Yeah, just a little bit. Maybe half an ounce. But I'll get over it, Father Jim. The truth is, I had more fun than a drunken sailor locked up all weekend in a Tijuana whorehouse!

Jack glared at him. "Now I really *am* scandalized, you canine Casanova. Go wash your mouth out with flea powder!"

With that, the two buddies broke into their famous "Joy to the World" dance around the kennel: ***Joy the fishes in the deep blue sea – joy to you and me!***

And they simply ignored the stares that followed them out the door and all the way to the car.

*

Feeling a little uptight and uneasy about describing his increasing suspicions, Jim nonetheless phoned Jay Spader early the next day to bring him up to date on his journey and his trips to the Indian battlegrounds. "Jay, this is really some country. I have no doubt that many of those Indian-US Army battles wouldn't have occurred in today's litigious world, however. No doubt, a law firm providing free legal help to the poor would have filed a 'stop order' or whatever to prevent the U.S. from violating the many treaties signed with the Indians. And then, even if the lawyers lost at the local level, why, they'd have appealed all the way to the Supreme Court . . . while also proving the Indians weren't given necessary counsel to interpret the treaties before they signed them.

"The lawyers also would have shown that the culture of the Indians didn't give the treaty-signers adequate authority over the members of their own tribes –

while proving conclusively that signatures from *all* the Indians should have been obtained, in order to make the treaty binding. And how about interpreters? Any good lawyer could have demonstrated that each tribe deserved a platoon of interpreters, in order to fully understand the documents at issue.

"Hey, I'm quite sure the ACLU would have filed a cease and desist order requiring the Army to let Sitting Bull and his tribe perform their ceremonial Ghost Dance in order to enter the spirit world."

Jay Spader listened carefully to all of this, then cleared his throat. "Jim, are you drinking any more than usual, out there on that river?"

Taken aback, Clark stammered badly. "Drinking? What are you talking about? I'm sober as a judge!"

"Okay, okay, no problem. It's just that you were . . . kind of *rambling* a little big there, big fella. I wonder if the stress of all that paddling might have affected your nerves?"

"I've never felt better in my life," was the icy reply.

"Okay, don't get touchy on me," said Spader. "I hear where you're coming from, and I hope you'll include some of those thoughts in your article about the Native American peoples of the Muddy Mo. I know our readers are interested in Native American culture; they can't get enough of it."

"I'm glad to hear that," said Clark, "because I've got some terrific photos and interview materials, along with dozens of tape recordings and videos. Thanks for hearing me out on the cultural aspects."

"No problema," said Spader. "I'll pass them on to the board and the CEO. Take care of yourself, Jim."

"Ten-four," said the paddle man. But when he hung up the phone, he was shaking his head. He still felt uneasy. Something wasn't right. Something didn't fit. Was he imagining things – or was there something dark hiding deep inside Jay Spader's cheerful words . . . hiding like a coiled and poisonous snake?

*

Early the next morning, Jack and Jim shoved off into the Missouri again. The river was like an old companion – not always friendly, but always there – and usually willing to help when needed. "Jack," said the big man, only a few minutes after they'd gotten underway, "I wonder if I might have a word with you?"

The dog made a groaning sound somewhere deep in his voice box: aggravation. ***Here we go again: River History 101. Doesn't this guy ever get tired of hearing his own voice?***

"Jack, I've been thinking about the Muddy Mo a good bit of late, and I've come to some rather interesting conclusions."

Interesting to you, maybe.

"Has it ever occurred to you that the misunderstandings and sufferings of the settlers and Indians were also inflicted on the river, itself, during the 1800s?

What? Jeez, you're making less sense with each passing day!

"Hear me out, Jack. Think about all those dams that got built across the water, during that period. Big dams like the Oahe, just north of Pierre, were

installed by well-meaning citizens – but in a way, they almost 'castrated' the once wild and free-flowing Missouri. They also depleted much of the rich `bottom land' in the river valleys, in every state where the backed-up water ate away at the earth. In the end, those dams took an enormous toll among the natural lives of fish and other wildlife. And what about the loss of recreational space and agriculture for our own citizens?"

Jack was gazing off over the water now, utterly lost. ***Ah, Jim . . . can you tell me where all of this is headed, please? Otherwise, I hope you won't mind an occasional snore now and then.*** **Already, the dog's weary head was drooping toward the bottom of the canoe.**

"All I'm saying, really, is that the river, itself, isn't immune from the same forces that so often warp and destroy human lives. The river suffers too, Jack!"

Uh-huh. Tell me about it. Pleasant dreams, Jim!

The Lab's head was resting on his front paws now, and he was already dreaming of his afternoon romps with Suzy-Q. But Jim blathered on, unaware of the fact that he was now talking entirely to himself.

"Jack, I figure it will be about 275 miles to Sioux City, Iowa, which translates to seven days of hard paddling. I expect to relax as much as possible – while trusting you to do the worrying and keep us straight in this fast current. There are too many barges and towboats and floating logs out here for me!"

No reply from Jack.

"Say, did you notice that huge bend in the river coming out of Pierre? It's called the West Bend and it was just full of Canada geese and several different breeds of ducks, including Mallards. The Lower Brule' Indian Reservation is on the west side of the bend and the Crow Creek Indian Reservation is on the east side. I don't know much about the Crow Creek Reservation, but the Brule' is Lakota."

No reply from Jack.

Jim paddled on. It took him another half an hour to discover that his buddy was sound asleep and snoring like a milk-fed lamb in the peaceful silence of the summer afternoon.

*****

The next seven days were a grueling test, as they paddled relentlessly toward Nebraska, and the toughest part was portaging around the four remaining dams. But there were plenty of other struggles, as well. They had to get off the river and take cover under the tarp twice from nearly golf-sized hailstones, along with driving rain. On those occasions, Jim imagined he had Joy in his arms keeping him warm through the onslaught. (When he discovered that his comforter was actually Jack, he felt thoroughly ridiculous.)

It was hard, grinding work at times. But the beautiful, richly hued rainbows made up for the hassle. And they also savored the wildlife and the scenery with its colorful rocks, blue skies and plush grasses. At times the sight of the riverbanks lined with wildlife was almost breathtaking. "I can't believe the interstate highway system is just a short distance away," Jim told Jack, "with all those crazed motorists traveling millions of miles in their tiny, claustrophobic cars." It was amazing, all

right. Although the two canoe-riders could often hear the roar of tires on concrete, they'd pretty much gotten used to it. And so had the wildlife.

It was remarkable, when you thought about it, how quickly the creatures of the wild could adjust to civilization. Back in downtown Baltimore, a peregrine falcon had made headlines by raising a family on top of a 40-story high-rise office building. Unbelievable! But nature was full of surprises, and Jim couldn't get enough of them. On the fifth day of their journey, they hoped to reach the first of two segments of "wild river," as listed on the National Register of Wild and Scenic Rivers. (Those segments run from Ft. Randall to Running Water and from Gavins Point Dam to Ponca State Park in Nebraska.)

"According to our South Dakota brochure," Jim lectured Jack at one point, "the two sections look much the same as they did during the Lewis and Clark Expedition. We'll be in those waters for 90 miles. If they're anything like the region around the White Cliffs of the Missouri in Montana, that stretch should offer us a very pleasant change of scenery. With no more dams to worry about, the current should increase and give us a break, also."

After going one-on-one with an especially large barge being pushed upstream by a jumbo tug, Jim had allowed the canoe to turn sideways. Struggling to move away from the monster barge, he'd unwisely allowed his attention to stray from the floating debris. A mistake! Suddenly, a huge tree floating faster than he was moving struck the canoe. Over they went! "Oh, my God," Jim shouted. "Look out, Jack!"

This was their first capsizing since tumbling through the rapids on their first day, weeks before.

"Where's the painter line?" roared Jim. "It has to be nearby!" The water was muddy, deep and cold. Of course, Jim couldn't see his hands in front of his face in the murk. He continued to search for a painter line but was unable to locate one, nor even to tell for sure if he was near the capsized boat. He was suddenly so tired. ***Maybe it isn't worth it,*** **he thought.** ***So many disappointments in my 31 years; it's so serene down here, and they tell me death by drowning is one of the most peaceful ways to go.***

But then an image of his brother Johnny appeared, as clear as a photograph. And all at once a familiar voice was booming in his ear: "Don't you dare panic, Jimbo! You can handle this. Your body will float as fast in the current as the canoe, so swim to the top and breathe. Do it!"

He obeyed. And sure enough, when he bobbed back up to the surface, he found the canoe floating beside him, even if upside down. The craft hadn't sustained any real damage – why, the dry bags were still tied to the thwarts! And then suddenly, as if from nowhere, the painter line was in Jim's hand.

As he pulled himself along the surface, he gagged and spit out muddy water. Nearly choking, he called out for Jack and tried to determine his distance from shore. He couldn't locate the dog . . . but he was at least relieved to find himself only about 100 yards from the shore. There was a sand bar ahead, and also a point on the river where fishermen were straining to see if they could help. "Hang on,

mister!" they yelled. "The river is quite shallow in this area, so force yourself to go to the bottom. Hold the boat if you can and don't let go of your rope!"

For a few anxious moments as he clung to the sandy bottom of the Mighty Mo, Jim believed the current was pulling the boat toward the bank. Was Johnny's spirit in control of the boat? He now found that he could hang onto the painter rope while swimming back up to the surface occasionally to breathe. Several men and women stood with linked hands at the shallow edge of the river. Their faces were masks of grim determination, as they formed a human chain and then sent one of their own wading out deeper to reach for him when he surfaced.

"I've never been so happy to see someone as I am to see you people," Jim said in a croaking voice. "You're wonderful! Look – my dog Jack is even here!" While the grateful dog coughed up at least a gallon of Mighty Mo, the men and women pulled Tripper to the edge of the stream and emptied out as much of the water as they could. "What do you want to do with the bags tied onto the canoe?" they asked. "They seem to be dry, which is pretty surprising, given the power of that river."

After asking them to unsnap the large dry bag and hand it to him on the bank, Jim opened it up and dug out some dry clothes and a towel. Excusing himself, he went into the woods, followed closely by the wet Lab. "What's the matter, Jack? Are you afraid they might have an appetite for fat dogs? They look harmless to me."

Oh, really, big shot? Well, you're not the one who'll end up being barbecued on the charcoal, are you? These folks look pretty hungry to me, and I want to be sure they don't have a hankering for dog-steak!

Sighing with frustration – "You're paranoid, Jack!" – Jim returned to the site of the overturned canoe, then arranged to treat the entire crew to steaks and drinks with all the trimmings at a local restaurant. A fellow who identified himself only as "White Hawk" accepted for himself and his daughter, whom he said he would bring along.

The guests all seemed to be having a wonderful time. All were in a happy mood and enjoyed a wonderful and boisterous meal – just the kind of shindig he and Jack needed after their scare. "I'd like to get a picture of you all eating, if that's okay," said Jim. "If you don't mind, I'd like to turn on my video camera on and learn some things about you I could share with my editor in St. Louis. I'll show one of you how to run the video camera, and I can then interview several of you, if you would. Some of this will probably get on television after the New Year."

The group of Yankton Lakoto Sioux all voiced their agreement. A good time was had by all! Jim asked what they thought about the vision he'd had of his dead brother, helping him find the painter rope. (He'd shared that he was part Indian as well.) "That sounds plausible to me," one elderly, wrinkled man said. "We believe it's possible to obtain such help from those who've gone on to the other side. Your Cherokee ancestry is in your heart and soul, Jim, and will never leave you. The river wasn't ready for you to join her at this time, either."

When Jim asked them to comment for the camera about saving his life on the Missouri, to a person, they modestly down-played heir part in the rescue. They also swore they wouldn't have done it if Jack hadn't threatened to tear an arm or two from each of them, if they allowed the big man to drown!"

"Are you laughing at me, Jack?" frowned Jim.

Who, me? Hey, I'm just praying I don't wind up on the menu here, pal.

It turned out that the Indians, Yankton Lakota Sioux, were quite well off, owning rather large cattle and sheep ranches, and were mostly college graduates or had children of their own in college. They enjoyed part-ownership in one or more ranches, restaurants, motels and many varied businesses in the state, also. "Jim, you just have to spend the night on my ranch," said one. "We'll treat you so many different ways, you're bound to like one of them!"

"I'd be honored – but Jack is rather shy and might have to be hog-tied," Jim joked.

"That'll be fine," said his potential host, "provided *you* do the hog-tying. That big brute looks like he could tear the head off a fire hydrant!"

As it turned out, Jack actually seemed to enjoy himself. He was even taken to a field where he was able to point and retrieve four rooster pheasants for shooters – which required only took one shot per bird by the crack marksmen. Jim, of course, carried the downed birds but did not shoot. And when the fun was over, the feisty retriever quickly became insufferably obnoxious: *Big Guy: didn't I tell you that you weren't much of a shot, back there in Maryland? Maybe I could live here from now on? These people seem to appreciate my special skills!*

Jim did his best to ignore this raillery, however, and soon sped off one of the tribe's fastest piebald pony stallions. Wow! What a piece of horseflesh! Jim had ridden a little, but this was better than anything he remembered. The gait was comfortable, yet consumed distance quickly. The wind in Jim's face was most welcome. White Hawk, the oldest son of Big Hawk (the leader of Jim's rescue team), accompanied him on a black-and-white paint mare. The ponies covered the miles as quickly and effortlessly as though floating. The hoof beats sounded muffled as they rode across the pastures and past herds of tame buffalo and cattle. It wasn't even necessary to shoe the horses for these unpaved and non-graveled lanes.

The speed and hushed sound of the footsteps brought to mind stories Jim had read in which Indian warriors approached buffalo and other game – and sometimes soldiers of the U.S. Army – without being detected. The horse herd was from Spanish stock that had been protected for centuries. He was asked if he would prefer to stay with Big Hawk and his wife in the main house, or to simply camp out in one of the bunkhouses. Jim chose to stay in a bunkhouse. This handsome building was painted brilliant white with blue trim and resembled the kind of sumptuous ranch so often featured in westerns. The bunkhouse was spotlessly clean, with comfortable beds. A large television, stereo and record player were also available for his use.

"Hallelujah!" Jim told himself when he saw the layout. "Let freedom ring!" The bunkhouse featured a well-stocked bar with leather stools and plenty of nutritious snacks. At first Jim thought he was getting special treatment as a guest – but he soon realized that hosts were accustomed to living in these luxurious digs.

As soon as he'd unloaded his gear, he jumped on the cell phone. "Joy, this is Jim. Believe it or not, I'm in a bunkhouse on a ranch owned by a Yankton Lakota Sioux. I was just getting ready to enjoy my `beauty rest' for the evening night, but I wanted to hear your wonderful voice. It's amazing the way fate works, isn't it? I mean, first I was rescued from drowning and then I was brought to this beautiful ranch. We went pheasant hunting and horseback riding. I feel like a new person and I just wanted to share my elation with you.

"After capsizing in deep water and being rescued by the Yankton Lakotas, all of this seems like some magical dream."

Joy could hardly believe her ears. "Are you serious? Did you really capsize again? Tell me what happened."

"Oh, no big deal. I flipped into the wash from a huge barge and couldn't find the painter or the boat and was deep in the water. My brother Johnny encouraged me to keep fighting and I think he must have placed the painter rope in my hand. Then Tripper was grabbed by a human chain from a point in the river."

"Jim, darling, it's so wonderful to hear your voice, and to know you're all right. I had a premonition something had happened, but I didn't know what. But I *do* know you love horseback riding and hunting. I bet Jack was happy to go pheasant hunting, also. Thanks so much for the call – you make me feel so needed, taking the time like this to give me a ring after such an amazing day! And I'm especially glad you got a chance to meet and relax with some 'regular' and successful Americans who also just happened to be Indians. I'm sure they were happy to meet such a wonderful white man as you, also."

They chatted for a few more minutes, expressing their deep and growing love for each other. Then they said goodbye and hung up. Jim had a warm and fuzzy feeling after speaking to the beautiful Joy, and she was meditating quietly: *Jim, my darling, please be careful and let us enjoy a wonderful life together. I am so afraid for you.*

After a refreshing sleep and a huge breakfast at the main ranch house, Jim video-taped interviews with White Hawk and two or three others and took shots of the ranch buildings and corral. The place looked like a post card. When the reporting was finished, Jim spoke to his host with enthusiasm: "White Hawk, I'd like to run something by you to get your take on it, if you don't mind. I'm interested in your thoughts about the relationships between Native American Indians, other tribes and the Whites.

"Of course, Jim. I'm always interested in such discussions. My major was agriculture, but I minored in sociology. What are your concerns or questions?"

"Well, back in Baltimore, about 90% of the 300 yearly murders are performed by Black African-Americans against other Blacks. Apparently, most killings take place over disputed drug territories. I have several friends who are Black and although they're concerned, they say they can understand to a large degree why this is happening. Their reasoning is that Inner City youth are more comfortable with challenging other Inner City youths in drug trafficking or competing for girlfriends or boyfriends. Angry words expressed by one Black against another Black are taken more seriously because they usually share much of the same environment.

"For example, they may call the other Black person a 'nigger' in jest and there is no comeback. But, don't let anyone else, Black or White, call him that. If an acquaintance angrily calls him a `MF White Man's Lover,' or tells him to `Stay off my street and out of my territory' or `leave my sister or girl friend alone,' or `My football team can whip yours any night of the week,' there could be spilled blood. They might accuse another of `kissing up' to White teachers or football or basketball instructors in school. When they fight, it seems the fights are with `no holds barred.' For one to call the other an SOB indicates he is insulting the other man's mother and it becomes a life and death struggle.

"Stay out of my (drug) territory is often a challenge that results in death to the weaker Black on the street. In studying for my canoeing of the Missouri," Jim continued, "it became clear that many of the Tribes in the Sioux Nation were fighting each other constantly – but seldom did they attack the White men. For example, Lewis and Clark were not attacked, although it almost happened once or twice. Was it because they didn't speak the same language as many of the other Tribes? Or, did they hold in awe the White man – with his more powerful firepower, his horses and his `Great White Father' in Washington?`

"The Blackfoot and your own Teton Sioux may have been an exception as they didn't seem to fear the White man as much and it was disease that bested them."

After Jim had finished, White Hawk sat silently for a minute or so. Then: "You asked a tough question, Jim. Like you and me today, I think my ancestors feared only what they didn't understand. Another Indian raised in similar

circumstances might have expected to have close ties with other members of the tribe and all could shoot an arrow or use an axe or hatchet, ride a horse or perhaps shoot a rifle. A brave from another Tribe may have believed he would have a chance to win the challenge as he, himself, had been taught in similar Indian warfare.

But if an Indian youth were to come up against a White man who had a modern rifle and had training in a different area, it might cause the young man to hesitate. He might not attack the White, but he might `test his strength' against another Indian. I think their different languages had something to do with it, as did the competition for furs, buffalo, deer and Indian maidens. Abductions of young women from one tribe to another for their squaws or slaves were quite common. Poor communication between Tribes and Groups within a Tribe would certainly have played a part.

"There was also anger against those who signed treaties with the White man at times, because some Indians didn't even believe their chiefs had the right to sign away their land and rights to another without their express signatures. Another consideration, I would think, is that when a group of youths get together without a strong purpose, sometimes problems involving violence occur.

Unless the group is organized for a positive purpose with somewhere to expend their energies, they might be like a powder keg waiting to explode. In our history, many of our young braves were renowned for leaving the village for weeks on end, looking for trouble, with a pretense of hunting for food.

"Thank you for bringing this up, Jim. I'll give it some more thought and we can discuss when you visit. All right?"

White Hawk then drove Jim and Jack back to Tripper. "My fellow Tribal members cleaned up the canoe and made everything ready for use."

"That was good of you, White Hawk."

Before Jim left, White Hawk made him promise to come back with Joy for a visit as soon as possible, when he and his family would personally escort them for interviews with especially interesting families in the Tribe. Waving so long with his paddle, Jim said his farewells, and Jack even let out one of his rare barks. Then Jim paddled out into the current and headed toward Sioux City, Iowa, another five days downstream. His heart was light, thanks to Johnny's spirit, which had come back from "somewhere else" to help him find the painter line. He was also feeling good about his wonderful conversation with Joy and the friendships he'd developed with the Indians.

The signs were good. Less than an hour after their departure, Jim spotted a watching gold eagle sitting in a treetop, a great blue heron and an osprey fishing along the shallows. He also noted a beautiful mule deer drinking from the river. Jim knew that if he stopped to explore the banks, he'd find tracks or slides of muskrat – along with the wily raccoon, weasels and maybe one of our American favorites, the beaver.

Geese and ducks were working on their lunches. It was a beautiful, nearly cloudless, low-humidity morning. This was just the kind of perfect day one lived for

in the great outdoors. How it made him long for the companionship of the perfect Joy!

As he paddled away, nagging thoughts began running through Jim's mind about the attempts to either delay his progress or actually injure him and the dog. Why would someone not want him to reach St. Charles by October 1? And what about that attack by Kip and Sam, who'd later had him arrested, costing him $500 plus a night in jail?

Apparently, Kip or Sam (or both) had been related to the judge at Jennings. Although he couldn't link that incident to the kidnapping of Joy for a three-week period, it seemed very possible that Joy's husband might have been contacted by Kip to arrange for such an attack.

And there was more. Angela clearly had tried to delay his departure from the hotel casino along the river. Perhaps someone had contracted for her to do so? She'd also told Jim that Joy's husband had called about Joy's location and made a serious threat to do physical harm to her. Shortly after that phone call from Joy's husband to Angela, Joy had been abducted for three nearly three weeks. Clark had gotten just a glimpse of two men who he thought might be Kip or Sam, as he paddled past an island. And not long after that, he'd been attacked with a net and tied to a tree along Fort Peck Lake for almost two days without water and food or protection from insects or bears.

What could all of these events mean? Not far from Bismarck, the "wolf-dog" had made his savage, unprovoked attack on Jack. After that, two men had fired rifle shots close to them. Were they trying to scare Jim off? He hadn't been able to

get a look at them – but wasn't it possible that they'd been following a third person's orders? And how in the world could Kip and Sam have obtained information about Jim's Muddy Mo journey and his deadline?

That information could only have come from the "Wild Rivers" home office! Was Jay Spader involved somehow*? I'd better go slowly in accusing Spader or his Organization*, Jim thought.

He was troubled by all these questions, but he made good time in the five-mile-per-hour current. After a few hours, they paused for a bite. "Isn't this thick-steak sandwich delicious?" Jim asked Jack. "Thank God for the Yankton Sioux," he exclaimed, while barely dipping the paddle deep enough in the water to keep them on a straight course. "Why, I'll bet old Seaman – the Newfoundland dog who accompanied Lewis and Clark – didn't didn't get a steak sandwich like the one I just gave you!"

Jack snorted derisively. *Maybe not – but then, old Seaman didn't have to listen to a paddling windbag prattle on for hours at a time, did he?*

Sniping happily at each other, the two voyagers paddled on. The current was fast, and they covered a lot of territory. By the end of the day, Jim had paddled 50 miles.

"I am soooooo sore, ole buddy, after all that horseback riding," the big man groaned with pain the next morning. "And I thought I was a natural cowboy! Hah! I can tell you one thing – I didn't get this sore from tackling running backs and fighting off linemen in college football, NO WAY!"

When Jack showed no sympathy, Clark sighed and got back down to business. "Well, it looks like we've entered the 39-mile segment listed as part of the National Register of Wild and Scenic Rivers in South Dakota," he said as they were laying out the canoe on the swift-running Missouri. "The Scenic segment runs from the Randall Creek Recreation Area at Pickstown to Running water. The second segment, which is 59 miles long, stretches from below Gavins Point Dam to Ponca State Park in Nebraska. I'm told these segments look much like they did in the early 1800s during the Lewis and Clark expedition. Look around, Jack. Is this some fabulous scenery, or what?"

The dog yawned grumpily. ***What's the big deal, Jimbo? As far as I'm concerned, if you've seen one wild river, you've seen 'em all.***

"And here's another piece of good news, Jack: The Lewis and Clark Lake is coming up. It's 25 miles long and it's the last lake. From then on, it's all river and 806 miles to St. Charles, Mo!" Grinning happily, he turned to confront his canine partner.

"Tell you what, Jack: I'm going to take us a short ways up the Niobrara River in Nebraska before we get onto Lewis and Clark Lake and the 59-mile Recreation River designated portion. I've read some interesting facts about that river. It has 79 miles of National Wild and Scenic River designation, although it's a couple of hundred miles west. I just feel the need to paddle in a smaller river for an hour or so, even though it will be upstream and perhaps somewhat difficult.

"The Santee Indian Reservation is also nearby, so maybe I'll drop in on them for an interview or two." Once again, he turned to eyeball his sidekick: "Tell the truth, Jack. You're impressed with how much I know about the river, aren't you?"

Riiiiigghhht! You're just a living encyclopedia, aren't you, big man?

"Yes, by your expression, Jack, I can tell you really do enjoy my sharing my new-found knowledge of the Missouri River area with you!"

After Jim had paddled up the Niobara River for a half-hour, they were waved in by one of three young adults, two of whom appeared to be Indian from their dress, complexion and mannerisms. The other one seemed to be a Southeast Asian. Things are changing, Jim thought. These three had been whittling on slender poles, perhaps in order to begin gigging large fish.

Jim paddled over to the bank and remained in the canoe. The young man who had hailed him sat holding the front painter line and the rather-large, sharp stick he had been cutting. All three wore denims that seemed to be seeking the back-of-the-knee level, and which dragged the ground. Of course they also wore baseball caps turned sideways. Young adults in this area probably got that from the East.

"Hey, mister. Where're you headed? You know, it's dangerous to canoe this close to the Reservation because there are some real rowdies around there. They don't like whites. As a matter, we don't like whites, either! What do you think about that? If we weren't so broke, we could probably buy something to relax us, and just hang out. Could you help us out?"

Jim didn't hesitate. "You fellas seem like hard-working and responsible citizens. Assuming you're 21 or over, I'd be glad to buy you a drink and a sandwich, if there's a restaurant located nearby. But I don't give out money when I don't know what it's to be used for."

"Well, maybe a white fella like you just don't understand we pore little Indian boys. We like money because it gives us independence! Why don't you just climb out of your canoe and join us?"

Jim stepped out carefully, still holding his paddle and thinking *This is getting to be a habit – attempting to stay alive.* But then the big man shouted: "Jack! Heel! Attention!" In a flash, Jack had moved to Jim's leg, and had gone into his attack crouch. Pointing at the leader, he gave a menacingly growl and showed his huge teeth. Looking at the spokesman for the group, Jim said, "I am one of these guys who appears to be white, but I am part Indian, with a Karate Brown Belt. My sidekick is a trained riot-control dog. I have to keep him under control, since he badly hurt some hoodlums in Baltimore, Maryland – they had to be hospitalized. Of course, way out here in the boonies, a bad dog bite would quickly become infected. Might even require an amputation or two! I wouldn't venture to guess how long it would be before you would be well, or even walk again."

The spokesman turned to the other two and they spoke in low tones for a minute or two. "Mister, we're just three guys having a little fun with a guy we thought was a `greenhorn.' We certainly don't mean no harm. My name is Ernest Fast Man and these two are John Looking Bee and Leonard Chan. If you're serious

about drinks, we'll meet you upstream a half-mile at the Last Chance Saloon and Casino. Those people know us, and they certainly won't give you any trouble."

"Of course I was serious, Ernest. Lead the way. Jack, all-aboard! I'm ready for a cool one."

Holstering their knives and picking up their poles, the three hurriedly walked upstream in the pathway that flanked the Niobara. After an hour and a couple of drinks at the Last Chance, Jim spoke to the three plus several others who'd gathered around and were enjoying the fun. "You fellas are all right. You may not know it, but my dog Jack and I have solo-canoed 1,500 miles from Three Forks, Montana en route to St. Charles, Missouri.

We aren't troubled by running into lively folks like you. All's well that ends well, right? Actually, I'd like to shoot some videotape and ask you each some questions about your life in this area, including on the Reservation, if you don't mind."

When they all said okay, Jim rolled the tape and they had a relaxed conversation about life in Nebraska and South Dakota and especially in and around the Missouri and Niobara Rivers and the Santee Reservation. After another round, Jim said, "Well, I have to go, guys. St. Charles awaits, and since it's much easier to paddle downstream on the Niobara, I look forward to it. I do appreciate your invitation to stay a couple of days, but Jack and I must be in St. Charles by October 1 and time's a-wastin'."

"So long, Jim, we enjoyed meeting you. I'm sorry for what we said on the river. Come back anytime." This from Leonard. As Jim paddled off, the words

from White Hawk came to him: "Gangs of youth are just kids full of energy with too much time on their hands. They may have been raised to tolerate pain and suffering with strong physical expectations and also to question the community's authority. If they don't have an opportunity to release that energy, their actions may be a problem!"

After camping out that night and preparing a hearty breakfast of bacon and eggs for himself and Jack, Jim schooled himself mentally for the run up to the Lewis and Clark Lake, which might present some wind-problems. "I feel good enough to tackle anything the Missouri can send me," he told himself. But the lake was calm when they got there and they zipped across the 25-mile expanse of water and then pulled into Yankton for the evening. "We're going to stay in a camp ground that has a good telephone, so I can get in touch with Joy about Omaha," he told his companion.

Sounds like a good plan*, thought Jack out loud, *provided that we get to eat supper first – and that it doesn't consist of dried dog-chow!

When he dialed Joy's number she sounded ecstatic. "Jim, I have a wonderful surprise for you! I'd planned on the two of us attending a baseball game – the Omaha Royals are playing – or maybe flying to Kansas City to see the *big*-league version of the Royals. However, knowing you played a little college football at the U of Mo, I obtained tickets to a very early Missouri-Nebraska game in Lincoln through their State Natural Resources Department. I don't mind telling you, they wanted blood for those tickets! Is that okay with you? The tickets are for Saturday, August 25 at 1 p.m."

Jim stared at phone. "Is it okay? Is the Pope Catholic? Does it snow in Minnesota in the winter? This is like a dream come true. I didn't think anyone could find tickets to a Nebraska game this close to kickoff."

She laughed merrily. "Well, I sold myself, that's all. I got the Secretary of Montana Natural Resources to personally contact the Secretary of the Nebraska Natural Resources and tell them that you will have canoed 1900 miles since May 15 by game day. I think he might have suggested you might want to interview the Nebraska Secretary on videotape about the Missouri River."

Jim shook his head. "You continue to amaze me, Joy! I was counting the hours until I could see you and now you enhance that with the game. That must be why I love you so much – you spoil me with your knowledge, your loving and your gifts."

*

"Hello, handsome," a woman's voice called. It was the Friday night before the big Mizzou-Cornhusker game and Jim was pulling into the dock in Omaha. "Hey, Joy! Is that you up there?"

"What do *you* think? Who else would come down here by the river bank and flag down a derelict and a dog?"

"Sounds good. Hey, I'm shedding my clothes as we speak, and I assume you're ready for me?"

"You'd better *not* be disrobing, Big Boy! Yes, I'm here but I have everything on but a flashlight," she said as she stepped out of the shadows and took the painter line Jim pitched her.

"Oh, am I hungry, Joy . . . for you *and* a steak. Jack is probably so tired from gazing at the city lights – I'm sure he'd rather just go right to bed than eat or make friends with some sweet female Lab!"

Jack glowered. *One of these days---bam!*

"Have you already arranged for an outfitter to keep Tripper for a couple of days?"

"Yes, and I have a reservation for only two at Coniglia's Steak House. Sorry, Jack. Unless you're a guide dog, you're not allowed in the restaurant."

Lifting one eyebrow again: *Really? Who do you think has been guiding this riverboat all the way from Three Forks, Montana?*

Within an hour, they had Jack placed in a nice private home, ready to feast on a t-bone steak with a female companion near the waterfront. Joy had rented a car and after some lengthy kisses and intimate touching, they sat down to the most beautiful huge salads, followed by baked potatoes and filet mignons . . . all washed down with vodka martinis-up. The Sheraton Hotel was only four blocks from the restaurant, so they were given permission by the head waiter to leave the car there.

"Let's walk to the hotel, Jim. It's such a lovely night and I'm so full, I must have some exercise. But you must promise to keep from caressing my fanny on the street. I think the vodka has convinced you that you're Casanova!"

"What do you mean, *I've* had a lot to drink? Didn't you match me drink for drink?"

Jim dodged her elbow. "Jim," she giggled," I wasn't going to tell you,

but when I went to the restroom, I told the drink waiter to bring me seltzer water with ice each time you were served a vodka martini. I haven't had as much exercise and sleeping and eating on the riverbank as you."

After arriving at the Sheraton and "working off" their huge meal and martinis, they dressed again and skipped happily back to the restaurant to pick up the Ford Taurus rental car. "Let's go dancing, Joy. We had such a beautiful night of dancing in Rapid City."

"Funny you should think about that. Just so happens, sweet man, I have checked out two very nice dance halls with excellent bands, very close to our hotel. I might even save you a dance if you play your cards right."

Dancing cheek-to-check to the dreamy music allowed them to experience more of the closeness they felt for each other, not only physically, but also in their conversations. "Joy, do they allow dancing in Great Falls, if we decide to live there?"

"Only in your private bedroom with the shades pulled, and fully clothed. Of course they do, silly man. Montanans are heavy lovers, hard workers, hard riders, hard drinkers and slow dancers. Just trust me, Easterner, and you'll never go wrong."

In the few minutes they had in their private bedroom with the shades pulled, Jim and Joy practiced more of the intimate love they felt for each other. "If heaven were better than this, Joy, I shouldn't go---it would be too much for my overworked heart. You are the most wonderful person in the world and I'm so in love with you."

"I love you too, Jim. I hope the future is really as bright as it appears right now. Maybe no one has a right to this much bliss, darling."

After a good night's sleep in each others arms, they checked on Jack and then visited the Omaha Zoo, one of the finest in the U.S. "We have to hurry, if we're to get to Lincoln and get seated before the 1:30 p.m. kickoff, sweetheart," Joy said. "I know you're hoping to have some flashbacks of your football days at Mizzou."

*

"What kind of weenie line-backers are you Mizzou coaches growing Missouri?" Jim's booming voice gave the nearby Nebraska fans a big laugh. "They're giving up five yards to anyone who gets past the defensive line. That offensive line should be in Sunday school, but they're blowing out Mizzou. In my time, we would have been in their faces as they came past the line. Uh, oh, Nebraska! Did you see that number 51 linebacker come all the way into the backfield and tackle the quarterback? Looked like the same number 51 Mizzou had when I was on the team!"

"Did you win the national championship many times, dear?" Joy asked grinning evilly.

Grabbing Joy in a half-nelson, Jim said, "Now you listen to me you misguided horsewoman from the no-football state of Montana! No, we didn't even win the Big 8 12, but we knew we could."

Jim seemed to relax after those outbursts and took pleasure in the game, which was quite close, considering Mizzou was unranked and Nebraska, as usual,

was ranked high in the country. The score ended up 20-3 – a moral victory for Mizzou, especially before a sellout crowd of 75,000 in Lincoln.

*

Jim interviewed the Director of Natural Resources on the telephone Sunday morning. Then Joy and Jim visited Boys Town and toured the beautiful downtown area of Omaha. "I hadn't realized it was so hilly here. Maybe Old Man River had something to do with that," Jim said. Too soon, it was check out time at the Sheraton and Joy's flight was scheduled to depart for Great Falls. "We've got to pick up that black weenie dog, also, while you have the car leased, Jim. Jack may have been having so much fun he won't go with us."

But, when Jim arrived at the door, Jack was ready for their famous dance. The kennel manager stood open-mouthed as Joy clapped and the pair circled in her yard. "You two should take this show on the road," she laughed.

"I'll have to leave you two here at the outfitters, Jim. I will be late for my flight if I don't move out. I do so badly hate to say good-bye, even for a month before we meet in St. Louis. But, my darling, we'll be together forever after that."

They kissed and hugged long and intimately, as Joy stood by her car. Then, Jim turned slowly toward the outfitters.

*

After the Tripper was brought to the water's edge, the outfitter left Jim and Jack. Jim checked over the ropes and painter lines and made sure he could reach the camera, water and snacks. Jack went at to "attention," pointing toward the dark area under the overpass. What Jack "pointed" were two blacks and a

scraggly-haired white man – a derelict? – all of whom appeared to be in their early 20s, walking menacingly toward them. Both of the blacks had dirty dreadlocks and one wore a green smock like those used by medical personnel. "Big Dreadlocks" carried a metal baseball bat and the white lugged a heavy chain. The speaker didn't show a weapon, but perhaps was carrying a gun or knife.

With an ugly snarl, the spokesman of the group, who looked like a weight lifter, said, "Did you pay your toll to pull in here, Big Man?
This is our land and we charge $20 for each put-in to the river. Pay us and we'll carry your canoe to the water."

"How come the Chamber of Commerce or the outfitter didn't tell me about a fee for put-in? I don't think I will pay any such fee, unless you have proof that you have a right to charge me."

"Let's take him, boys!" The three made a circle, swinging the bat and chain while the speaker took a stance as though he had something in his pocket.

The man with the baseball bat stepped toward Jim and swung the bat. "Here's what I think of you guys." Jim quick-stepped, turned completely around and swung a foot with all his might and hit the bat-holder full in the face, knocking him backwards, with blood flowing. The chain-holder twirled the chain as Jim spoke two words to Jack, "Take him." Jack hit the man flat in the chest, bowling him over as he angrily went for the thug's shoulder.

That stopped it! "Please, mister! We don't want no trouble. If you don't think you owe us anything, let it go. Just call off that maniac dog. We'll be on our way." The three put on their best hangdog expressions, with their open hands in a

pleading sign in an attempt to show they were sorry for mistakenly trying to hurt Jim.

"None of us have fathers and we all work to support our mothers. You wouldn't want to deprive our younger brothers and sisters from of food, clothing and a place to live, would you?"

"It's odd that you don't think of jail until you get hammered by someone or the law, isn't it? If you were to go to the Nebraska Unemployment Office, they would help you find jobs that would fit in with your family needs, I'm sure. And you're not going to get away so easily from us, gentlemen. I just hit a button to call 911 and the cops will be here within minutes."

They were.

"Well, what do we have here? Are you guys trying to strong-arm another victim from the river? These three are still on probation, and now you'll serve some time, I'll bet," said Sergeant Whitaker of the Omaha Police Department. "They could have gone to Boys Town and learned a trade a couple of years ago, but that didn't fit in with their drinking, drugging and girlie plans, did it?"

After Jim signed the complaint, Sergeant Ross and his assistant, Corporal Johnson, helped Jim put Tripper near the river's edge. When Jim told them he'd solo-canoed for 1900 miles, they whistled in appreciation. Then, with his sidekick proudly sitting in front, Jim paddled off, calling out, "Next stop, Plattsmouth Marina!"

"Hello. Angela, is that you? My goodness, it seems a long time since we've seen each other."

"It seems that way to me, also, Joy. Have you seen Jim Clark lately?"

"As a matter of fact, I flew to Omaha to meet him a week ago. We went to a Mizzou-Nebraska game and had a ball. Why do you ask?"

"Oh, no reason. I know you seemed to really care for him. I hope he's the one you've been looking for..."

"Why are you being so secretive, Angela? What do you have on your mind?" Also, her supervisor was pressing her to finish her late report on the Missouri River across Montana.

"Well, I guess Jim told you we `saw' each other while you were missing, didn't he?"

"No," Joy replied, feeling her heart sink. "He didn't mention it. Did something happen?"

Veronica gave her friend a simpering smile. "Well, I didn't plan on telling you, but we did kiss some."

"Nothing more?" Joy held her breath.

"You have to realize, Joy, Jim and I didn't know if you had returned to your old boyfriend or former husband, during those several weeks when you were gone. And, of course, we were both kind of lonely. I just went downriver to get him a hot meal and maybe boost his morale after his many days on re-heated or thawed rations."

"Don't play games with me, Angela!"

"I stayed for two nights in the motel in Judith and we had a wonderful steak. Jim used my room to shave and shower and we hugged and kissed a little. Both of us were quite lonesome, I tell you. I'm not sure who seduced whom, but you probably understand how such things can happen, don't you?"

"Oh, Angela! Why are you doing this? Look, we don't know each other well enough for you to try and save me from destroying my life over a man! Did someone put you up to this?"

Angela smiled sweetly. "No, Joy. I swear---I just want to get this off my conscience and not hurt you or Jim, either. You and I were building a great friendship before Jim Clark came along, and I've really come to care about you. I wanted to protect you from the heartache of a potentially destructive relationship, if I could. Sometimes men can be so thoughtless and crass. Trust me, I know!"

"I don't want to talk any more, Angela. Thanks for your concern."

Joy's eyes were full of tears and her heart was heavy as she returned the receiver to the cradle. Was Angela lying? ***Why was she even telling me this stuff? How can I approach Jim about it, or should I? Perhaps I should just get on with my life and find another guy, and never open up my heart and soul for another man!***

*

The e-mail Jim received from Joy stunned him as he read: "Jim, why did you NOT tell me you met and spent two nights with Angela in Judith, Montana? Please call me immediately when you get this. You must know, I am very disappointed and upset! I thought we had developed a more loving, open and trusting relationship. Joy."

Jim heart shrank as he read the e-mail. His mind raced. He was innocent here . . . although he now realized that he should have told Joy about meeting Angela. My God, I hope I haven't ruined another relationship!"

Later that evening, with his heart in his mouth, Jim called Joy and blurted, "Joy, this is Jim. I hardly know where to start. I did see Angela at Judith Landing, but, except for one kiss she initiated, I swear, not a blessed thing happened. I was missing you badly, and at first I was tempted. It's usually an ego-builder for a man to have a pretty woman come-on to him, and I was no exception, for at least a moment. But I did climb back in my canoe – and I left almost immediately after spending the night (alone) with Jack in my tent before she walked me back to the River.

"I certainly didn't stay there that night. I hope you believe me . . . but I can only tell you what's in my heart and head. I realized I loved you, and I sure wasn't ready for a relationship with your friend, Angela.

"I questioned her later about your ex-husband contacting her about your whereabouts. I believe Angela has become involved in the attacks on me, as well as in your abduction. Actually, I believe her meeting me was a set-up, if you want the truth.

"Where I went wrong, Joy, was that I let Angela and the detective I hired to find you plant a seed in my mind that you might have stayed for those three weeks with your ex – voluntarily. And yet I was so happy to have you back with me! I guess I felt somewhat guilty for kissing Angela in her hotel room, so I just remained silent."

Joy hesitated. Her mind was whirling. "Jim, now I realize I should have been completely open with you about the abduction. It was clearly a crime. I was taken and held against my wishes. Later, however, I came to realize my ex had a mental problem and just might kill me and bury my body somewhere. He had both a gun and a knife and he would have used them. I believe someone was paying him to do what he did."

Joy continued, "For the first week, he kept me locked in a line shack deep in the Wild and Scenic portion of the Missouri south of Loma. He even put handcuffs on me and tied my feet to the chair. I was provided a straw to drink soup and water he set out, and a hamburger was placed on the edge of a table.

"After two weeks, he began to soften his tone with me and told me he had always wanted to stay married to me and was now thinking he would let me go soon, if I showed some understanding of him and his needs. But he said that if he let me go, he might get life in prison, and that he would never let himself be captured alive. When he said that, his eyes became wild and I was frightened for my life. That man was sick!

"After the second week, I decided I didn't want to die and asked him to remove my handcuffs and let me eat with my hands. I wanted to see you and my mother again. He left and then returned after drinking alcohol heavily, and he finally agreed about the handcuffs. As he was removing the cuffs, I reached out and touched his hand and his face and asked why he couldn't tell me he loved me before we split up. He said he was raised to assume that woman was put on this earth to please a man or men and a man should not have to ask for anything. He claimed he

never came to me unless he was drinking heavily when we were married, which was probably true.

"He believed I should have offered more to him to keep him happy and sexually satisfied.

"I wanted to live, so I said something like, 'If I tried to make you happy now, would you let me go?' Again, he left the room, but only after replacing the handcuffs. When he returned, in bikini shorts and with a hard on, and apparently, after drinking more alcohol, he had shaved and put on my favorite aftershave. Without attempting to kiss me, he knelt before me, and unbuttoned my blouse and began kissing my breasts and sucking on my nipples. He whined as he asked if I would remain still if he loosened my ankles so he could go between my thighs. I replied that I guess I didn't have a choice?

"He laughed and loosened my ankles and put his tongue in me, while he was breathing heavily and masturbating. He made no move as though he was going to put me on the floor and enter me. I acted as though I was really enjoying it, but Jim, I was miserable. The man is a mentally deficient pervert and I thought only of returning to your arms.

"He climaxed himself while he was working on me, and immediately staggered out of the room, weaving badly. He returned to stand in the doorway, drinking from a fifth of whiskey or rum, leering at me and saying things like he always knew I was a slut who liked any man in me.

"He apparently forgot my feet were untied and slid down in the doorway and continued to drink.

"I watched him until he finished the bottle and closed his eyes and rolled over on his face. Then, quietly, I stood with my hands still locked in the handcuffs and stepped through the doorway. I found his key chain and gun and knife on a table and glancing back at him, I very quietly went out the front door. Out of sight of the cabin, I lay down on the ground and wriggled my body through my arms until my hands were in front of me.

"I took the keys, tossed the gun and knife on the floor of his truck. I found the key to his truck ignition and got in and locked the doors. Then I put the key in. Thank God I locked the doors first, because he staggered out right then. But I got the truck started and put it in gear. He tried to open the door, but couldn't. He tried to climb in the back, but I speeded up and whipped the truck back and forth, making him fall off.

"When I looked in the rear view mirror, he was sitting at the side of the grassy lane, staring bleary-eyed at me. After an hour, I arrived at the Choteau Sheriff's office and told them. Of course, I had difficulty in making them believe what had happened until they checked their records and found I was telling the truth.

"I then called my work and asked them to locate you on the river – and the rest was easy!"

Clark just stared at the sky for a few seconds. "Joy, you are remarkable! I was so frightened that you were going to be killed. I was, and am, so in love with you. Angela was doing her best to seduce me, but I just couldn't go along. I left

immediately after shaving, while she sat on the dock and cried. I had nearly accused her of consorting with someone to harm me. "

He wanted to touch her arm. Softly. "Can you forgive me for doubting that you loved me – and can you forgive me for kissing Angela? I swear on my grandmother's grave, I never did more than return her kiss!"

Joy was smiling now. "Yes, Jim. Like I said, I should have been more open in explaining what happened. I was afraid you wouldn't believe me or think I was a slut, just as you were afraid I wouldn't believe you about Angela. I love you desperately and want to be in your arms forever."

He grinned. "And I love you, Joy. I will be able to put my words together better when we meet in St. Charles on or about October 1. Now I can sleep. Good night, darling."

"Me, too, sweetheart. Good night and give Jack a hug for me."

*****

"Jack, I've had severe back spasms for the past 24 hours. I'm going to pull into St. Joseph, Missouri. This used to be a really thriving area. The Rosecrans Army Air Base was located there throughout WWII."

Jack frowned. ***Jeez, will you stop complaining? All you've done is paddle a canoe for 2,000 miles, you wimp!***

But the doctor did find Jim to be suffering from exhausted muscles – the cause of the spasms. He immediately prescribed two cortisone shots. "My God, doc, what's in that medicine---gasoline? Hurts like hell!"

"Are you telling me you have paddled 2000 miles and portaged around 14 dams, and you're surprised that your body is screaming? I'm also prescribing some muscle relaxant for you. You need to stop for at least 48 hours and not lift anything. Pamper yourself. Let that big dog drag the canoe and its equipment to wherever it must go! He'd probably make a good sled dog, come to think of it.

"Actually, I'm rather surprised the Indians in South Dakota didn't eat him, considering how fat he is!"

Jim felt desolate as he listened to the doctor. Was this the beginning of failure? Would he be able to bounce back in time to make it to St. Charles by the first of October?

"Joy, I thought I'd give you a call and let you know the doctor told me to rest a couple of days with a cortisone shots. I'll be off a couple of days with some back spasms. The doctor here in St. Joseph gave me two cortisone shots and prescribed some relaxant meds and some rest for at least 48 hours. Jack thought *he* was the one who needed rest, just for putting up with my speeches, can you believe it? However, I am only going to rest one day."

Joy caught her breath in alarm. "I've been concerned about something like this, Jim. If you want to finish the race by October 1, you must pay attention to the doctor. You're past the lakes now and the current is with you, so you can make up for lost time later, I expect.

"Besides," she suddenly giggled, "I want your body to be in good shape when it meets mine in St. Louis!"

"Don't you worry your pretty head about that, Joy. I'm lean and mean! Actually, I was surprised that the Mizzou football coach didn't try and recruit me to come back and play against Nebraska the weekend we met in Omaha. He probably didn't have my cell phone number, that's all."

Joy howled. "I miss you, darling. Take care of yourself---seriously. Your body can wear out. Drink plenty of water and other liquids and rest as often as you can."

"I will, Joy. This muscle relaxant is putting me to sleep while I'm sitting up talking to you. Take care, sweetheart. You'll be in my heart until I have you in my arms."

*

"Hello, Jim. This is Veronica, your `throwaway' from Baltimore. Remember me? Jim, I guess my PMS is acting up, but I'm pissed off! I just don't think I should back off and let you have a fling with that beautiful Indian maiden, while Henry and I have to sit by the phone waiting for some well-heeled male to call and invite me to dance and dinner!"

Jim closed his eyes. He'd been dreading this call for several weeks, and now it was here.

"I expect you're going to make a `killing' on your paddling – and to think how I stressed out myself making a home for you for two years. I'm the one who prepared you for this trip, both mentally and sexually!"

Jim was tired of biting his lip. "Hey, you gotta be kidding, Veronica! Just how many flip-flops are you capable of? First, you act as though you can't stand the thought of my being away, then, you drop me hard. Then you try and sweet-talk me back; then you help me make up with Joy. I'm getting the bends' from all your shifts in direction!"

"I'm not flip-flopping, Jim. I can only be sweet for just so long, and then I lash out, I guess. We women are unpredictable, you know. I suppose I sound somewhat confusing to you, but I just want a fair deal, that's all. Probably one-fourth of your bonus for completing that trip – I think that would be fair compensation, don't you? I'm sure you'll give Joy that much."

Jim gritted his teeth. "If you hadn't dumped me so unceremoniously, Veronica, I would gladly have given you half my bonus. But I'm just not in the mood to agree to share anything with you, given your treatment. I'll think about it and get

back to you when I'm nearing the finish line."

Veronica sneered. "You're pretty much a loser, Jim. You're just not a responsible person, that's all. Your first wife pushed you out and kept your son. Then you couldn't make Henry and me happy for very long. Now, you're pulling the wool over the eyes of that naïve Indian lass. I don't know what made me step in and get you two back together. Your mother and father ought to know exactly how you've messed up the family name. Don't you have any integrity at all?"

Jim was dangerously close to exploding now. "Leave my family out of this, Veronica. This hurts! I am not the same man I was when I began paddling the

Missouri. The river has changed me by giving me ability to see myself in a positive light, and by building my self-confidence. The river gives and the river takes away.

"And let's get the record straight. I gave you all of me---but then, when you rejected me, like the river, I took myself away from you. I'll be in touch."

She gasped with surprise. This sad sack was actually standing up for himself! "Jim, are you saying, don't call me, I'll call you?" Veronica had begun to sob.

"You got it, babe. Take care."

*

After a days of rest in an elegant St. Joe motel room – while also enjoying the built-in Jacuzzi to the max – Jim's spasms had disappeared. At this point, even Jack seemed to be in a pretty good mood . . . and Jim was absolutely convinced that he could now paddle without pain.

Even better, the sun had finally come out again. The big man was ready to roll on. "Here we come, St. Charles!" he roared as he pushed off from the dock in St. Joseph. "My gosh, I didn't think it would feel so good to pick up a paddle again, but it's wonderful," he told the cavorting Lab. "Why, it almost fits my hand! The river is running swiftly now, perhaps 5-6 miles per hour, and there will be no more dams. We'll have to watch out for barges and speedboats, and fog will be a problem at times, but I'm ready to rock!

"With my trusty double-ended kayak paddle at the ready, I'm going to kick us up to 45-50 miles a day. All aboard for the St. Charles Express!"

*

"Boy, these rocks are heavy," Sam complained out loud as he huffed and puffed his way along, rolling several large stones above the dolomite cliffs. "If I'm not careful, I'll send them down into the Missouri River. Kip told me pretty much what he wanted to do, and as always, I do what he says wants. What the Hell! I have to do something with my life, and I might as well do it making some trouble for someone. Man, these damn rocks are driving me crazy. I sure wish Kip would get back.

"I expect Clark and that damn dog to paddle along here later today, so I gotta get my stuff together. Gonna push this pile just a little further and then go find a pry pole to get the whole pile set to fall down on the canoe. Whoa! I almost fell over myself. Wait a minute – hang on – NO! NO!"

Now Sam's calloused hands and short fingers clawed for a grip on the rocks and small bushes as he slid down faster and faster toward the dolomite cliff edge above the river. He couldn't stop himself, as the bushes tore away and his heels scrabbled for purchase against the earth.

He fell silently for 100 feet – and then his head splattered open on the rocks like a smashed watermelon. A moment later, he was tumbling another 50 feet to a rock-shelf, before bouncing away and plummeting into the depths of the Missouri River.

*

Kip drove on. No sign of Sam. Where the hell was he? After a while, he pulled into the narrow lane off the county road and drove slowly toward the river. He left the lane near some heavy sumac bushes and put the Chevy van in park and

set the emergency brake. Insulated bags packed with food, jackets and hats were neatly stored in the back of the van. Beneath them, hidden in a false bottom, Kip had hidden two rifles, three pistols and some hunting knives.

"Here's his cache," Kip said, parting the bushes and picking up a pack that contained Sam's sleeping bag, small tent, some food and water and his cooking equipment.

"It doesn't appear to have been used since I dropped him off," Kip thought out loud. "And yet I dropped him off four days ago, didn't I? Strange."

Kip walked toward the river. He was an excellent tracker. "Here's a cigar butt like Sam smoked. Here's where he moved some rocks to the top of the dolomite cliffs. These cliffs are well over 100 feet high, and run straight up from the river. Uh, oh! Boot skids and finger scratches, small bushes yanked from the ground as if someone had slipped and was sliding toward the cliff edge!

"You were a good man, Sam! What a shame to lose you!"

Without expression, Kip swept away the evidence of his tracks and returned to put Sam's equipment in the van and vamoose as soon as possible. "I need to be in Washington, Missouri, within the next week." He picked up the bags and other personal gear of Sam's, did his best to erase all evidence of tire tracks, and drove off quickly.

Approximately 50 miles from St. Charles, and not far from Washington, Kip found a small, narrow island backed up by a heavily wooded hillside, where concealed parking was available. On the afternoon of Sept. 29, he prepared for a

showdown with Jim Clark. He'd managed to find a replacement for Sam, because he couldn't handle Clark alone.

"What is this?" Jim was asking Jack, a few hours later. "Someone is waving me in, Jack. I don't recognize him, so it may be perfectly okay. This could be a bad situation, but I'm going to pull in and face it. Maybe I'll get some answers."

I'm going to do the same, pardner,* thought Jack, *because I've just picked up the scent of Kip and the wolf-dog, hidden in the woods.

"I've been waiting for you, Clark! I'm going to see just how well you can protect yourself from one of the best college judo experts and a darned good boxer. Only one of us will walk away," the six-foot, 250-pound, bearded jock said. He took the judo *en garde* position, with his hands up and rocking back and forth on the grassy island. But before Jim could pull the canoe up onto the bank, Jack leaped to shore and ran helter-skelter into the woods, growling viciously and loudly.

A moment later a pistol shot rang out. A man screamed, and the gun sounded again. Apparently a strange thing had occurred: the wolf-dog had decided not to fight Jack! Instead, he watched Jack and Kip fight. "Your dog just got shot, smart guy! Now, it's just you and me," the attacker grunted as he threw a quick kick at Jim's head, but Jim leaned backward and there was little effect from the kick.

"This is just what I want, fellow!" Clark spun and his kick landed solidly over the man's heart. He clutched his chest and attempted to catch his breath. But Clark immediately followed that kick with a left-footed kick to the groin and then an elbow to the side of the huge face.

The attacker grabbed Clark's elbow and grasped Clark around the shoulders to keep him close and avoid the heavy blows from his feet, elbows and head. Clark rolled backwards and pitched the man over his head, throwing him hard into the shallow river among some jagged rocks.

Dazed, but angrily determined that he was going to win his battle with Clark, the big fellow staggered into the shallow but swift water and attempted to pick up a large rock to attack Clark with. Off-balance, he pitched into a large sharp rock, hitting his head hard. His head made a sickening sound, like a wet gourd cracking open, and then he slipped soundlessly beneath the dark, deeper Missouri River water. The Missouri River had claimed him!

For a moment, Clark hesitated, then quickly he removed his life jacket and dove into the water where he had seen the man disappear. He was able to grab onto some cloth and pull and push the man to the edge of the river. He dragged the unconscious man to the cleared area where the battle had begun. Earlier, Jim had heard a man scream and gunshots from the direction Jack took into the woods. Leaving the limp body, Jim then ran into underbrush, where he found Kip, bleeding and clutching a broken leg, his pistol several feet away. The wolf-dog was just sitting watching, but Jack was bleeding and apparently badly hurt. Still, he managed to remain between Kip and the pistol.

Jack's jaws were clamped on one of Kip's arms. Jim picked up the gun and then Jack and brought him down to the island. He then returned for Kip. Calling 911 for help on his cell phone, he explained where he was to the best of his GPS

directions and that medical help was needed immediately. The EMS people called back and gave him tips on how to help the injured Kip and Jack. Thankfully, Jim had been trained in life-saving techniques.

"I've got to give artificial respiration to this man as soon as possible." He worked feverishly at mouth-to-mouth resuscitation for five minutes. At last the big fellow, still bleeding badly, groaned and spit out water and seemed to be breathing on his own, although very roughly.

"What happened to you, Kip?"

"That monster, vicious dog attacked me," groaned the minor-league thug, "so I shot him. But he just kept coming. I never saw such an animal--- he must be half-bear! I went to shoot him again, and accidentally shot myself in the hip. I think the bullet broke my hip bone."

*

Sheriff Nolan brought two deputies followed by three people from Emergency Medical Services (EMS), along with two stretchers. Sirens and emergency lights were whirling up the hill from at least three vehicles. Jim filled out a complaint of attack by Kip and the unidentified fellow. He also told them what Kip had told him about shooting Jack.

After learning that possibly $100,000 might be in jeopardy if Jim didn't reach St. Charles by 12:00 midnight on September 30, the EMS officer assisted the bruised and bleeding Clark into his canoe. The wolf-dog followed and curled up where Jack always stayed. Jim pushed the canoe into the downstream current. The EMS man and woman had agreed to come back down and pick up Jack on a

stretcher and give him a transfusion until they could drop him off at a veterinarian's clinic near the hospital. Of the three, Jack was the most seriously injured---he had been shot in his lower back and would require surgery to walk, if he ever walked again.

Although the big fella must have been in pain, he only groaned and whimpered when lifted. "Jack, I'll be there to see you as soon as I check in with Spader at St. Charles. If I can, I will paddle twice as far and fast to get back to you. Okay?"

Jack looked at Jim and licked his hand: *Okay. But all I can say is: There'd best be some filet mignon in that prize money for yours truly. You hear? Seriously, Big Guy, you're okay to paddle the Mighty Mo with! Don't want to do it again, but you're okay.*

*

Early the next day which was Sept 29, Jim called Spader and told him he would be docking at St. Charles in 24 hours. True to his promise, Spader was there, with his CEO, George Wellmann and CFO Gene Kerrey. The news media were represented by the St. Louis Post Dispatch, St. Louis News Press and KMOX and KXOK-TVs, and a bevy of radio and public television and cable reporters, US News & World Report, the Chicago Tribune, Great Falls Press, Philadelphia Inquirer, Baltimore Sun, Kansas City Star and representatives of the Lewis and Clark Bi-Centennial.

Beautiful Joy was also there, looking like a million bucks, and dressed in her lovely Native American cream-colored buckskin dress with even more stars in her

eyes than normal. Jim took her in his arms and kissed her deep and long and the news media people applauded. Joy told him that she would take him to see Jack at the Animal Hospital as soon as possible. The Wild Rivers staff had called her.

Surprise greeters included Jim's ex-wife, Jeanne, and their 11-year-old son, Sean, from Boston, whom Jim had not seen for three years. "Come here, Sean, and let me give you a hug," Jim said with tears streaming down his face. His former girlfriend, Veronica, and her son Henry were also there. Veronica had apologized in an e-mail to Jim for her phone call, brought on by her PMS and a big argument with her supervisor, she said.

"Hey, that's all right," said Jim. "I think I get the male equivalent of PMS quite often, myself."

From the edge of the crowd, a middle-aged couple pushed forward and reached out to touch Jim. "Dad, Mom! How did you know about this? I am so happy to see you. You came all the way from Switzerland to meet me? This is almost too much!"

"Why, Ms. Jennifer Long of the Wild Rivers staff contacted us to tell us you would be here no later than today, so we took a little vacation and came," his mother said.

"It isn't every day one's son paddles 2500 miles on the longest river in the U.S. by himself with just a dog," his father said.

The six of them surrounded and hugged Jim and Joy and congratulated them on the successfully completed trip. "I have dinner reservations tonight for all six of us in our hotel dining room – and I'll pick up the tab!" Jim's father said.

Another unexpected greeter was George Fender, the man who had attacked Jim and whose life Jim had saved. Choking back tears, Fender clasped Clark's hand and asked his forgiveness for all he had done or tried to do. Apparently, he had been contracted to hurt Jim's arm so he couldn't continue his paddling, but he did not intend to injure him badly or to kill him. He thanked Jim for saving his life and said he wondered if he would have saved him had the circumstances been reversed.

Fender had confessed, been charged with several assaults and was free on bond. He had implicated Kip, Sam, Angela and Joy's former husband, all of whom were to be charged with crimes. Spader's, CEO and CFO were there with a cashier's check in the amount of $100,000 made out to Jim Clark. The media had a field day, even though the back-up STAR, Jack wasn't there. Many poses featured CEO Williamson and CFO Kerrey with Jim holding his double-ended paddle and Joy by his side, backed up by Tripper.

The CEO and CFO requested a meeting with Jim for the next day but he requested to bring Joy as well. The executives agreed that he should most certainly bring Joy Price with him, since she had done much of the important photographic work that would be used in displays for Wild Rivers. "I wonder what that meeting is to be about," Jim mused.

Jim and Joy visited Jack in the animal hospital where he was doing quite well, considering the seriousness of the wound. The veterinarian didn't know what the aftereffects and his ability would be to walk and run normally, but he said, Jack was one heckuva dog! Which came as no surprise to Jim and Joy.

The next morning, before the 10 a.m. meeting with the CEO and CFO, Jim and Joy filled every available display board in the long conference room/library of Wild Rivers with glossy blown-up pictures of the trip. "If I do say so, myself, this is a most impressive display!" Jim intoned, as he gave Joy a gentle kiss. Duplicates had been made of the taped conversations and videotapes of interviews

"Jack will be happy, when he sees how many pictures there are of him. The one wearing a Mandan warrior headdress will, undoubtedly be his favorite," Joy said. Messrs Wellmann and Kerrey quickly reviewed the displays before huddling in the CEO's office preceding the 10 a.m. meeting with Jim and Joy.

"We are very pleased with the work you and Joy have done, and of course, what we have seen doesn't include the tapes. Wild Rivers has purchased two other outdoor magazines and will have spreads in both of them as well. As your contract provides us with the first basic information, we understand you will retain the rights to the photos and videos.

"There will be a number of interviews with the media, already set up. Mr. Spader is no longer with us, but we request that Ms. Jennifer Long attend the media interviews with you and Joy, if that is all right with you."

"I will want to discuss this with my attorney," said Jim, "however, I see no reason that would be a problem. We had already anticipated making beginning and ending `trailers' for the videotapes that would give full credits to Wild Rivers. Certainly, without the confidence your Magazine showed in us, this trip would not have been possible."

"Gene and I have discussed offering you the position of Vice President for Exploration, Jim. A review of your experience told us you have traveled worldwide in your work and would be a great addition to our staff as we expand. We would pay you $50,000 per year at the beginning, complete with benefits. What do you think?"

With his heart in his throat, Jim said, "You sure don't waste time, do you? I am overwhelmed at the moment, George. On the one hand, it would give us a chance to put to use my extensive experience in the outdoors. However, on the other hand, I do want to remain active in outdoor activities. Can I have the next two days to consider it? There's this certain young lady I know with whom I wish to discuss it first. "

"By all means. We hope we have a long and successful relationship. Joy's background will be important to us as well. We will pull together a proposal for her as well, if she's the 'certain young lady' you are referring to," Gene Kerrey said, smiling broadly.

The five of them rose to their feet, almost in unison, as if the pressures of the huge decisions awaiting them couldn't allow further delay. Shaking hands all around, and answering a few questions about the displays, they concluded the meeting.

Two hours later, sitting outside the Animal Hospital in the rental car, Jim turned to Joy and said, "Joy, if Jack agrees, would you marry me? I love you so much and promise to be a loving and caring mate for as long as we both shall live. I have had plenty of time to think about what I was going to say. I would like to make

our home in Montana. If we don't agree to work with Wild Rivers, I will contract with only those publishers who agree that you can travel with me and receive professional recognition for work in which you participate. And, the next time---no solo paddling---we do it together!! We can put our `papooses' on our backs as they come and home-school them.

"Joy, the Mighty Muddy Mo released me from my doubts and fears of the past and I am ready for whatever comes. I saw Johnny in my sleep last night and he bid me farewell and Godspeed!"

Joy responded, "Don't tell Jack, but even if he *disagrees*, I will marry you, you big lug! With a proposal as sweet as that, how could anyone say no? Probably no woman in history has received a joint marriage proposal from a wonderful man and a wonderful dog! We will truly have a marriage made in Heaven or at least in the Great Above, and watched over by the Old Man, as the Indians call their God."

A moment later, Jack finally gave them his blessing. *You don't have to say anything, you two. I know you have decided to get married, regardless of my opinion. But, I am going to surprise you--- I approve of Joy. Just not sure about the Big Guy--- but I'll give him time to mend his ways.*

Joy and Jim put their faces down to Jack and gave him gentle kisses and hugs and thanked him for his support.

He groaned impatiently. *Will you knock off the sickening sentimentality, please? Now go ahead and kiss her, you big lug!*

Jim did. And did . . . and did . . . and did!

THE END